The Golden Sellout

A Luca Thriller

A Luca Mystery
Book 16

Dan Petrosini

Print ISBN: 978-1-960286-41-3
Naples, FL
Library of Congress Control Number: 2024926427

Part One

Naples, Florida

Chapter One

I hung up and went into the kitchen. Mary Ann was unloading the dishwasher. She asked, "Who was that?"

"Pembroke, from the Treasury Department. He needs help on a case involving a Jay Adams who used to work there. They think he's tangled up in a Wall Street scheme."

She paused, putting a dish away. "What did you say?"

"I wouldn't mind doing something to raise the heartbeat, but the financial markets? All those suits? No way."

"You've been in Florida too long."

Grabbing a handful of spoons out of the dishwasher, I said, "Not long enough."

"We should go to Miami for the weekend."

"You want to put the Spanish we're learning to a real-world test?"

Mary Ann's cell phone rang. It was the call that would change everything.

"Hey, Patti, I was just going to buzz you . . . What? Oh my God!"

The color drained out of Mary Ann's face. She was shaking

her head. "I can't believe it. How terrible. Joe and Sue must be devastated . . . Where did this happen?"

She moved the phone away from her mouth and whispered, "Steve Ryan died of an overdose."

My stomach turned. The neighbor's kid had wanted to be a police officer. Steve, Jimmy, and my daughter, Jessie, had palled around when they went to middle school. I'd brought them to the office several times. Stevie was a good kid and the closest thing to the son we never had.

THREE DAYS LATER, I reached for Mary Ann's hand and walked into the Fuller Funeral Home. The lobby was packed with people in their late teens and early twenties. Jessie and another neighborhood kid were sitting on a couch. Both were clutching tissues.

We weaved through the crowd. Our daughter jumped up and hugged us. "Mom, Dad, I can't believe this, it's surreal."

It was. This sorrow-filled lesson held a stronger message than all the things I had warned her about growing up. I hoped like hell that all the people in the room got it. Drugs were not only dangerous; they were deadly.

Mary Ann said, "Did you go in yet?"

Tight-lipped, Jessie shook her head.

I put my arm around her shoulder. "Come on, let's pay our respects."

We stood in line, inching toward the casket. I tried to distract myself by thinking about the origin of the phrase, *paying your respects*. Paying was a weird thing to say. Was it the travel required in past centuries? For me, the payment was the discomfort I felt. It didn't matter that I'd seen scores of dead bodies, my stomach was a pit of snakes.

Joe Ryan, the father, was hunched over. His brother was

patting him on the back. Standing next to the coffin was his wife, Sue, who was stroking her dead son's face.

My legs were cement. Every fiber in my body was telling me to turn around. A tear rolled down my cheek. I swiped it away with the back of my hand.

Mary Ann handed me a tissue. We were next in line.

The mother, Sue, saw us and her face crumpled. Mary Ann and Jessie wrapped their arms around her. Sue wailed. Crying openly, I joined the group hug.

"We're so sorry, Sue."

"What am I going to do? He's gone. My baby is gone."

Closing my eyes, I knelt by the casket. I stole a look at the boy I'd known for fifteen years. He was a good kid, and I appreciated that he'd watched out for Jessie.

Though I hadn't seen Steve in two months, the way he looked told me he wasn't into hard drugs. The rumor was that fentanyl-laced coke had caused the overdose.

Jessie knelt beside me and began sobbing. I put my arm around her and cried with her. Mary Ann grabbed my hand. She whispered, "Come on, Frank. It's not good for Sue to see us like this."

I staggered to my feet. Joe Ryan stared blankly at me. I squeezed his shoulder. "I'm sorry, buddy."

"Steve looked up to you, Frank."

My voice cracked. "He was a good boy."

"You're the reason he wanted to be a cop."

The Ryans' next-door neighbor approached the casket and Sue started wailing again. I tugged at my collar. "What can we do for you?"

He muttered, "Nothing, not a damn thing can bring Steve back."

"Try and hang in there."

He moaned, and I said, "We're going to sit in the back."

I nodded silently at friends and neighbors as we made our

way to the last row. The girls sat. The room was quiet. I said, "I have to use the bathroom."

It wasn't true. Space was what I needed. Passing through the lobby, a teary-eyed family came through the door. A suit, still in the cleaner's plastic, was draped over the mother's arm. A twenty-something girl was carrying a large picture of another young man.

Bile splashed the back of my throat. I ducked into the bathroom. A boy, washing his hands, was talking to a friend taking a leak. I went into the stall and sat on the bowl.

I tried coaxing piss out of the bladder they made for me when one of the boys said, "I can't believe it, Adam's funeral is going to be here, too."

"I heard he had one of those test kits."

"I guess he didn't use it."

What kind of world were we living in? People who used cocaine tested it for the presence of fentanyl. Wasn't knowing that there were test kits enough to tell you that you were playing a deadly game?

Chapter Two

Mary Ann said, "Yes. She really feels bad about not going to the burial."

"She flew in for the wake, and she's got a final tomorrow."

"She took it better than I expected."

"I'm completely drained."

"I know. I'm going to get changed."

She disappeared into our bedroom.

A couple of minutes later, she whispered, "Are you sleeping?"

"No. Just thinking."

"I still can't believe it. What a nightmare."

"I can't imagine what tomorrow is going to be like, but it'll be worse than today."

"I feel so bad for Sue and Joe. I don't know how they're going to get over this."

"They're not gonna get over it. We're not supposed to outlive our kids, especially when they're only twenty years old."

"How did this happen?"

"Kids take risks. They think they know what they're doing."

"He was such a good boy. Remember how he used to look out for Jessica?"

"Yeah. He and Jimmy were the only ones I trusted. Look at this picture Jessie put on my phone."

"Wow. The Three Musketeers. They were so cute together."

"And innocent."

"It took a while for you to warm up to Steve. Remember when he wanted to help you paint and spilled the can all over himself?"

I chuckled. "He was so interested in what a detective did. He'd ask questions; some of them were good ones, like he had an insight or something."

"Jessica and he got so excited every time you took them into the station."

I choked up. "A ton of memories. Steve would've made a great cop."

"It's so sad. It's like everything's changed." Her voice trailed off.

I got out of the recliner. "Over time we'll get back to normal. We'll have scars, but Joe and Sue will never fully recover."

"You think they'll move?"

"I don't know if I could live in the same house; you're surrounded by memories."

"It's a parent's worst nightmare."

"Too many lives are being destroyed by drugs. I overheard that another kid overdosed, and the wake is going to be in the room next to where Steve's was."

"It's out of control. Why can't the government stop some of this?"

"There's too much money in it."

"Do you really believe that?"

"Absolutely. Look, the Mexican government is essentially run by the cartels. I hate to say it, but we're no angels either. If we had the will, we could put a dent in the supply getting into the country. And the chemicals to make fentanyl come from China. We should be leaning on them like crazy."

"Why aren't we getting them to help?"

"That's the trillion-dollar question. I'm not saying it'd be easy; we'd have to make tough decisions on what's important, but we've got a damn crisis on our hands and it's getting worse."

"What is the sheriff's office doing about this?"

"Last time I had lunch with Gesso, he mentioned they were forming a special unit to work with Lee and Broward counties."

"I'm not naïve, but I never thought we'd have drug issues in Naples. I mean, marijuana is one thing, but this fentanyl is killing our kids."

"It's a hundred times more powerful than heroin."

"They say something good comes out of everything bad that happens. Let's hope it does."

That was nonsense. It was something we told ourselves to mitigate the pain of an event or loss.

I couldn't sit around waiting for something good to happen. Things happened because we made them happen. And I was going to do my part to make sure something happened.

Chapter Three

He said, "You look like crap."

I signaled a server holding a coffee pot. "Thanks, pal. Only caught about an hour of sleep last night."

The waiter filled my cup, and I ordered two fried eggs and toast.

Derrick said, "The Ryan kid is on your mind."

"It's disturbing, Derrick. You know we were close to Steve."

"Trust me, at least Jessie is an adult. I'm worried about what my baby is going to be facing when she's a teenager."

"She'll be okay."

"Let's hope so, but that's what the Ryans thought. Who knows what the next thing being cooked up in some lab is going to be?"

"I just don't get it, Derrick."

"The chemical compounds?"

"That and why people take chances with it. I don't understand anything about it."

"Nobody does."

"Well, if we don't understand it, we have no chance of stopping it."

"Everybody understands money."

"It makes the world go round."

"No doubt it makes the drug world what it is."

The server slid my breakfast onto the table.

I grabbed the pepper shaker. "The influence that money has is huge. The cartels have used it to corrupt governments. They're buying protection. And taking a page from the Carlos Escobar book, they get in favor with the poor, providing jobs and putting up parks in their neighborhoods."

Derrick shook his head in disgust. "Regular people protecting the cartels. That's as crazy as it gets."

"It's back to the money. These people are poor and uneducated. Where else are they going to get a job that pays that kind of money?"

"It's the same with the street dealers in this country."

"To a degree, but don't forget we have an educational system. These kids are choosing to drop out, and there's usually no parent to kick them in the ass before they do."

"I read the other day that in the United States, two million kids drop out of high school every year."

"That's an ugly statistic with far-ranging consequences."

"Maybe with AI you won't need too much of an education."

"Yeah, can't wait until machines run everything."

Derrick said, "We're not going to be around to see that."

"Maybe, but I'm seeing too much damage from drugs. There needs to be a real war, and the Feds have to lead it."

"You ever hear from that top dog at the Treasury?"

"Yes, he wants me to get involved in an operation they're concerned about. It's a big hedge fund run by someone who used to work at Treasury."

"You were looking for something to do."

"I'm looking for something exciting to do, but the stock market is a world I don't know and don't want to be in."

"It's not much different from anything else, you just follow the money."

"Money, the common denominator."

"According to the Bible, it's the root of all evil."

Swallowing the last of my breakfast, an idea hit me. "I wouldn't go that far." I stood and dug a twenty out of my pocket and put it on the table.

Derrick said, "Something I said?"

"No."

"What's going on, Frank?"

"I have to go talk to Jimmy, the kid Ryan was with when he OD'd."

"I heard he was interviewed. He said he wasn't there when the buy was made."

"I don't believe it. I knew Steve, he wouldn't go alone."

Chapter Four

Jimmy Pearson opened the door. "Oh, hi, Mr. Luca."

"Hey, Jimmy. You have a couple of minutes to talk?"

"Uh, sure. Come in. Mom isn't home; she ran to Publix."

I knew she had left the house. "Tell her I said hello."

The TV was paused on a video game. Two real-looking thugs were lying on the street in a city scene.

He clicked the remote and said, "It's about Steve, right?"

"Yes. Whatever happened, happened, okay? I know you were there, and all I want is what you know about who you bought from."

"I'm never doing that again, I swear."

"I hope so. Now, who sold it to you?"

"I didn't buy anything. It was Steve, he—"

Pinning the blame on a dead man was as old as the pyramids.

"Hold on, Jimmy. You can trust me. I'm not going to tell anyone, not your mother, the police, no one. I don't care who did the buying. All I'm interested in is identifying the supplier."

"I don't know. It's probably the same guys everybody gets it from."

I put my hands on my knees and leaned forward. "Who is the dealer?"

He chewed on a fingernail.

"Jimmy, no one is going to know you told me."

He shrugged.

"You want another friend to die?"

He shook his head. "No, no. But I'm, I'm . . ."

I sat next to him. "It's okay to be afraid. I'm scared all the time."

"But you were a detective."

"Everybody gets scared. You have to push the fear away and do the right thing, the thing that needs to be done."

"I know, but . . ."

"Just tell me. Don't you want these guys to pay for what they did to Steve?"

He frowned.

"They poisoned him. It could've been you."

He whispered, "They said if anyone opened their mouths, they'd, uh, kill them, gut them like a fish."

"You think the sheriff's office doesn't know who the dealers are?"

"Then why do I have to say anything?"

"Jimmy, you, Steve, and Jessie were close growing up. You kids were over to our house a lot and came to the station a couple of times."

"Steve and me wanted to be cops, a detective like you."

"His life was cut short by drugs. If we do nothing, we're telling the world it's acceptable. Do you think it's okay to do nothing?"

"No, of course not."

"Then tell me who it was."

"What, what are you going to do?"

"I have trusted sources in the department. I'll make sure they give the dealers a hard time; you know, disrupt their practices. If they catch them in the act, arrest them, that kind of thing."

"You won't tell them who told you?"

I put my hand over my heart. "No one will ever find out."

He nodded. "Okay. There's like three guys: a little short guy, they call him Nino, a big black man with a scar on his cheek, but I don't know his name. He never says a word."

"And the other guy? You said there was three of them."

Jimmy frowned. "Yeah, the other guy was the boss. They call him the Fisherman, but I'm pretty sure his last name is Ruiz."

"How do you know that?"

"First time we saw him, he was standing off to the side. We didn't know if it was cool or not to make the buy, and Steve asked Nino who he was. You know, it could've been a cop or something. But Nino said it was okay, he was the boss.

"One day we were getting some, and this guy pulls up in a SUV. We thought it was the police, but the driver said something like, 'Yo, Ruiz,' and you should have seen the look the Fisherman gave him."

The truth about buying coke regularly had slipped out. "I don't know if that means it was his last name."

"Oh, it had to be, because the next time, Nino and the other guy weren't there. I don't know where they were. So, Steve and I walked up, and he said, 'What the fuck you want?' and Steve said, 'Mr. Ruiz, we'd like a gram, if that's okay?' The Fisherman said, 'You say that name again, I'll slice your ass up. Feed you to the effing alligators.'"

"Any idea on his first name?"

"No."

I remembered a dealer named Manny Ruiz. But he was low-level when I was on the force. "Was he there every time you bought?"

"No, not all the time."

"Who handled the drugs?"

"You gave the money to the black guy, and then Nino would go around the side of the house and get it."

"How about the Fisherman? Did he handle the drugs or money?"

"No, he was just there. Watching. Like I said, he was like the boss."

"Where do they deal from?"

"They hang out by a convenience store on Golden Gate Boulevard, not too far from the middle school."

"They're dealing in a school zone?"

"You meet up there, but you follow them to a house on Forty-Seventh Street."

"Where is that?"

"Kinda behind the middle school."

"It's close?"

"There's a couple of streets and a canal in between."

It seemed outside the area where the penalties were higher. "Do you know the address?"

"No, but it's a little blue house about a quarter mile after the road makes a turn."

"Okay. Look, I'll pass it along. Maybe we can shut these guys down."

"Don't tell them I told you."

"You don't have to worry."

"Okay."

Standing, I said, "I hope you learned your lesson about doing drugs. There's nothing recreational about taking that garbage. It's deadly, and the people peddling that crap are dangerous."

"I swear. I'll never go near that stuff again. No way."

I left knowing people, especially younger ones, had short memories and, combined with peer pressure, would rationalize the risks they took.

Chapter Five

I turned around and smiled. "Hey, Sarge."

Sergeant Gesso bear-hugged me. "Good to see you, Frank."

"Same here, my friend."

"How's Mary Ann? Is she doing okay with the MS?"

"She's good. It hasn't flared up in a long while, so it's manageable. There's less stress in retirement, and that helps."

"Good. And Jessie? How's it going in college?"

"She's doing well."

"That's great. Now what about you? Since you don't golf or play tennis, what have you been doing to keep busy?"

"Not too much, but me and Mary Ann are learning Spanish, and we're both pretty fluent with it."

"You mentioned that before, but is it enough?"

"I'm still trying to figure things out."

"Are you bored enough to come back?"

I smiled. "Some days I'd like to, but Mary Ann would kill me."

"I'll take that as a maybe. Come on back, we'll talk in my office."

His office was filled with sunlight. Gesso slid behind a desk, and I sat in a chair with fraying fabric.

As he turned to adjust the blinds, I said, "How are things here?"

"Same old problems, fighting for the resources we need to keep a growing population as crime-free as possible."

"People think it happens with magic. They don't know how much work it takes."

"You know me, I'm for giving every citizen a ride-along in a patrol car."

"At night."

He smiled. "Naturally. So, what's on your mind?"

"My neighbor's kid, the one who overdosed."

"Damn shame. These kids are playing with fire."

"It's not only kids."

"You're right."

"Any leads on the dealer?"

"Not yet. We put some pressure on a couple of them."

"It was Manny Ruiz, the Fisherman."

"Ruiz? Sounds vaguely familiar."

"He's been around. I spoke to narcotics, they know Ruiz."

"How do you know it's him?"

"I talked to a neighbor's kid. He was with Steve when the buy was made."

"Who? We interviewed the deceased's friends. Everyone said he was by himself."

"He wasn't. Jimmy Pearson was with him."

"Pearson, yeah, we talked to him. You sure you can trust him?"

"Absolutely. He didn't want to say anything because he was scared. I had to pull the information out of him."

"Does the narc unit know where they're operating out of?"

They did, but I still gave him the details of what Jimmy relayed.

Gesso said, "We'll scout it. If it checks out, we'll raid the bastards and shut them down."

"You know, I used to bring Steve here when he and Jessie palled around. He was a damn good kid."

"I'm sorry, Frank."

"If it's okay with you, I'd like to go along for the ride when you take them down."

"Of course. We'll jump on this lead. I'll let you know what's going on, and we'll get them off the streets."

Chapter Six

The driver shut the headlights and announced, "Safety is number one. Watch out for each other. We don't believe they'll be more than three, four max, in the house. But be prepared for anything."

A chorus of affirmations rang out.

Another van came into sight. It was headed toward us. We converged in front of a one-story blue home.

The driver of our vehicle said, "Okay. Let's do this!"

The doors of both vans popped open, and a dozen officers spread out, surrounding the house. I followed a pair of them to the front door.

Two officers banged on the door. "Collier County Sheriff's Office! Open the door!"

After a second round of knocking, the lead officer pointed to a cop with a battering ram. He and another officer held on to either side and rammed the door.

As the door splintered, I scurried to the side. Five officers rushed in. After hearing three 'all clears,' I stepped over a sliver of the door into the house.

A couch, whose better days were when the Beatles came to

America, anchored a room littered with fast-food wrappers. A card table and folding chairs were the only other things in the space.

A voice came from another room. "All clear. The house is empty."

I rushed to the rear slider. Three officers were guarding the backyard. The door groaned as I forced it open. "You see anybody leave?"

"No."

I walked into a bedroom. Bedding was balled up on a mattress on the floor. A large-screen TV was catty-cornered on a stand, with a pair of gaming controls off to the side.

The closet held a couple of shirts, two pairs of jeans, and a worn set of sandals. I went into the second bedroom. It was empty. My gaze settled on a bank of light switches.

It had four buttons, unusual for a bedroom. Using a pocketknife, I unscrewed it from the wall. There were no wires.

The large cavity in between the beams was being used to store drugs.

I notified the lead, who took pictures and headed into the kitchen.

I pulled open the fridge. A six-pack of beer sat in front of three cartons of Chinese food. The food wasn't moldy.

The freezer held two pints of ice cream. Neither had freezer burn. The house was being used.

Mary Ann was in the pool doing laps. I watched her, wondering if I would be able to fight MS the way she was. She pulled up and stripped off her goggles. It took her a couple of seconds to catch her breath.

I said, "You're ready for the Olympics."

"Yeah, right. The senior ones."

She dipped under the water, pushing back her hair. When she surfaced, she headed to the stairs. I handed her a towel.

"Thanks. How'd it go with Gesso?"

I shrugged. "Let me ask you, you think Sarge is dirty?"

"Gesso?"

"Yes."

"What makes you think he's on the take?"

"I'm not saying he is. We raided a drug house."

"We? Who's we?"

"We think it's the dealers who sold to Steve. I tagged along."

"You did what? Are you crazy?"

"It was nothing. I laid back. There was no one at the house."

"And if there was? What if they started shooting? You could have been killed."

"Hold on, this was a low-risk situation."

"Anytime you're in the field there's risk."

She was right. "Take it easy, I was out of harm's way."

"I can't believe you went on a raid and you didn't tell me."

"I wasn't sure I was going. Gesso called me when they were setting up. He knew how close we were to Steve and invited me. I didn't think twice about it."

"And that's the problem right there. You thought about yourself, not me, not Jessica."

Stress wasn't good for her MS. I calmly said, "Of course I did. I was the last one in the house. I stood in the van until the house was cleared. I should have told you before. It's not like I was trying to hide anything. Okay?"

"I don't want you taking chances, no matter how small you think they are."

"All I was trying to do was nab the dealers who killed Steve."

"Let the sheriff worry about that."

"I wish I could."

"What are you talking about?"

"They didn't know who sold it. I got Jimmy Pearson to spill it out."

"You talked to Jimmy?"

"I figured he was there when they made the buy and was right. When he was interviewed, he claimed not to be present when the coke was bought."

"He was afraid his mother would find out."

"Exactly."

"These kids, it's hard to believe they're using drugs. They seem so normal."

"I don't know if they're ignorant or it's peer pressure, but I have to do what I can to stop this crap."

"You're retired, Frank."

"I know that. I just want to get the guys who cut the coke with fentanyl behind bars, where they belong."

"Be careful, Frank."

I nodded. "But back to Gesso, you think he could be protecting dealers?"

"If he was, then we're no better than some crummy Mexican town."

That was true. "You know I like the Sarge and believe he's clean. But I wanted your opinion. You were here before I moved to Naples."

"He's a good man. It could be a coincidence . . ." Her voice trailed off. She knew I felt coincidences were rare and a poor excuse to discount evidence. "It could be someone else with knowledge of the raid."

That was obvious. "It's delicate. I'll have to root around."

"Don't get involved."

"I'm afraid if I don't push this along, it'll go nowhere. I can't let that happen to the Ryan family."

Chapter Seven

Sergeant Gesso's wife was strict when it came to food. He referred to her as the food Nazi. She always made lunch for him, and though she was a nice lady, we'd razz him over the hummus and salads he ate at his desk.

I dialed his cell. "Sarge, how are you?"

"Hey, Luca."

"I'm in the neighborhood. You want to grab lunch?"

"My wife made—"

"Come on, we'll grab a pie at LowBrow."

He hesitated before saying, "It's been a while since I had pizza."

"I'll meet you there in ten minutes."

"Sounds good."

The place smelled like baking bread. I grabbed a corner table and watched the parking lot.

Gesso backed his cruiser into a space and got out.

He smiled when he saw me.

"Hey, are you happy to see me, or is it that you're eating real food?"

"I haven't been here since the last time with you."

I stood. "Are you good with a Margarita pie?"

"Definitely. Make sure it's well-done."

I put the order in and came back to my chair. "Is there any progress on the dealer who killed Steve Ryan?"

"I would've told you."

"We can't let this go cold."

"Frank, I know how important this is to you, but you know the resources we have. Our narcotics unit is small and has more than they can handle."

"Believe me, I get it." I put up a palm. "Now, don't get offended, but who knew we were raiding the house on Forty-Seventh Street?"

"You're insinuating there was a leak?"

"Just checking the possibilities."

"The protocols, as far as I know, were maintained; nobody on the team was aware of the operation until they were in the vans."

"So, just Scotty and Behrens knew?"

"Yes. I mean, of course the DEA was apprised to make sure we weren't stepping on an active investigation."

The DEA. That could be where the leak was.

"Is Dillon still running things for them?"

"Yes."

A pie man came from behind the counter and put an aluminum tray holding a steaming work of art on our table.

We slid slices onto the paper plates he provided. Sarge folded his piece and inhaled. "It smells incredible."

Mouth full, I nodded.

Reaching for a second slice, I said, "Dillon is a good man, but I don't trust the rest of them up there."

"That's not a fair thing to say."

"You're right. I was too general. Call me crazy, but the DEA has been around for over fifty years, and things are worse than ever."

"It's a complicated world."

"The DEA has over ten thousand people. How come they can't make progress?"

"You know you can't measure it that way. They do some great work."

"I'm not saying they don't, but I think we have to consider that corruption has to be a major factor for why we don't shut down a lot of this."

Gesso put his half-eaten slice on his plate. "Come on, Frank. You know you can't say stuff like that. It's not fair smearing people who are working hard."

"I know. I'm talking between us. I don't say this to just anybody."

He picked up his piece of pizza. "Good. I figured it was the frustration speaking."

"You mind if I reach out to Dillon? See if they know about where the supply originates?"

"You're getting back in the game?"

"No, I just want to ask a few questions, make sure they know the kid was a neighbor and all."

"You're a private citizen, you can do what you like, but let me give you a little advice, okay?"

"Sure."

"Don't start hitting them with allegations, it's insulting."

"You know me better than that, Sarge."

<hr>

As soon as I got home, I closed the door to the den and dialed the DEA office in Fort Myers.

"Dillon Rogers."

"Hey, Dillon, it's Frank Luca."

"Luca, it's been a while. How are you?"

"Good, and you?"

"Not bad. I thought you retired."

"I did. I'm helping out on a case involving a neighbor."

"What can I do for you?"

I realized I should have visited him in person. "I want to talk to you, it's kind of delicate. Can we get together?"

"I'm swamped and heading to North Carolina for two weeks."

"I see."

"Can it wait?"

"Uh, not really."

"I've got fifteen minutes before a Zoom with my masters in Washington."

"My condolences."

Dillon chuckled. "You ain't kidding. What's going on?"

"A neighbor's son overdosed. The sheriff's office identified the dealers and conducted a raid on a house in Golden Gate. We gave your office a heads-up to be sure we weren't stepping on something the DEA was working on."

"We appreciate the notification. That's the Ryan case, where the Pearson kid provided the information, right?"

My stomach snaked. They knew about Jimmy Pearson. "Yes."

"What did the raid yield?"

"Nothing. The dealers were tipped off."

He cleared his voice. "And you think the leak came out of here."

"We had a complete blackout. I'm not saying it couldn't have leaked out of the sheriff's office, but only two people, Gesso included, knew about it."

"That doesn't prove anything."

"Of course not, but, and don't take this the wrong way—I have a ton of respect for you and the agency—but there's been several breaches by DEA employees over the past two years."

Dillon hesitated before saying, "It only takes one bastard to undermine the reputation of all the hardworking men and women that make up the DEA."

That was tantamount to an admission. But rather than say it was more than one person who betrayed their fellow officers by taking money from the cartels, I said, "I realize this type of thing is best handled in-house, but since we go way back, I felt it important keep you apprised."

"Okay."

"I'm sure you have an idea who it might be."

"You know I can't comment on internal investigations."

And, right there, I had confirmation someone had tipped off the dealers.

Chapter Eight

As I approached, he said, "Hey, partner."

"This is getting to be a habit, buddy."

I signaled the server for coffee and sat. "You know, I don't think we ever went out for breakfast when we were partners."

He smiled. "What are you talking about? I picked up plenty of doughnuts for you."

"I miss those raspberry ones. Mary Ann catches me eating one of those, she'll have me eating asparagus."

"Lynn is the same way."

The server poured coffee and I ordered waffles. "It's a good thing. If it was up to me, I'd eat fast food all day."

"Lynn's new, favorite saying is eating clean."

"Talking about dirty, I talked to Dillon at the DEA, and he basically admitted they have a dirty agent."

"Bingo, that's where the leak was."

"It looks that way. I'm going to talk to Gesso. Maybe there's a way we can set up another raid to expose the leaker."

"I don't know, Frank. Why not leave it to their internal affairs? They're pretty good at surfacing that crap."

My cell vibrated. It was Mary Ann. "Hey, I'm out for breakfast with Derrick. I'll—"

She said, "It may be nothing, but Connie Pearson just called. She said Jimmy never came home last night."

I stiffened.

"Frank?"

I was lightheaded. "Yeah. He probably got drunk with friends and is sleeping it off somewhere."

"Connie said he's not answering his phone, and she called all his friends. She said he hasn't been the same since, uh, Steve died. And he's depressed. You think he might have done, uh, drugs or did something to himself?"

My stomach dropped. "Did she file a missing person report?"

"She called the sheriff's office, and they're going to send a car."

"I'm heading to see Gesso after breakfast. I'll make sure he gives it priority. I'll call you as soon as I talk to him."

I hung up. Derrick said, "What's going on?"

"A neighbor's son, the one who was with Steve when he overdosed, didn't come home last night."

"I don't understand why these damn kids don't call their parents."

I dabbed a bead of sweat on my upper lip. "I got to get going."

"Wait until you eat. Your waffles will be out in a minute."

I stood. "I can't."

I KNOCKED on Gesso's open door. "Hey, Sarge."

He peered over his reading glasses. "You sure you're not back on the payroll?"

"I promise not to take too much of your time."

"Sit down. You want a coffee?"

"No. Look, the kid who told us about the dealer who sold drugs to the Ryan kid went missing."

"How long is he missing?"

"Just overnight, but my neighborhood is skittish, to say the least."

Gesso nodded. "The parents file a missing person report?"

"I think a car is on the way to them."

As he reached for the phone, I said, "It could be nothing, but we'd appreciate it if you could do whatever you can."

He spoke into the phone and hung up. "A patrol car is at the Pearson residence. They'll update me ASAP."

"Thanks, Sarge. Being a parent isn't easy."

"I don't need the reminder. How did it go with Dillon?"

"The DEA is leaking like a pasta strainer."

Gesso shook his head. "I hope you put it more delicately when you spoke to him."

"I'm no politician, but don't worry, the call went well."

"I'm sure you handled it like a real diplomat."

"Let me ask you, how many other raids have you conducted that came up empty?"

"We don't do many of them."

"Out of the ones you did since I left, how many came up with zeroes?"

"Two of them."

"And you pre-advised the DEA, right?"

Gesso nodded.

"There's your proof. The leak is on their end. Unless you think it's coming from inside here."

The phone on his desk rang. Gesso picked it up. He pulled his lips in. "Where?"

After a pause, he said, "All right, get homicide down there and the medical examiner. I'm on my way."

The sergeant looked me in the eye. "A body was found in a canal."

I tensed. "What's the description?"

"White, male, eighteen to twenty-five."

Heat flashed up my neck. "I'm coming with you."

"I don't think that's a good idea."

"Why not?"

"The body was mutilated."

"In what way?"

"The person who called it in said it was gutted."

I put my head in my hands. "Please. Please, don't let it be Jimmy."

Gesso stood. "If you want to come along, I'll let Donovan know."

Donovan had taken over homicide when I left. "I don't want to step on anyone's turf. If he doesn't mind, I'd like to see the crime scene."

"Donovan thinks the world of you. He'd welcome any help you can give him. Let's go."

Chapter Nine

As we drew nearer to the crime scene, the vise in my stomach tightened.

A detective held up the crime tape. We drove under and parked. Gesso handed me gloves and booties before getting out of the car.

He stuck his head back in the vehicle. "Are you coming?"

I'd been to hundreds of crime scenes, but I hesitated to get out of the car. Was it because I wasn't on the force any longer, or was it the possible identity of the victim?

Raindrops bounced off the windshield as I opened the door. Pulling gloves on, I followed Gesso.

"Hey, Luca!"

I turned around. It was Detective Grimes of the Special Crimes Unit. "Hi, Eddie."

"What are you doing here?"

"Tagging along."

"It's an ugly one. The kid is ripped wide open."

I swallowed. "How old do you think he is?"

"Eighteen or so."

Approaching the canal, I squinted. Slowing my steps, I tried to equate Jimmy's height to the figure laid out on the grass.

The corpse looked taller. Dr. Bilotti was bent over the body's head. The medical examiner was studying the victim's mouth.

Bilotti stood. Donovan, who'd replaced me, asked him, "Can you estimate a time of death?"

"Based on the bloating, if he wasn't moved, twelve to eighteen hours."

The pair separated, exposing the victim's face. I collapsed onto my knees. It was Jimmy Pearson.

Gesso said, "Are you all right?"

I struggled to my feet. "Slipped on the wet grass."

He whispered, "It's your neighbor?"

"Yes."

"All right, listen up. We have an ID. The victim is Jimmy Pearson."

Pressing my lips together to keep what was backing out of my stomach from leaking out, I stepped forward. Jimmy was sliced open from his rib cage to his groin.

Donovan sidled up to me. "Whoever did this is a frigging psycho."

Nodding was all I could manage.

"I'll bet you don't miss this."

Through clenched teeth, I said, "The Fisherman did it."

"What?"

"Manny Ruiz, the Fisherman. He did this to Jimmy."

"How do you know that?"

I walked away.

"Frank, hang on."

I hurried to the side of a patrol car and threw up.

A hand rubbed my back. It was Dr. Bilotti. "Are you okay, Frank?"

Wiping my mouth with the back of my hand, I said, "Yeah. I know the boy, he's a neighbor."

"I'm sorry, Frank. This is as nasty as it gets. Whoever did this should be in an institution."

"It was a drug dealer, a guy they call the Fisherman."

"Interesting, my initial assessment was a fishing knife was used, but I'll have to confirm it."

I bent over and dry heaved. "This is a disaster. I have to nail the bastards."

"Frank, I understand why you're here, but you know better than anyone, catching killers is an all-in affair."

"I want to help, I have to."

"You're retired. Leave it to the younger men."

"What? I'm an old man now?"

"That's not what I meant. Donovan is good and getting better every day."

"He's got a long way to go before he sees what I've seen."

"You know I have tremendous respect for you as a friend, as well as professionally, but this isn't good for you. And if you bring the stress home, Mary Ann is going to be impacted. You can't fool around with MS."

Bilotti was a valued friend. And he was right. "I know, but it's just too close to home." My eyes teared up. "Jimmy's been in my house a thousand times."

He reached into his pocket and came up with a set of keys. "Go sit in my car and try to relax. I'll drop you at your house when I'm finished here."

"I came with Gesso. My car's at the station."

"That's okay. Go to my car. I'll let him know you're leaving with me."

I took the keys and looked toward Jimmy's body. Donovan was talking to Gesso. With the information I gave them, they'd get the Fisherman.

Bilotti's car was stuffy. I turned off the classical music the medical examiner had playing and opened the windows. After cranking up the air-conditioning, it cooled down. Palming my phone, the home screen picture of Jimmy, Steve, and Jessie smiling made me curse. I turned toward the crime scene.

It was weird being on the outside. My neighbor's kid, a boy I'd taken to work with me, had been murdered, and I was a bystander.

My gaze drifted to the army of officers combing the area for evidence. I should be out there. Putting a hand on the ignition, my cell rang.

It was Mary Ann. I waited for the third ring to answer. "Hey, I was just going to call you."

"What did Gesso say about Jimmy?"

I blinked away a tear. "It's bad, Mary Ann."

"What is? What happened?"

My voice cracked. "He's, he's been murdered."

"What? Jimmy? He was killed?"

I exhaled. "Yes."

"Are your sure about this?"

"Yes, I went to the scene and identified the body."

"You said he was murdered. But why would they kill Jimmy?"

Because I forced him to rat on the dealers. "I've got to go. They want my help."

"Oh, Frank, things are spinning out of control."

"Everything will be okay."

"Does Connie know?"

"No, not yet."

"She's going to be devastated. Jimmy was her whole world."

Tears streamed down my face. "I'll call you later."

<hr>

THE FRONT DOOR OPENED. Sitting in my recliner, I looked at my watch, it was 11:32 p.m.

Mary Ann said, "Frank? What are you doing sitting in the dark?"

"Just thinking."

"What time did you get home?"

I fudged it. "An hour ago."

She turned a lamp on. "You should have come to Connie's, everybody was there."

"How is she doing?"

"A complete mess, but what can you expect?"

I flicked away a tear rolling down my cheek.

Mary Ann said, "Are you okay?"

I shook my head. "I never should have gotten involved."

She put her hands on my shoulders. "What are you talking about? It's not your fault."

"It sure is."

"How can it be? Tell me."

"I went to Jimmy's after Steve overdosed. The two of them were best friends, and I didn't buy the story Jimmy wasn't there when they bought the drugs. He told me who the dealer was, and I passed it on to Gesso."

"So? That's a good thing."

"He was scared. The dealers threatened them, that if they ever said anything, they'd gut them."

"Gut them? Like a fish?"

"Yeah."

"You think the dealers got to him because he said something?"

"Yes."

"How can you make that connection?"

"Because Jimmy was gutted."

She put her hands over her mouth. "Oh my God."

"And it's my fault."

She sat on the edge of the couch. "How can you say that?"

"Because I discounted the threat. I figured he was just scared of his mother finding out, and . . it's so screwed up, I don't know what to think."

"It's not your fault. All you were doing was trying to help; you did the right thing."

"You think so?"

"Definitely. Stop blaming yourself."

I shrugged.

She pulled my arm. "Come on, let's go to bed."

Whether I was directly or indirectly responsible didn't matter. What was important was doing something about it.

Chapter Ten

She got out of her chair. "Wait for me."

"You don't have to come."

"I can't leave her alone."

"What am I? A ghost?"

"She needs a woman."

We were two houses away when an unmarked car pulled up. A pair of detectives got out.

I whispered, "They had to send McMillan?"

"You never liked him."

"He's a hard-ass. He never cuts anybody a break."

"Oh, right. He's the one who gave Marilyn's mother a ticket for going five miles over the limit."

I waved to them and quickened our pace, meeting them as Connie opened the door. She looked twenty years older than last week.

McMillan and his sidekick, a new hire named Flores, introduced themselves and we stepped inside.

I chatted up the detectives to give Mary Ann a chance to settle Connie down.

McMillan looked at his watch. "Let's get going, we have a busy afternoon."

We sat around Connie's glass kitchen table. McMillan pulled out his notebook. "Mrs. Pearson, the department is sorry for your loss."

Connie closed her eyes and nodded.

"Mrs. Pearson, do you know anyone who could have done this to your son?"

She wagged her head. "No. Nobody. He was a good kid, everyone loved Jimmy."

"The nature of the crime indicates it was something personal. Are you sure you don't have any idea?"

"No. This whole thing doesn't make any sense."

"What about your son's drug use?"

"I didn't know he did drugs until his friend Steve overdosed."

McMillan raised his eyebrows. "How did he support his habit?"

"Jimmy was a good kid, the best son anyone could have. He made a mistake, but he wasn't an addict."

"Was he stealing from you?"

I said, "I knew Jimmy very well. If he used narcotics, it was purely on a recreational basis."

"Mrs. Pearson, what did you do to stop his drug use."

I stood. "Detective, I'd like a word please."

McMillan sighed as he followed me into the foyer. I said, "Look, I know you have a job to do, but the lady just lost her son."

"You think I don't know that?"

"Well, you're making it look like the kid was an addict or something."

"Whether she likes it or not, her kid used drugs."

"She is aware of that."

"Well, that usage led to his murder. It's high time people started accepting responsibility for their actions."

I leaned into him. "He was seventeen years old. Teenagers do stupid stuff, just like we did growing up."

He hissed, "I never did that crap."

"You want to take the high road? Well, how about the fact it's our job as adults, and especially as law enforcement officers, to do our part to protect kids."

McMillan said, "You of all people know we can't protect everybody. Drugs are all over the place."

"And whose fault is that?"

"If there was no demand, there wouldn't be a drug problem."

"You sound like a politician."

"It's true."

"Yeah, well, we can do a much better job of stopping that garbage at the border."

He shrugged.

I stuck a finger in his face. "Don't forget Jimmy was a minor. And his mother, who is a widower, is mourning the loss of her only son."

McMillan toned his act down a notch and finished the interview. Connie showed him and Flores out the door. When she came back into the kitchen, tears were streaming down her cheeks.

Mary Ann jumped up and embraced her. Connie sobbed, "Jimmy was a good kid, the best. He was so caring; he took care of me."

"I know he was a special boy."

Her shoulders heaved. "They think he was a druggie."

I stood. "They don't. McMillan is a jerk."

"They blame Jimmy for what happened. How can they?"

"Don't worry, I'm going to make sure you and Jimmy get justice."

Mary Ann said, "You want to come over for dinner later?"

"No. I want to stay here."

"I'll make something and come back. What do you feel like eating?"

"I'm not hungry."

"You have to eat. I'll make something and see you in a couple of hours. If you need anything before that, call me. I'll be right over."

As soon as we stepped outside, Mary Ann said, "McMillan is a bigger ass than I thought."

"Empathy isn't his strong suit."

"What did you say to him?"

I relayed our talk.

She said, "I'm glad you said something. How he was talking to her was ridiculous."

"If you can believe it, he doesn't think we can do a better job cutting off the supply of narcotics. Thinks it's all about the users."

"Of course, the border matters. At the very least, you cut down how much is coming in, and the price on the street rises. A major part of the problem is how cheap and available drugs are."

"With people like McMillan around, it's going to get worse, not better."

"Don't exaggerate."

"I'm not. If I didn't tip them off, who knows if they'd ever catch the killer."

"What's going on with that? They have a read on where the Fisherman is hiding?"

"If they don't grab him, believe me, I'll catch the bastard."

"Come on, Frank, give Gesso and Donovan a chance."

Chapter Eleven

Mary Ann said, "I'm exhausted."

I said, "I don't think I've ever been this tired. Oh, it's starting to come down."

"Every funeral we go to, it rains."

"It fits."

"It feels kind of weird, but I'm glad they didn't do a repast lunch."

"Connie said his friends were going to do something next week at the high school."

"Yeah, she mentioned that. I'm getting changed."

I followed her into the bedroom and got out of my suit. I hopped into a pair of shorts and put on a T-shirt with the sheriff's logo on it.

"I need a coffee, you want one?"

"No, my stomach is upset."

Mine was too, but I had to do something to keep my mind from bringing up the picture of Jimmy in the coffin.

I headed into the kitchen, stopping to pick up the remote in the family room. I flicked the TV on and started the coffee.

WINK News was on. I went into the family room. The

newscaster was talking about an arrest at Miami Airport. I turned the volume up.

"We're going to Miami International Airport, where Melissa Andrews is reporting live."

A blonde woman in her thirties was standing in front of an airport terminal. "Just under an hour ago, Miami-Dade police officers apprehended three young women about to board a flight to Cartagena, Colombia. The trio were arrested on suspicion of money laundering. TSA security personnel observed the suspects acting nervously as they passed through security. They flagged the ladies and alerted the Terrorism Task Force.

"The women were interviewed, reinforcing the suspicion they were up to something. The question was what. They asked the airline to delay the departure to give them time to investigate further.

"As background checks were being run, they pulled the women's luggage off the plane and discovered something surprising. It wasn't drugs or weapons but close to ten million dollars in cold, hard cash. The women were taken into custody and transported to federal court for arraignment. We'll follow this story as it unfolds."

Mary Ann came out of the bedroom. I said, "They just caught three women at Miami Airport trying to fly to Colombia with ten million in cash."

"Has to be drug money."

I went into the kitchen to get my coffee. "I'm sure it is."

"I wonder how many people get through each day."

"Good question. I'm sure it's a lot more than you'd think."

"I thought all the airports had x-ray machines to detect cash hidden in luggage."

"They do, but there's the human factor; an operator has to catch it. There are millions of bags going through every day."

"Maybe they can program the machines with AI to make it automatic."

"Finally, something I can get behind with this AI stuff."

"You never liked change, Frank, and you're getting worse the older you get."

First it was Dr. Bilotti, and now my wife was telling me I was old. "Yeah, well, you better watch out, or I'll replace you with a young avatar or whatever they call those AI beings."

A RINGING CELL phone woke me up. I'd fallen asleep watching TV. Mary Ann was talking and hung up.

She said, "That was Connie. She asked if you could go over there to change a light bulb."

"Now?"

"It's only four o'clock."

"Did you hear from Jessie?"

"Not yet."

"Text her. Make sure she's all right."

"I just did. Are you going to Connie's?"

I pinched the bridge of my nose. "I'm dead tired."

"It's the light in her closet, she can't see a thing in there."

"Okay. But you have to come with me."

"Why?"

"Because she's a wreck, and I, uh . . . just come with me, okay?"

"You need an emotional barrier?"

"No. I'm an old man and need your help."

"Old man?"

I got out of my recliner. "That's what you said earlier."

"Look, everybody is stressed out."

"Let's go."

Connie lived four houses down. As we walked, I said, "I know it's early, but she should consider moving to a condo or something."

"She'll be fine. She just needs to adjust."

"You're going to jump on me for saying this, but she's a woman living alone. Every little thing becomes a major ordeal."

"Changing a bulb isn't an ordeal."

"No, but she needs help doing it. I don't have a problem doing stuff like this, but she's going to be embarrassed calling for help when something little goes wrong."

We waved at a neighbor walking their poodle and turned up Connie's walkway.

She opened the door, and before we could say a word, she burst into tears. Mary Ann embraced her, and we stepped inside. The foyer was lined with flowers from the funeral. My sinuses reacted to the lilies.

We trudged into the kitchen. The sign-in book from the wake was on the table. Mary Ann got a glass of water for Connie.

She sipped it and said, "I'm sorry, but I just can't help it."

"It's okay, Connie. You must get it out. The worst thing you can do is to hold it in."

I swallowed. In a minute I was going to start crying. Mary Ann took her hands and the two of them sobbed. I headed for the bathroom.

Splashing water on my face, the reality came into focus that every crime, especially homicide, had many victims. Jimmy's life ended too early, and his mother's would never be the same.

What do you do when the worst possible thing that could happen to you has already happened?

Crazy as it seemed, his father, who had died ten years ago from a heart attack, was the lucky one.

I dried my face with a towel. The passage of time usually dulled the pain of whatever happened. But in this case, the past would never be more than an inch away from Connie.

I went back into the kitchen. The door to the microwave

was open. Two cups with tea bags sat on the counter. Connie wiped her nose. Mary Ann said, "Do you want some tea?"

What I wanted was to run. "I'm okay. Connie, where do you keep the bulbs?"

"Jimmy put them in the laundry room cabinet, they're up really high."

"I'll get the ladder out of the garage."

"Jimmy hung it on the wall."

The ladder was behind the bodyboard I had bought him on his sixteenth birthday. I moved it out of the way and saw his baseball mitt and aluminum bat. I'd taught Jimmy how to hit. When Jessie and Stevie and he were kids, we'd go to North Collier Park and practice every spring weekend.

I brought the ladder into the house and went into the laundry room for a bulb. Stepping out, I looked into Jimmy's room. Two suits were laid out on his bed. The thought of Connie picking out the clothes to bury Jimmy in sickened me.

The pain being caused by drugs had to end.

Chapter Twelve

When I went to John Jay College in Manhattan, I commuted. But it was a different era. Going away to college was something most kids wanted to do. But Steve and Jimmy would never get whatever kids got out of a college experience.

Life wasn't fair, but there was no way to rationalize two neighborhood kids dying before eighteen. Both boys had been in our house more times than any of the female friends Jessie had.

Both were fascinated that I was a detective. They repeatedly professed a desire to follow in my footsteps. Steve drifted away when he became a teenager, but Jimmy was steadfast about going to the police academy.

"Frank? Are you okay?"

Mary Ann popped her head in the den.

"Yeah, just thinking."

"I'm going to Publix. You want anything special for dinner?"

"Whatever Jessie wants."

"Okay. Why don't you sit on the lanai? Get some sun. It'll be good for you."

"Maybe in a little while."

"I'm going to the cleaners as well, so I'll be back in an hour."

The sound of the garage door opening prompted me to power up my laptop. It fired up, but the low battery warning came up. Fishing out the charging cord from the desk drawer, I saw a dish Jessie had made to hold my keys.

Running my finger around the edge, the day came rushing back. It was a Saturday, and Mary Ann always had an activity planned for Jessie. That week Jessie and Jimmy went to a ceramics place on Airport Pulling Road.

It was my job to pick them up. I remember how excited they were as they came out of the store. Jessie couldn't wait to give me what she had made.

I remembered taking a picture of them. Rummaging through the drawer, I found the photo. When I took the shot, Jessie and Jimmy were sitting in the back seat, giggling and talking about what they were going to create the next time. They were so happy, so innocent. I swiped away a stream of tears running down my cheeks.

"Dad? What's wrong?"

"Uh, nothing."

"You're crying."

I held up the picture. "You and Jimmy—" I began sobbing.

Jessie wrapped her arms around me. "It's okay, Dad. Get it out. You guys were close."

"I'm sorry."

"There's nothing to be sorry about. Everyone is upset about what happened to Jimmy . . . and Steve."

"I've seen a lot, but these two really hit me."

"It's so sad, so tragic."

"That's the right word. It makes paying the tuition a bit easier to swallow." I forced a smile and stood. "I need some water."

"I'll get it. Why don't you wash up?"

I nodded and put the photo in my pocket before heading to

the bathroom. Crying in front of your kid wasn't ideal, but it was better than holding it in.

Jessie was sitting in front of my desk. I picked up the glass she got for me. "Thanks."

"Are you feeling better?"

"Oh, yeah. I'm sorry you had to fly back, but I'm glad you came home again."

"Me too. Are they close to catching the killer?"

"I think so."

"Mom said it was related to drugs. Is that why he was murdered?"

"It's complicated, but it looks like it was the dealer who did it. Promise me you won't touch that garbage, Jess."

"I never tried it and never will. I don't understand why so many kids feel the need to get high."

"I wish I had the answer, honey."

"Why isn't the government doing more to stop it from coming into the country?"

"I hate to say it, but there's just too much money involved, and it corrupts people into looking the other way."

"But it affects everyone."

"I know. It's a vicious cycle. The money makes the cartels stronger and extends their power with political contributions to—"

"They're payoffs, not contributions."

"You're exactly right."

"It's corruption, Dad."

"I know."

"I hope things don't have to get much worse before people wake up."

I couldn't say that if corruption spread any further, it'd even be almost impossible to root it out. "Let's hope not."

She smiled. "I remember you saying, 'Hope is not a strategy.'"

"It certainly isn't."

"Be honest, Dad. You know the law enforcement world, do you think they can turn this drug problem around?"

"It's going to be tough, but if there is the will to do it, they can."

"Sounds like they need the right leadership."

She hit the nail on the head. The issue was, I didn't see anyone capable of stepping up. Politicians would talk about it, but we needed to move from issuing sound bites to concrete action.

Chapter Thirteen

"Hi, Donny. It's Luca."

"Hey, Frank. What's on your mind?"

"I'm not pushing, but I'm looking to see where you are with the Pearson case."

"I was going to call you, but it got busy."

And politicians have your best interest at heart. "That's okay. What's going on?"

"During a canvass we found a witness who places Ruiz at the park."

"Good. When are you picking him up?"

"We're waiting on the DNA results from the autopsy."

Jimmy had been in the water for hours and hours. I wasn't sure what DNA or fibers might have been left for forensics to collect. "When is it coming back?"

"Bilotti said they'd have it this afternoon."

"Good. Do you have anyone else on the radar who might have been on the scene?"

"No. The witness who saw Ruiz at the park said he was alone."

"What time was that?"

After hesitating, he said, "We got this, Frank. I'll call you when we get the DNA back."

"Okay. Thanks, I'll wait to hear from you."

I ended the call and made another one.

"Medical Examiner's Office. How may I help you?"

"Dr. Bilotti, please."

"One moment, sir."

"This is Dr. Bilotti."

"Hey, Doc, it's me."

"Frank, how are you?"

"Good. Look, Donovan tells me he's waiting on the DNA recovered from the Pearson autopsy. What did you find?"

"Not much, the body was submerged in water, and a good deal of any external DNA has been lost."

"When will you get the results?"

"The lab promised they would have it before two p.m."

"Do you know if they're running whatever was found on Pearson against Ruiz's profile?"

"That's outside of my domain."

"Yeah, I know. Can you do me a favor and text me when you get the lab results?"

"Sure. I'd be happy to."

"Thanks, Doc. I owe you one."

"Frank, are you doing okay?"

"Yeah, just, you know, my neighbor and . . ."

"It's been a while since we drank wine together. I have a couple of bottles of Barbaresco that are ready to drink."

"I just drooled all over the phone."

He chuckled. "If you're free Friday, that works for me. If not, we can look at next week."

"Pencil it in before you change your mind."

I KEPT CHECKING MY PHONE. Mary Ann said, "Take it easy, Frank. If Bilotti said he'd text you, he will."

"I know."

Ping.

I swiped. "You're my good luck charm, Mary Ann. That was Bilotti."

"Okay, but don't call Donovan right away."

"How long do you think I should wait?"

"A couple of hours."

"That's crazy."

"He could be in the field."

"So? All he has to do is—"

She got up. "Do whatever you want."

I walked around the pool ten times and went inside to relieve the bladder doctors had replaced my cancer-ridden one with.

When I came out of the bathroom, I called Donovan.

"Hey, I'm not pushing, but I was talking to Bilotti about wine, and he mentioned—"

"Yeah, we have the results, and we're going to run it against the Codis database and Ruiz's profile."

"That'll take too much time. Use the RapidHit system."

He said nothing.

"Donny?"

"Yeah?"

"Sorry, I'm just trying to help."

"Look, I realize you knew the victim, but, uh, you're retired, and I'm handling things now."

"Of course I know that. We both want this cretin off the streets, and my suggestions are only to get him behind bars as fast as possible."

"I have to go, Frank."

And just like that, decades of experience was shoved aside.

Mary Ann came out of the bedroom, giving me a 'I told you so' look.

I SLAMMED the phone down and stormed into the kitchen. Mary Ann was reaching inside the fridge. She said, "Who were you talking to?"

"Gesso. I can't believe they still haven't located the Fisherman."

She squinted.

I said, "The dealer who killed Jimmy, Manny Ruiz."

"I know who you meant. They have a line on where he is?"

"Who knows if they're even looking."

"What makes you say that?"

"I feel like I'm getting the runaround. They can't even confirm what cartel is supplying Ruiz's gang."

"Maybe you should back off a little, give them a chance to—"

"Ruiz is a cold-blooded murderer. How long should we wait? Until he kills another one of our kids?"

"Frank, you were a homicide detective, you know it takes time to catch a killer."

"Not when you know who it is!"

"They're probably vetting what you told them."

"Then why the hell haven't they questioned him?"

"Not having DNA on the body complicates things."

"I had plenty of cases without DNA evidence. If you work the case properly, you don't need it."

"You always said Donovan was good. Now he's not?"

"He has no sense of urgency. It seems like they're dragging their feet."

"Why would they do that?"

"Because it's drug related. You know a lot of people don't

sympathize when drug use is involved. It's the same thing with prostitution."

"To a degree, but not everybody feels the same as McMillan does."

"Maybe, but it's a lot more than you think. People don't value the lives of sex workers or drug users like they should. They're someone's son or daughter."

Chapter Fourteen

The headline read, "Seizures of Counterfeit Designer Goods Rises."

I read the article. The news wasn't as good as it looked. Seizures were up, but the smugglers were brazen. An informer quoted in the piece said contrabandists were flooding border crossings with vehicles filled with knockoffs.

The organized crime gangs were sending ten trucks a day, knowing one or two would be stopped, but eight or more would get through to the United States.

The strategy worked because the markups on handbags were so high they could afford to lose 20 or 30 percent of the goods shipped.

It reminded me of the Miami gang we'd busted at Waterside Shops. Posing as shoppers, a gang of them would swarm the high-end pocketbook department. Some would distract the sales staff while others would grab expensive bags and run.

Smugglers shipping over the border were using similar tactics. What made both approaches work was the margins. I set the magazine aside.

Selling drugs had even higher profit margins. Probably the

highest in history. It was why so many got into that world. But all the cash it generated created a problem of its own.

You could only buy low-value items with cash. You couldn't buy a car or a house with suitcases full of currency. And banks no longer accepted large cash deposits.

The other issue with it was the money was trapped in the United States, and the people whose cash it was lived south of the border.

A buzz ran along the base of my skull. I envisioned the border, and an idea began to form. It could be a way to make a difference.

Chapter Fifteen

I moved my gym bag to my other hand and shook his. "How's it going?"

He said, "I was just thinking how nice it is that we can work out together since we're not working anymore."

"One of the benefits and negatives of having time on your hands."

"Oh, come on, you're in the best shape since I've known you."

"It's from not eating doughnuts from the cafeteria."

He chuckled. "I'm glad we get to do this together."

"Yeah, instead of making life tough for criminals, we torture ourselves."

"It's not that bad. Today is a leg day."

"Ugh. I hate them."

"It's critical, especially as you get older. And you know, you're not getting any younger."

I punched his shoulder as we went into the locker room. "Thanks, pal."

Derrick opened a locker saying, "I'm afraid to ask, but you hear anything on the Fisherman?"

"Nothing. I'm trying to keep my cool, but I'm about to lose it."

"Why don't you go to Gesso, tell him Mrs. Pearson is going to go to the press about the lack of action."

"That's the best idea you've ever had."

After the workout, Derrick went to shower. Not one for public showering, I headed for the sunshine. I stepped outside and pulled my phone out.

Gesso answered his cell on the first ring. "Frank, what's going on?"

"I wanted to give you a heads-up."

"On what?"

"The Pearson case. The mother, Connie Pearson, is frustrated, and she's threatening to go to the media about the lack of progress."

"I figured sooner or later it would happen."

"You know Mary Ann and I are close to her, and if you could give me something to give her, I might be able to convince her to hold off."

"I wish I had something, but . . ."

His voice trailed off.

"What's going on?"

"I hate to say it, but we can't locate Ruiz, and we've gotten word he's in the wind."

My chest tightened. "What?"

"We hear he skipped into Mexico."

"How the hell did that happen?"

"He was spooked."

Blood pounded in my ears. "This is unacceptable. It's a disaster."

"The DEA is working on locating him through their contacts."

"I got to go."

Hands on my knees, I drew in several deep breaths. A passerby stopped, asking, "Are you all right, sir?"

I STORMED INTO THE KITCHEN. "They blew it!"

Mary Ann said, "What are you talking about?"

"They let the Fisherman get away. He's in Mexico."

"Oh my God. How did that happen?"

"I have ideas."

"He had to have help. You think he was tipped off?"

"Definitely."

"By whom? The DEA or someone in the sheriff's department?"

"I hope like hell it wasn't the sheriff's office."

"Who told you?"

"Gesso. An informant said Ruiz ran, and the DEA confirmed he was in Mexico."

"If they have a bead on him, they can get the Mexicans to grab him, and we can get him extradited."

"Good luck with that. Besides, he's probably in Colombia by now."

"When Connie finds out, she's going to be devastated."

"I have to do something."

"What are you going to do?"

"I don't know, but I can't just sit here."

"Did you forget you're retired?"

"No, but —"

"And that Ruiz is out of the country?"

"We're supposed to just sit here and take this crap?"

"We've put our time in, it's up to the next crew to do something about it."

"That's bullshit. Everybody has a responsibility to do what they can."

"And you have a responsibility to our family. You did more than your part, now it's our time to enjoy the rest of our lives."

"How the hell am I going to enjoy myself when our kids are getting picked off one by one?"

"Stop being so dramatic, will you?"

"I'm not being dramatic. Something has to be done about this, and if they're not going to, I have to."

"Here we go again. You're the only one who can save the world."

I wagged my head and said, "I'm going for a walk."

BACK IN THE GARAGE, I stripped off my sneakers and went into the house. Mary Ann was on a raft floating around the pool. I ducked into the den and made a call.

"Treasury Department."

"George Pembroke, please."

"Who shall I say is calling?"

"Frank Luca."

The call was passed through, and Pembroke said, "Frank, how are you?"

"Pretty good."

"You change your mind on helping out with the Wall Street investigation?"

"No, but there is something I have an interest in, given the right circumstances."

"And what would that be?"

"Taking down a drug cartel."

Pembroke chuckled. "You shoot for the moon, don't you?"

"Look, I think I've proven myself by finding two million nobody else could. That's why you reached out to me when I retired about going after financial crimes."

"Yes. What you did was incredible, and it caught my attention, but going after a cartel?"

"Going after drug money fits the bill better than anything I can think of."

"In conjunction with the DEA and Homeland Security, we're running several operations."

"And none of them are making a dent. If anything, more drugs are entering the country than ever before."

"It's a challenging arena, but we are having some success."

"Look, I think some of the measures you've instituted, like preventing the cartels from depositing large amounts of cash into the banking system, have worked, but they've adapted, using mules and other methods to get the cash out of the States and into South America."

"The newest generation of equipment is catching an increasing amount of cash at airports."

"They've already changed tactics; my bet is they're using the border."

"Our intelligence suggests they may be using seaborne options."

"I'd look at what you have and see if there is anything actionable, but my initial focus would be concentrated on the surface crossings."

"I'm uncertain whether another operation in this area is warranted."

"For me, this one is personal, I've lost two young men who meant a lot to me from drugs. I'd really appreciate a green light."

Pembroke hesitated before saying, "I'm not discounting your attachment, but if you recall the situation I mentioned about a financial group I wanted your help with?"

"The hedge fund one?"

"Yes. I don't want to make it a quid pro quo, but if you agree to work on that one, I could find a way to authorize this."

"Tell me a little bit about that case. Who and what is the target?'

"The firm is Adams Capital Management. It's a hedge fund of hedge funds, and there are, shall we say, whispers of impropriety. We don't want to have another Madoff-type event."

"It's a Ponzi scheme?"

"We believe so, but possibly on a scale that would make Madoff look like a lemonade stand."

"I don't know much about the finance world."

"You don't have to be a wizard. It's better you're not from the Treasury. Plus, you're a New Yorker, maybe we can attach you to a team of auditors up there and have you look around. If there's anything, you'll pick up the scent."

"If I agree to do it, it'd have to be after I'm done with the drug case."

"That's fine."

"If we can come to an agreement . . ."

"We can offer ten percent of whatever you discover or confiscate."

"I'm not referring to the money. No disrespect intended, but for me to do the investigation I want, I'd need complete autonomy and authority, as well as access to the surveillance tools the government has."

"Our mission of safeguarding the economic security of the US provides us with broad authority, and, combined with executive orders that came out of the war on terror, we shouldn't encounter an issue. We also have some of the best assets in the federal government, and if needed, can marshal resources from other agencies."

I wanted to say that for the tens of billions being spent on resources, what they were missing were results. "I'd need full access to them and any intelligence you have. I'd report only to you, but I would need the authority to check into individual financial records, internet—"

"We use the Patriot Act as coverage for those type of searches."

"I don't know the legal terms, but I'd need the powers of an inspector general or a special prosecutor, but limited to investigating, not prosecuting."

"I'll speak to our counsel and draft a memorandum of understanding."

Chapter Sixteen

He said, "What's the story with the secrecy?"

"You have to promise to hear me out."

"What's going on, Frank? You're scaring me."

"There's nothing to be afraid of. Come on, let's walk."

"You remember how you used to tell me to get to the point?"

I smiled.

Derrick said, "Spit it out already."

I took a deep breath and said, "I going to work with the Feds to bring down the cartel selling drugs here."

"Have you lost your mind? Bring down a cartel? How the hell do you think you're going to do that?"

"By going after their money. The biggest problem drug dealers have is the cash. We disrupt that flow, and we put a serious hurt on them."

"Number one, it's not going to be easy, and number two, there's a good chance you'll end up dead."

We stepped aside to let a golf cart carrying beachgoers pass. "Sure, it'll be tough, but I have an idea, and it's never been done before."

"What is it?"

"Right now, they look for cash being smuggled out of the country, but when they find it, they confiscate it and arrest the mule carrying it. Then they try to get the person to talk, offering them a deal."

"Standard operating procedure."

"Right, except it hardly ever works."

"Why is that? Everybody wants to save their ass when they get caught."

"They're afraid of the cartels. If they talk, they know they'll be killed, along with their family. So, they keep their mouths closed. And if they get convicted, the maximum penalty is only five years. Most of the time they don't serve all five, making it an easy decision to keep quiet."

"And what's your plan?"

I gave him the rundown.

"I have to admit, it's a good idea, but do you realize how dangerous this is?"

"It's not dangerous if you're careful. Look, there's a couple of otters." I pointed to the creatures who were playing with each other in Clam Bay.

"Cool. But don't fool yourself on the danger, Frank."

"My eyes are wide open."

"They better be. I can't believe the Feds are going to let you do this."

"Well, I had to agree to help on that Wall Street case they wanted me on."

"Which one?"

"Adams Capital Management. It's run by Jay Adams, who was a big shot at the Treasury Department."

"So, you scratch my itch, and I'll scratch yours."

"Kind of. So, do you want to work with me on this?"

"No, thank you."

I knew money influenced most people, including Derrick.

"There's a lot of money to be made here. The agreement provides for ten percent of whatever we seize: cold hard cash, bank accounts, homes, whatever."

He shook his head. "Lynn would go nuts if I jumped back in."

"It'd easily be in the hundreds of millions. Our end could be forty or fifty million. Tax free."

"I can't believe Mary Ann was okay with you doing this."

She didn't know yet. "She'll come around."

"She must have given you hell."

"It's something I feel I have to do."

"It'd be something if it worked."

"You in or what?"

"The money is very tempting."

I wanted to ask where the danger had gone but said, "I'm leaving for Washington the day after tomorrow. Let me know what you decide."

MARY ANN THREW her hands in the air. "I can't believe you're doing this. And you didn't think to talk it over with me beforehand?"

"You know I've been itching to do something. I can't just lay around the house."

"We're taking Spanish lessons, and you go to the gym. Plus, we do a lot of things, like going to the beach."

"It's not enough."

"I asked you a hundred times to travel. Didn't we have a good time when we went to Italy?"

"It was great, but we can't be traveling all the time."

"All the time? We went away once since you retired."

"We'll go again. Wherever you want. Pick somewhere and start planning it. We'll go right after this is over."

"How long is this going to take?"

"Not long. A month or two."

She put her hands on her hips. "You have to be honest with me. How dangerous is this operation?"

"I told you, it isn't. I'm just quarterbacking this from an office."

"Are you sure?"

"Absolutely. And when it's over, we'll take a nice, long trip."

"Okay. So, where do you want to go?"

"Wherever you want."

"I always wanted to go to Lake Como or Venice, and the Amalfi Coast is supposed to be gorgeous. We could probably do both on the same trip."

"Check it out and see if it makes sense."

"I think there's a train from Venice to Naples, which is close to Positano. And maybe we can go to Capri."

"Look into it. I have to call Derrick."

Dialing his number, a bad feeling that the travel trade-off was manipulation, settled on me. Derrick answered. "Hey, Frank."

"Did you decide what you want to do?"

"I'm on the fence. Lynn isn't thrilled with the idea."

"She'll come around. Mary Ann is on board."

"I don't know, she's talking about having another baby."

"At your age?"

"Lynn is younger, and as I recall, you were a year older than me when you had Jessie."

"You're right, sorry."

"I'm not sure I want another kid, but I'll lose that battle."

I held back from saying, 'Tell her you'll agree in exchange for joining me,' and instead said, "You'll work it out. I'm leaving on the United seven a.m. flight tomorrow. I told Pembroke to have a ticket waiting for you. If you make it, great—if not, I understand."

Part Two

Washington, D.C

Chapter Seventeen

After hopping in a cab, we drove down Pennsylvania Avenue. It felt surreal being in a city plastered all over the news but one I hadn't been to since a middle-school trip.

Believing the combination of money and boredom would entice Derrick to join me had been a miscalculation. Rolling around my adage that you never really knew someone, I realized I was in this alone. If this mission was going to succeed, avoiding mistakes was going to play a major role.

We pulled up to a neoclassic building with massive, fluted columns. It looked familiar.

The driver said, "This is you."

"Oh, I'm trying to place the building. I've never been here, but I kind of remember it."

"It's the one on the back of a ten-dollar bill."

"Right." I paid and took my time taking the steps to the Treasury Department.

Seated on the couch in his office, Pembroke was talking to a rail-thin man. The Treasury chief stood. "Frank, it's good to see you."

I reached for his hand. "Same here."

"Frank Luca, meet Romney French."

Suit hanging off him, French stood, extending a bony hand. "Good to meet you."

"I asked Romney to join us. He's in charge of HSI, Homeland Security's Investigation unit."

"Okay. I thought this was going to be a Treasury operation."

Pembroke said, "Considering the scope of what you're going for, counsel advised it has to be multi-agency. This would cover jurisdictional issues and comply with existing protocols covering special agents."

"I understand, but to have any chance at succeeding, the fewer people involved, the better."

Romney said, "Point taken, Mr. Luca, but HSI has broad legal authority to conduct transnational criminal investigations. As a special agent, you'd have as close to carte blanche as there is."

Pembroke said, "It'd be another agency to draw resources from, and as Romney said, their legal authority is as broad as it gets."

There was no question that having the legal protection and authority was a grand slam, but it irked me that Pembroke had brought them in without talking to me first. Was this the way Washington worked?

"All right, I understand."

We discussed the goals of the investigation, deciding to give it the code name of Project Omega. I liked the name; Omega was the last letter in the Greek alphabet, and it correlated with cash being the end result of drug dealing.

After meeting with Pembroke and Romney French, I was ushered into an office to be sworn in as an agent of the Treasury Department, the Drug Enforcement Agency, and Homeland Security's Investigations unit.

Repeating the various oaths, seeds of doubt crept in. But rather than water them, I forced them aside.

Then it was on to the registration process, where my picture was taken and ID's issued. Housekeeping done, Pembroke said, "I'd like to get you down to surveillance before meeting with the DEA."

"Sounds good."

I was shown into a cavernous room whose walls were covered in video screens. The displays were grouped in threes, each section monitored by someone wearing headphones and sitting behind a curved desk.

The words just tumbled out of my mouth. "Man, this looks like something you see on TV, like a giant situation room."

"It is special. I'll let Mr. Sears, who's responsible for this division, know you're here."

It was quiet for a room with dozens of people at work.

A barrel-chested man approached. Shoulders back, he had a military air about him. He stuck his hand out. "Mr. Luca, Mike Sears, I'm the head of the Civilian Recon Intelligence Branch."

We shook hands and Sears said, "Mr. Pembroke was clear on extending every asset we have to ensure the success of your mission."

"Thank you. I'll try not to get in the way of the work you're doing."

He swept his arm. "There's a tremendous amount of technology in this room, and you're going to need assistance in navigating it."

"No doubt, I'd appreciate the help."

He turned around. "Bradley! Mr. Luca is here."

A man in his thirties with messy hair and dark-blue glasses hurried over. The poster child for a techie extended his hand. "Cary Bradley."

After talking for ten minutes, Sears brought us to a half-moon-shaped desk in front of a group of wall-mounted monitors.

"You can work from here. I've commandeered four screens

for your sole use. Bradley knows every inch of this place. He'll show you how it all works. Bradley's been assigned to you for as long as you need him."

I thanked him, and Sears left. I said, "Is it okay to call you Cary?"

He smiled. "Around here, everyone calls me Bradley."

"Bradley it is. So, you're the technology wizard?"

"I've been here ten years and basically know all there is to know about the equipment and our capabilities."

"Good. I'm not so hot with the tech stuff."

"No worries, I can do it in my sleep."

"Is that right?"

He nodded. "It's nothing magical. In fact, things are kind of boring around here."

"Really? With all that's going on?"

"It's super-routine. By the way, Mr. Sears never told me what you are looking to accomplish."

"We want to observe the border crossings into Mexico. Mr. Pembroke told us there is a direct contact between the Home-land Security officers at the border and this command center."

"We have the ability, but the southern border is just under two thousand miles long. What crossing or crossings do you want to monitor?"

"It's my understanding the largest land crossing is the San Ysidro one."

"It is. San Ysidro handles more than seventy thousand northbound vehicles a day."

"How many of those are inspected?"

"A tiny fraction. We rely on intelligence to focus on certain transports."

"That isn't working too well, is it?"

He looked over his glasses but said nothing.

"I'm interested in the southbound traffic."

"Into Mexico?"

"Exactly."

"Okay. The busiest would be El Chaparral. San Ysidro used to have two-way traffic, but the southbound lanes of Highway Five were relocated when new inspection facilities were built."

"You do know your stuff. Can we look at that crossing?"

Bradley rolled a chair to a keyboard and made a couple of strokes. "Here's an aerial view, along with three ground feeds."

Presto, the screens were filled with mile-long lines of cars and trucks inching their way to the crossing facilities. Uniformed officers walked along the lanes, talking to drivers and checking paperwork.

I said, "That's impressive." I studied the lines of traffic. "Is there an agent or two with the best nose?"

Bradley looked up from the keyboard. "I'm sorry?"

"Somebody with great instincts. Someone who believes smuggling is going on and turns out to be right."

"When there is suspected contraband, the vehicle is pulled out of the lane and visually inspected. If that raises further suspicion, it can be sent for a Vacis exam."

"Vacis, that's a huge x-ray machine, right?"

"Yes. But as far as the agents go, I don't know offhand who has the best record southbound, but I can find out."

"Good. If you don't mind, get two names and we'll go from there."

"I'm on it."

Bradley went to his station and picked up the phone. I scanned the room. Were we keeping an eye on everything? There had to be at least two hundred screens being watched by fifty or sixty technicians.

It was a ping-pong match between assurance and creepiness.

Bradley scurried over. "We have two officers with seizure rates thirty percent higher than average."

"That's what I'm looking for. Who are they?"

"Blake Gulch, they call him Mad Dog, and Ann Florenze."

"Are they on duty now?"

"They sure are." He pointed to a pair of monitors sitting below a large display. "Florenze is walking lane two, and Gulch is working the fifth. I'll zero in."

He tapped a keyboard, and the large screen displayed an image of a small-framed woman. Her ponytail stuck out the back of her baseball cap. Hand on her hip, she was pointing to a dark sedan.

Bradley said, "Good timing; she's pulling someone out of the line."

Was it weapons, drugs, or money?

I said, "Can we see who is in the car?"

He nodded, moving the camera to the driver. "He's alone."

Bearded, the driver had a prison tattoo snaking around his neck. He was talking to Florenze.

Bradley said, "He's trying to sweet-talk his way out, but once you've been tagged, there's no stopping the protocol."

"From what I recall, half of the seizures are firearms and weapons, right?"

"It's higher than that, around sixty percent, followed by bulk currency, which runs about twenty-five percent. The rest is all kinds of contraband, including stolen goods and the occasional fugitive."

I thought of the Fisherman, who fled to Mexico. How many other killers left the country either openly in a car or hidden in a trunk?

Florenze pulled her radio out and spoke into it. She pointed at the driver and then toward an area to the right.

The sedan followed Florenze's instruction, rolling slowly to the side. I leaned toward the screen as two agents met up with Florenze.

Chapter Eighteen

With Florenze watching, an agent opened the car door, and the man behind the wheel got out. The driver put his hands on the roof of the vehicle and the agent frisked him.

A canine unit came into view. The handler steered the dog toward the driver. Man's best friend sniffed and moved away. The canine officer circled the auto with the dog. Florenze reached into the car.

The trunk popped open. A dog sat inches from the rear bumper. Florenze walked around the auto and lifted the trunk lid.

Her arm shot into the air.

"Can you zoom in any further?"

"Let me see."

The trunk was filled with long, wooden boxes.

I said, "Looks like it might be weapons."

Two officers converged on the driver and handcuffed him.

"I wonder how many vehicles Florenze stops a day, and out of them, how many have contraband."

Bradley picked up the phone. "I can find out."

As Bradley talked on the phone, I watched a flatbed truck load the sedan.

He hung up. "The average number of vehicles pulled out of line every day is forty."

"And how many have issues?"

"A dozen a day."

"That means there's a hell of a lot of contraband pouring over the border every day."

Bradley nodded. "The focus is on what's coming into the country, not what's leaving."

"That's understandable, and I mean no disrespect, but we're not doing anywhere near enough of a good job stopping drugs and illegals from getting in."

"We can't stop every car. You know Texas did that, and the lines were all the way to Austin. It took six to eight hours to cross."

"If it were up to me, I'd deploy as much manpower as possible and send the message that we're done with letting the cartels poison Americans."

"It's not practical."

"I didn't say it was practical, but it'd work. You know, when Reagan was president, a DEA agent was kidnapped. Mexico wasn't cooperating in finding him and stonewalled us at every turn. So Reagan shut down the border. To get their attention."

"I didn't know that. What happened?"

"They cooperated, but, unfortunately, they killed the agent, and the trail led all the way to the highest offices in Mexico."

"There is a ton of corruption in Mexico."

"No doubt about it."

"That's what has me worried. We've got to find a way to combat that."

"We're increasing the use of technology to catch some of the smuggling, but the cartels keep changing tactics."

"That's okay, two can play that game."

"I'm not sure I understand. What are you referring to?"

"My plan is to attack the problem from a different angle."

His face brightened. "You have my attention. How exactly?"

Sears appeared out of nowhere. "How are we doing here? Is Bradley taking good care of you?"

"Yes. He's been extremely helpful."

He gestured toward the screens. "What do we have here?"

Bradley said, "A possible weapons seizure, sir."

Sears shook his head. "Hard to imagine any more violence taking place across the border."

I said, "The cartels are better armed than the Mexican police."

Sears said, "Well, part of our mission is to prevent more weapons from getting into their hands. I've made a request for an increase in the inspection ratio, and catches like this bolster the chances the administration will approve it."

I said, "Why wouldn't they?"

"Anything that slows commerce down is a tough sell."

"Maybe we ought to put together a truckload of corpses, overdosed kids, and send it to the White House."

Sears smiled. "Believe me, I've thought of pulling similar stunts to get the attention of the political class. But business interests and their lobbyists have tremendous influence on how we operate."

Bradley said, "And the powers that be are worried about how the Mexican authorities react to our efforts; they say we can't infringe on their sovereignty."

"They're infringing on ours by allowing drugs to flow into America."

Sears said, "They claim it's a demand issue, and though I hate to admit it, they have a point."

"Well, I'm not going to wait to see who wins that debate. I'm here to take action."

Sears said, "We're here to support your efforts. Whatever you need, we'll provide."

"I appreciate that."

"It's my duty. There's a meeting I must attend. I'll check in with you later."

I watched Sears walk out of the room and said to Bradley, "Where do you stand on the responsibility issue?"

"My opinion doesn't play a role; I took an oath to serve my country, and that is exactly what I'll do."

"So, you think it's the users who are the problem."

"It's a complicated issue, sir."

"Please, we're going to be working closely together. I'd really prefer being called Frank."

He flashed a grin. "Frank it is."

"I'm an all-in type of guy. I have to know you have my back."

"I figured that."

"What made you think that?"

"When we heard Mr. Pembroke had authorized the mission, I did some research."

"And what did you find out?"

"You are ex-homicide and had retired after locating a cache of drug money that had been hidden for years."

"And what did that tell you?"

"You're determined and principled."

"I'll take that as a compliment."

Bradley looked at his shoes.

I said, "What?"

"Nothing."

"If we're going to work together, we have to be honest with each other."

"It's just that, exciting as this may be, it kind of feels like Don Quixote."

"The story about the dreamer who chased windmills?"

He nodded. "Yes, I mean it's not exact, but—"

"You either think it's hopeless or I'm crazy."

"I'm not saying you're crazy, it's just difficult to make a difference."

"It sure is, but what's the alternative? Doing nothing?"

Bradley shrugged and I asked where the bathroom was.

"I'll be right back, and then we'll get to work, even if you think it's a waste of time."

Turning around before he could respond, I walked away.

I needed to think and take a leak. Sitting on the throne and tickling my abdomen to get a flow going, I wondered whether I should ask Sears for someone else. Upending a cartel was tough enough. Why make it harder by working with someone who didn't believe in what we were doing?

Washing up, I resolved to press ahead. If Bradley got in the way, I'd go to Sears. No, I wasn't playing here; I'd go straight to Pembroke and get the help I needed.

Bradley was sitting at his desk, scrolling through his phone. I rolled a chair over. "Are you ready?"

He pocketed his phone. "Yes."

"Here's my plan; I need to talk to Florenze. We're going to need her cooperation."

"What about the other agent, the one they call Mad Dog? You want to speak to him as well?"

"No. We'll work with Florenze."

"I'll reach out to her."

"Do it using Zoom or whatever you use for video."

"We use Google Meet."

"Whatever."

"Can I ask what we're looking for? Is it weapons?"

"No, cash."

He smiled. "Interesting."

"We're looking for large volumes of cash being moved by the cartels. Specifically, the La Familia cartel."

"They're very dangerous."

"Set up the video call. I've got a meeting with the DEA, and I'll see you later."

Chapter Nineteen

I waited in reception until the chief analyst for South America, the region the DEA called the Southern Cone, came out to get me.

Jack Pierce was fifty. Both in age and waist size. He waddled toward his office, and I followed.

Pierce squeezed into his chair. "I hear you're from Florida."

"I'm originally from New York City, but I moved down to Southwest Florida twenty-something years ago."

"Do you like it?"

"Yes, never been happier."

"We talked about moving there when I retire, but I don't know about the heat."

"You get used to it, but nothing is for everyone."

"That's true. So, I'm told you're looking for background on the La Familia cartel."

"Anything you can tell me would be appreciated."

Leaning back, he said, "You're going after a tough crowd."

"I'm aware."

He fingered his tie. "Cartels are brutal organizations, but La Familia is an unusually violent one. The group has a quasi-religious tone to it, and its leaders describe the beheadings and assassinations they carry out as divine justice."

"Divine justice?"

"That's what they call it. Recently, they tossed five severed heads onto the dance floor of a nightclub along with a note. They claimed they didn't kill for money, saying they didn't kill women or the innocent, only those who deserve to die. They called it divine justice."

"Interesting way to frame it."

Rolling a pen between his thumb and forefinger, Pierce said, "La Familia is cultlike. The leaders make members read a book called *Wild Dreams*. It's written by an American."

I jotted down the title. "I'll take a look at it."

"The founder of the cartel believed that every man must have a battle to fight, a beauty to rescue, and an adventure to live."

"He really tried dressing up his criminal enterprise."

"It's an easy sell when you're uneducated and don't have many employment options."

"They're not that close to the border. How did they become such a player in the US drug market?"

He pointed to a large map hanging on the wall. "They started on the southwestern coast of Mexico, right on the Pacific Ocean. Like other cartels, they imported drugs from Colombia and Peru via sea into the port city of Lazaro. Then, they moved into methamphetamines in a major way. They partnered up with the Sinaloa cartel for distribution, but those alliances never last too long."

"When did they get into fentanyl?"

"A couple of years ago. With the experience they had making meth, they put up a significant number of labs to process chemicals from China into fentanyl. Most of them are in the highlands of the Sierra Madre." He jabbed a finger toward the map. "It's the green area, by the red pin, north of Sinaloa."

"What kind of efforts are being made to shut down the labs?"

"We try, but La Familia is heavily armed and controls the area. Anytime a raid is planned they're tipped off."

"By the Mexican police or . . ." I let my voice trail off.

"Operations of that type are large-scale in nature and involve a lot of people."

"Including the DEA."

"We have a dedicated group, but nobody ever said we were perfect."

I stuffed what I really thought back in my mouth. "Perfection doesn't exist."

"Truth. Another unusual thing about La Familia is they insist that their members don't use drugs."

"They know that crap screws with your judgment along with your health."

"La Familia is deeply involved in politics in their home state of Michoacan, and as a result, legally have tremendous influence over large swaths of the area."

"Following the Pablo Escobar playbook."

"True, but not with the 'in your face' brash opulence of Escobar. The days of *Miami Vice* are a thing of the past. La Familia is relatively low-key. They're not driving Ferraris and living large."

"They don't want to attract attention."

He nodded. "And they're disciplined about it. La Familia puts out a manual telling its members how to blend in. They even tell them how many barbecues a month to hold with their neighbors."

I shook my head. "Great, make it harder to find the bastards. What's the DEA's estimate on the number of members they have in the States?"

"That's impossible to guess, but safe to say it's in the thousands."

"Two thousand, five or more?"

"On the lower end."

"It has to be more. During Project Coronado, the Feds arrested over three hundred members in a couple of states."

"That was a successful operation, and we followed it up with Project Delirium where we arrested over two hundred-plus La Familia members operating in a dozen states. The Mexicans picked up almost two thousand of them as well, on their side of the border. We put a hurt on them."

"Yet, the volumes of drugs coming over the border have increased."

"That's not a fair picture of the situation. We've got a two-thousand-mile border and—"

Standing, I said, "Thanks for the background on La Familia. I appreciate it."

"If you need something, I'll try my best to help."

Extending my hand I said, "Thanks, again."

Pierce took my hand. "Anytime."

As I tried to break the shake, he looked me in the eye. "You be careful now, these guys are as dangerous as they come."

I CLOSED my laptop and called Mary Ann.

"Hi, Frank, how is it going?"

"Good. I had a busy day."

"You're not tired?"

"No, I'm actually pumped up."

"Really?"

"Yeah, you have to see the surveillance room here. The place is huge and there are screens everywhere. I had no idea there was so much tech involved, it's incredible."

She chuckled. "Tech and you? How are you going to survive?"

"Very funny, wise guy. But seriously, they gave me a kid, Bradley, who's amazing. I bet he can tap a couple of keys, and I could watch you do your laps."

"That good, huh?"

"Yes, he's a really smart, nerdy type. He went to George-town for computer science and knows how to use all the tools they have."

"That's a big plus."

"It's incredible. We watched a border agent nail a guy with a trunk full of weapons that he was trying to smuggle into Mexico."

"Wow."

"And in real time. After that, I had a meeting with the DEA on the cartel that the Fisherman is connected to."

"How'd that go?"

A call came in. It was a restricted number. I swiped it away. "Good. It's the La Familia cartel, and these thugs are a different breed. I was just reading a book their members are required to read."

"Sounds more like a cult than a cartel."

"With a self-help component. The book talks about embracing a life of courage, adventure, and freedom. It says you have to take risks to find true meaning."

"Running drugs certainly rings the risk bell."

"Amen."

"How long do you think you're going to be up there?"

The restricted caller tried again. I swiped it away. "I'll know better tomorrow."

"Did you eat?"

There was a knock on the door. "I ordered room service. In fact, they just came to the door."

"Go eat, we'll talk later."

A young man set the tray on the table. I gave him a five and closed the door. My cell rang again. It was the restricted number. Maybe it was someone from one of the agencies.

"Hello?"

A gruff voice said, "Go back to Florida."

"Who is this?"

"You're going to get hurt if you keep it up."

"Who the hell is this?"

"You've been warned."

"Don't threaten—"

The line went dead.

Chapter Twenty

I pulled out the business card Sears had given me with his cell number listed. I punched in the area code but exited the call. Sears was highly regarded, but he'd ask someone else to hunt down the caller.

There was a leak in either Homeland Security, the Treasury Department, or the DEA. I'd call Florida in the morning and ask Gesso to check it out.

I'd come in close contact with Pembroke, Sears, Pierce, and Bradley. They knew why I was here, but how many others had they told?

Pembroke had tried to recruit me for various projects he was running. Why would he undermine me? It made no sense, plus he was at the Treasury Department. Money laundering was in his wheelhouse, but the threat had come right out of the gate. What were the chances he had a direct connection to the La Familia cartel?

I sat on the bed reviewing every person I'd talked to today. Just the fact Pierce worked for the DEA and knew a lot about La Familia made him a suspect. And he'd warned me the cartel was dangerous.

Pierce hadn't asked about my plans. Was that purposefully? And the Fort Myers DEA, innocently or not, had probably tipped off the Fisherman, leading to Jimmy's murder. Was the DEA culture one of betrayal? I'd try to stay clear of them.

Sears ran the surveillance division. The cartels had to know the unit existed and who worked there. Sears had an impeccable record. He didn't know everything about my plans, but he knew it involved the border, and that meant it would impact the cartels.

As I rolled thoughts around, Bradley came into focus. Most leaks weren't from the top but came from day-to-day operators. Bradley was a techie, and we had discussed my plans. He also had the technical skill to send an untraceable signal.

How the hell was Project Omega going to be successful if it was undermined from the inside?

AFTER STAYING in the shower an extra five minutes, I called Gesso and asked him to check the number of the caller. He sent the Verizon release form, and I completed it.

Riding in a cab along K Street, I couldn't shake the feeling Washington was worse than I'd imagined. Getting out of the taxi, I went to my temporary work quarters.

Sears was on the phone. I told his secretary I had to see him and waited for him.

His desk was framed by the flags of the United States and the Treasury Department. "Come in. I have an extraordinarily busy day today. The Michigan governor is in town, and she wants a dog and pony show."

"This won't take long."

"Sit."

"That's okay."

"What is on your mind?"

"I received a threatening phone call last night."

"From whom?"

"They didn't identify themselves and the number was restricted."

"A burner phone?"

"Yes. I'd like to replace Bradley."

"You believe he leaked something?"

"I don't know."

"Being cautious is the right move. Give me an hour or so. I want to be sure I choose the right replacement."

"I'd appreciate it if they're as good with the technology as Bradley is."

"No worries, I'll get it covered."

"Thank you."

I headed over to where, Bradley, headphones on, was typing on his keyboard. I tapped his shoulder, and he pulled the headgear around his neck. "Good morning."

"Morning. Look, uh, I asked Sears to get me someone else to work with."

"Really?"

I nodded.

He shrugged. "Okay, whatever you want."

My gut screamed. It wasn't Bradley. He wasn't defensive at all.

"Don't you want to know why?"

"I figured it was the Don Quixote reference. I shouldn't have said that."

I rolled a chair over, looked him in the eye, and whispered, "I received a threatening phone call last night."

Behind his blue-framed glasses, his eyes widened. "From who?"

"I don't know."

He smiled. "Wait, you don't think it was me?"

"No, but there's a leak in here or the DEA."

"It's got to be the DEA. Everyone here has the highest clearance you can get without going to top-secret."

It was useless to get into how often clearances were breached. "Do you have contacts with or know someone with contacts to any cartel?"

He pulled his chin in. "Of course not! How can you even ask that?"

I stood. "Do you want to work with me?"

"Yes. Is this a weird test or something?"

"Set up the Google Meet with Florenze, but don't do it here. Find a conference room or something. I want privacy."

"Can I ask you something?"

"Sure."

"What's driving you on this case? You're being threatened, and you're still going full steam ahead."

I told him about Steve and Jimmy, and he said, "Wow. I understand now. You're a good man, Frank."

"Trust me, I've got plenty of pimples. Now, set up that call."

"You've got it."

"I'll be right back. I'm going to tell Sears we're staying together."

Chapter Twenty-One

My cell vibrated. It was Gesso. "Hey, Sarge. What did you find out?"

"It was a burner phone, but the strange things is, it looks like one that was distributed into South America."

"That makes sense."

"The numbers assigned were either out of Chile or Peru."

"Is there anything on the activation?"

"Yeah, that's the funny thing, it was activated in Detroit."

"Detroit?"

"Yes. It could be a criminal gang buying in bulk from South America or—"

"I know who it was."

"You do? Who?"

"The La Familia cartel controls a corridor along Route 75, all the way into Detroit."

"Frank, you better watch your ass. These cartel guys will come after you in a heartbeat."

"This isn't Mexico. These bastards can't do whatever the hell they like."

"Don't take the risk, Frank. I'm telling you, get out of there and back into the sunshine. You did your time."

"Don't worry, I'm not taking chances."

"Really? You've been gone a day and you're already being threatened."

"They're trying to scare me off."

"If it were me, I'd listen."

"Who are you kidding? Getting a call like I did would fire you up."

"Maybe in the old days, but neither of us are young bucks. Leave it to the next generation."

"Right. The next generation is what has me worried."

"You have Mary Ann to worry about."

"I'm in Washington, the nation's capital, not a Colombian jungle."

"Okay, Frank. I'm just saying be careful. You have a lot to lose."

"Don't worry, I'll be home in a couple of days."

A HALF DOZEN empty coffee cups littered the conference room table. I moved one aside and pulled out a chair next to the one Bradley had settled in.

The room had no windows and was small. Claustrophobia had me eyeing the door.

"Are you okay?"

I nodded.

"Here we go."

Google Meet's logo melted away, and the petite face of Ann Florenze filled the screen.

"Hello, Miss Florenze. I'm Special Agent Frank Luca. I want to thank you for taking this call."

"No problem. I understand you're heading up a southbound

project."

"Yes. We'd like your help in ensuring its success."

"Be glad to. How can I help?"

"You have an excellent record picking out who's trying to scoot over the border with weapons and currency. Our particular focus is finding cash being smuggled into Mexico."

"We're focused on that already."

"Yes, but we're going to approach this a bit differently than you've been used to."

"I'm all ears, sir."

"Drug money is what were after, but we're not going to seize it."

"I don't understand, sir."

"We're going to follow the money. I want to disrupt the banking system they're using to launder the money. The banks helping these cartels have got to pay a price, and it's going to be a high one."

"You're going to fine them?"

"They have too much money for fines to be effective. The Treasury unit that deals with foreign assets is going to sanction them, preventing them from using the banking system. They'll be cut off; no banks will deal with them. It'll send a powerful message not to do business with the cartels."

Crow's-feet wrinkles highlighted her almond-shaped eyes as she smiled. "That sounds interesting. How do you want things handled?"

"Did you get the package we sent?"

She held up a bag. "Yes, they're trackers."

"Good. When you feel someone might have contraband, I'd like you to run them through a Vacis machine and check the x-ray. If there's a substantial amount of cash, you stick a tracker on the vehicle and let them go. We'll take it from there."

"Any particular place?"

"Wherever you can hide it without being seen."

"Okay. What next?"

"We're going to be watching your shift, and when you pull someone out of the line, Bradley is going to tap into the Vacis feed."

"What if there are weapons or other contraband, not cash?"

"Do as you would normally do. We're only interested in cash, large amounts of it."

"If it appears to be a borderline amount, what should we do?"

"Let it go. If it's some sort of test run, I want them to be as confident as possible."

"All right. But weapons we can seize?"

"Absolutely."

She nodded. "Okay, let's see how this goes."

"And, uh, Miss Florenze . . ."

"Yes?"

"It's important that you don't tip off the driver when you find something."

"I'm a poker player, sir."

"Good. And one more thing."

"What's that?"

"You should know that we're not going to track the first couple ones you find with cash. Let's say the first three. We'll let them go wherever they're heading to. That way they'll let their guard down a bit. So don't put any trackers on those cars."

"That makes sense."

"If we have to wait a couple of days, that's okay. We're playing the long game here."

"Understood, sir."

"I'm sure you realize the need to keep the circle small on this operation. Don't tell anyone what we're up to."

"My lips are sealed."

"Great, let's get to work."

Bradley ended the video call. "Maybe I shouldn't be asking,

but why did you tell her not to tag the first three she found trying to smuggle cash?"

"Because I don't trust anyone."

"I don't understand."

"You said you can track a vehicle with satellites and drones, right?"

"I sure can."

"Well, we're going follow the first car carrying cash."

"We're not going to use GPS on them?"

"No. This is between you and me."

He nodded slowly. "You're fooling our own people?" Then he broke into a wide smile. "This sounds like fun."

Chapter Twenty-Two

Staring at a monitor, I pointed to a sky-blue car. "Zoom in on that beat-up Toyota."

Bradley moved the joystick and tapped a key. "Here you are."

I leaned into the screen. An old lady was behind the wheel.

"That's okay, zoom out." Usually, my instincts were good, but that was the third car I'd been wrong about.

I kept my eyes on Florenze as she slowly walked down a lane of cars. She looked at the Toyota and continued past it.

I stood and arched my back. "You want a coffee?"

"Nope, I'm good."

"I'll be right back."

I took two steps and Bradley said, "Hang on." He waved me over. "Looks like she may have one."

Head shaking, Florenze was standing by the driver's door of a dirty, white van. She motioned for the driver to pull out of the line.

Bradley focused in. "It looks like he's refusing to pull over."

Looking over Bradley's shoulder, I said, "I wonder what he's got in the back of that van."

"I'm betting on machine guns."

As the van crept forward, Florenze radioed for help. She banged the side of the vehicle, but it continued to roll ahead. Three agents, carrying M14 rifles, rushed over. An officer in riot gear raised his weapon and walked in front of the van.

The man behind the wheel put his hands up. Florenze opened the driver's door, and an officer pulled the man out of the car.

"I don't know what these idiots think they're accomplishing."

They forced him to his knees and cuffed him. In a T-shirt and jeans, the driver was scrawny.

Traffic was diverted into another lane. Florenze opened the doors to the van.

I said, "What's in there?"

"It looks empty."

"That's crazy."

"Here come the dogs."

Two canine units approached the vehicle. They circled the van but didn't stop in any spot. One of the dogs was brought to the rear. Its handler tapped the floor of the vehicle, and the dog leapt in. Five seconds later, it jumped back down.

An agent got behind the wheel. Bradley said, "They're going to run it through the Vacis."

"Maybe there's a false bottom to the van and it's lined with cash."

Bradley navigated to the Vacis feed. "We've seen those numerous times."

An officer stopped a truck from advancing, and the van cut in front of it. It inched under the machine's arc. The screen's light-gray image showed the dark outline of the vehicle.

I leaned in. "It looks normal."

"It does."

"Can you get Florenze on the radio?"

"Sure." Bradley punched a number in and handed the handset to me.

"Agent Florenze, it's Frank Luca. We've been watching this van. What's going on with it?"

"It appears clean."

"Why did the driver resist?"

"He said his wife was in labor and he had to get back to Tijuana. I've heard that one before, but it looks like he was telling the truth."

"Good work. I hope he makes it in time."

"We'll get him on his way as soon as possible."

"Okay, let's get back to it."

I disconnected the call and told Bradley the driver's motive. "Poor guy almost got himself arrested."

"He could have gotten hurt."

"Every now and then, a suspect is telling the truth."

"It's got to be more often than that."

I snickered. "Not the first time. People always concoct some kind of story, thinking it will keep the heat off them, whether they did something or not."

"Yeah?"

"Definitely. Sometimes it's to keep something secret, like an affair or an unrelated crime, or to protect a family member. Trust me, it's endless."

"I guess so."

"I'm going for that coffee."

"Hold on, it looks like Florenze didn't waste any time."

I peered at the screen. The border agent was talking to someone in a burgundy-colored Buick SUV.

"Let me see the driver."

Bradley zeroed in. The woman behind the wheel looked to be in her early thirties. Dark-haired, she was frowning. She said something and put her hands on the wheel.

As the SUV pulled out of line, Florenze spoke into her radio.

Bradley said, "She's directing it to the Vacis."

Two trucks were in line ahead of the Buick. As the first truck rolled forward, an agent put his hand on the driver's door and opened it. The female behind the wheel of the Buick got out.

Wearing sneakers and shorts, she was no taller than Florenze. Another border agent stood beside her as a third agent got behind the wheel.

The SUV inched toward the upside-down, U-shaped x-ray machine.

"Tap into the feed."

"It's already open on another tab."

"I have a good feeling about this one."

Bradley smiled. "You've had a couple of hunches this morning, haven't you?"

He was busting my chops, which was a good sign. "Don't count me out."

I stared at the screen as the Buick entered the detection zone.

Bradley said, "Doesn't look like anything is in the passenger area."

"Hold on." I pointed at the screen. "What's that?"

Bradley zoomed in on a darkened area of a rear quarter panel. "Interesting."

Chapter Twenty-Three

"The resolution is going to degrade."

"I don't care."

The picture got bigger and grainy. Leaning in, I said, "It's cash. No doubt." I jabbed the screen. "You see it?"

"Yep. We got one. Let me check the other side."

I stood. "We have to tell Florenze to let her go."

Bradley reached for the radio.

I said, "Make sure she doesn't tip the driver off."

"She knows to let the first ones through."

"We have to be sure. I don't want them screwing this up."

Bradley got in touch with Florenze.

The Buick was driven outside the range of the Vacis and released.

I softened my voice. "Make sure the satellite feed is only on the laptop."

Bradley tapped away. The screen filled with a fifty-thousand-foot image of the border crossing. He zeroed in, centering the image on the Buick.

"There we go."

"Can't we get it any closer?"

"Sure." He pressed a button, and the SUV image grew from pebblelike proportions to LEGO block-sized.

"That's good."

The burgundy vehicle snaked its way in the bumper-to-bumper traffic to the Mexican border. The driver handed her papers to the agent in a booth, and a minute later they were handed back.

The Buick crossed into Mexico, and I said, "Okay, here we go. I'll keep an eye on this, and you watch the crossing. We'll see how long it takes Florenze to find another car carrying cash."

"You got it."

I stood. "Oh, I want to let Sears know the first one is through."

"You better call him. She's getting off Mexico's Highway 101."

I picked up the phone as the Buick took the Ave Frontera exit. The car stopped in a long line of traffic waiting for the red light to change. I informed Sears that the first of three cars had passed through, and hung up.

"What did he say?"

"To tell him when we started the GPS tracking."

I watched the line of traffic start moving. The Buick drove along Ave Fonterra, making a left onto Ave de La Amistad.

"You think she's going to hand off the cash?"

"Maybe, but it seems risky to do it so close to the border."

"They're in Mexico, they wouldn't be afraid."

The car eased into the entrance to a Pemex station. "She's getting gas."

"Probably needs it."

I said, "She passed a couple of stations already."

"Maybe they gave her a certain credit card for fuel."

The driver pulled up to a pump and got out. She locked the

door to the vehicle and headed to the station's convenience store.

Bradley said, "She might have to use the bathroom."

As she disappeared into the store, I said, "I don't care how bad you have to go, it's super risky leaving a car loaded with cash unguarded. Tijuana is the worst spot in Mexico for car theft."

A male walked out of the store. He surveyed the area and went straight toward the pump where the Buick was parked. He put a hand on the roof and a key in the door. The driver's door opened, and he got in.

"Bingo. She passed the car off."

I said, "And we don't know anything about the guy she gave it to. We need to know who the first driver was. We'll get the info from Florenze—I don't want her to stop now, but get a tail on her and find out where she is going."

"I'm on it."

The new driver pulled out of the station and navigated back onto Highway 101. He stayed with the flow of traffic. Where was he going?

"If this guy is heading to Mexico City, we're going to be up all night."

"We should split this up; one guy keeps on eye on the car and the other watches the border."

I said, "That's good by me."

An hour later, I said, "He's getting off. Check Google Earth."

Bradley said, "That's near La Coma. He's getting onto Route 180."

"Where does that lead?"

"Hang on." His fingers flew over the keyboard. "Looks like Tampico."

I pulled out my cheat sheet. "The Gulf Cartel is active there."

"Good old Tampico. Have you ever heard of the Tampico Affair?"

"No, what is that?"

"In 1914 a handful of US Navy sailors came ashore for supplies and were detained by the Mexican authorities. The United States demanded they be released, but the Mexican government refused."

"That's unbelievable. Why would they do that?"

"The Mexican president had taken power in a coup, overthrowing the democratically elected president, and the United States had suspended diplomatic relations."

"How did it get resolved?"

"We seized the port of Veracruz and held it for six months until the conflict was resolved. A ton of anti-American feelings were generated from the situation, and it lingered through World War I, when Mexico refused to join the war against Germany."

"I can't believe I never knew that."

"We learned about that in middle school."

"Middle school? And you remember that?"

He shrugged. "People say I have a photographic memory."

I only remembered the bad things. "That's a good attribute. You'll never wonder where you put your keys."

"He's getting off."

The Buick made a right turn, then a left onto an unpaved road. Dust clouded the feed.

"I hope we don't lose him."

Bradley zoomed in. "Don't worry, we won't."

"He's slowing down."

The Buick turned onto a road leading to a home with a slanted, metal roof. The SUV stopped. Someone came out of the house holding something.

"That's a rifle, looks like an AK-47!"

"Is he going to kill him?"

The man waved at the driver and went around to the passenger side. He laid the weapon on the back seat and climbed into the seat next to the driver.

"Looks like he's the protection."

The Buick got back onto the highway and continued south. After an hour the road veered east, toward the Gulf of Mexico. They drove along the coast for hours, passing Tampico as darkness closed in.

I said, "They have to turn toward Mexico City pretty soon."

The Buick traveled in the dark for two more hours, approaching Veracruz.

"Where the hell are they going? It can't be Mexico City."

"Maybe Chiapas, and that's why they have protection, because there's a war going on between the cartels."

"Why would they go there?"

"Maybe they owe one of the cartels money."

I pulled up a map of southern Mexico. Nothing made sense. There was Cancun, but why? I stared at the map.

Bradley said, "They're getting off."

The Buick made a left toward a smattering of buildings. It drove slowly, pulling onto the side of a junkyard filled with piles of tires. They came to a stop in front of a roofless building.

Two men carrying rifles approached the car. The driver got out and they shook hands.

"What is this place?"

One man got in the rear and the other behind the wheel. The Buick turned around and headed back onto Route 180.

Bradley said, "It's either a team of drivers, or it's going to get rough."

"They're heading into Central America."

"I don't get it. What's down there?"

Chapter Twenty-Four

Swinging my legs off the couch, I tried to figure out what the Buick was doing in Peru. It was almost four thousand miles from the US-Mexico border.

It popped into my head that the South American nation was the place where the burner cell was purchased, the one used to make the threatening call my first night in Washington.

I flipped open my laptop and put Peru in the search bar. Peru was the largest producer of coca, the plant used to make cocaine. Were the cartels funneling cash earned from the streets of the United States to buy the raw materials needed to make cocaine?

It made sense but didn't feel right. The cartels had vertical operations. They didn't farm out processes to competitors, fearing they'd strengthen them.

Cartels had expenses like any enterprise, but physically moving cash this distance was mystifying. I snapped my laptop shut and hustled to the surveillance room.

The Buick drove down a dirt road lined with one-story structures defaced with graffiti. A roofless building sat at the end of the street leading to a fenced compound. Half a dozen cars were parked near a low-slung, concrete building.

The Buick SUV stopped at the gate. A guard holding an AK-47 spoke to the driver before opening the gate.

I squinted. "This can't be a bank, could it?"

Bradley said, "I doubt it."

"What the hell is this place?"

"I'm going to grab the GPS coordinates and see if any agency has any information on it."

"Good idea."

"Oh, by the way, the first driver, the woman, her name is Anna Carioca."

"Does she have a record?"

"Yes." He pointed at the screen. "She was convicted for smuggling about two years ago."

The SUV drove toward a metal structure. Two barn-like doors swung open, and the Buick disappeared inside. The doors closed, and two men with rifles stood guard.

Bradley said, "I don't have anything on this place or on the town itself. I'll reach out to a couple of agencies, see if anybody does."

He looked tired.

"After you're done, go get some sleep. I'll keep an eye on this."

"I only need an hour or two, at most."

"Whatever you need, get it."

Bradley was on his third call when the armed men opened the doors. As they stepped aside, the Buick SUV rolled out of the building. It went straight to the gate and drove in the direction of town.

Bradley hung up the phone. I said, "You have any luck?"

"Not initially, but we'll see once they dig in some. What's going on?"

"The Buick left. I'll keep my eye on this place. Go take a nap."

Bradley left. I pulled out my phone and made a call.

"Hey, Mary Ann, how are you doing?"

"Just reading. What's going on with you?"

"Looks like we hit a dead end."

"Oh. Sorry."

"It's okay, I'm getting tired of Washington anyway."

"You're coming home?"

"I think so. Maybe tomorrow."

"Good. Rita is having a little party on Saturday for Paul's fiftieth birthday."

"Sounds good."

A four-door black Toyota drove up to the gate. The guards swung open the gate, and the Toyota entered the compound.

"Did you book your flight home?"

"Not yet. I was going to . . ."

"Frank?"

The Toyota headed for the same building the Buick SUV had gone into. I squinted. The vehicle had American plates.

"Let me call you back."

"Is everything okay?"

"Yeah, yeah, I'll call you later."

The black sedan rolled inside the building and was hidden from view. Was it also carrying cash?

The door to the conference room banged open.

It was Sears.

It was timely. I wanted to ask him who we had on the ground in Peru. "I was just coming to see you."

Face reddened, he said, "What do you think you're doing?"

"Excuse me? What do you mean?"

"I've bent over backward for days to accommodate you, and now I've got people running all over me."

"I'm not sure I understand what the problem is."

"The problem is you're creating a diplomatic crisis. The ambassador called saying the Peruvian government is complaining we're violating Peru's sovereignty."

Something wasn't right. "We haven't done anything more than follow—"

"Stop whatever you're doing or we're going to have to cease cooperation."

"But Mr. Pembroke—"

"He doesn't run this operation, I do. Shut down whatever it is you're doing or it's over."

"No problem. We weren't onto anything, just poking around a little."

"Where is Bradley?"

"Taking a nap."

"Tell him I want to see him as soon as possible."

"I'll go get him now."

Sears stormed out.

I looked at the feed from the compound. Two men were running. One toward the main house, the other to the building the Toyota and Buick had gone into.

Pushing away from the desk, I hustled to the room where Bradley was sleeping.

He was breathing deeply.

Shaking his shoulder, I whispered, "Bradley, get up."

"What's the matter?"

"I need you, now." I pulled his arm. "Something is going on."

Chapter Twenty-Five

I pointed at the screen. "See?"

Bradley asked, "What's going on?"

"They're bugging out."

"They're leaving? Why?"

I lowered my voice. "Sears sold us out."

Bradley's eyes widened. "Are you sure?"

"A thousand percent. Right after you made those calls trying to see what this place is, he came down and told us to stop."

"I can't believe it."

"Believe it."

A black Jeep Renegade followed the Toyota out of the building, leaving a cloud of dust. Pointing to the Jeep, I whispered, "Follow that vehicle."

"But Sears said to—"

Pulling my cell out, I said, "I'm going over his head, right to Pembroke."

He surveyed the room and shook his head. "Okay, let's do this."

"I'll be right back, let me call Pembroke." I stepped out of the room. There was no way I was calling anyone at this point. It didn't feel good lying, but Bradley needed assuring.

Five minutes later, I came back in. Sidling up to Bradley, I flashed a thumbs-up. "Everything is good. What's going on with the Jeep."

"It's heading toward the highway."

"Does it lead to any place we know the cartels control?"

"Nothing I know of. They could be heading to Lima."

"How far a ride is that?"

"Tough to say, some of these roads are barely paved. But it'd be at least six, if not eight hours."

"It's going to be a long night."

"Go grab some sleep."

<hr>

SIPPING my third cup of coffee, the Jeep pulled onto a driveway to a walled compound. The driver waited for the gate to open. The sign on the fence said the facility was home to Santos Empresa Exportadora. It was an export company.

The Jeep drove in and parked in front of a two-story building. The driver closed the car door behind him. Two men came out of the front doors and followed the driver to the rear of the Jeep. The driver opened the hatchback and each of them took out two duffel bags.

They had to be filled with cash, American dollars smuggled over the border. But why deliver them to an export outfit?

I whispered to Bradley, "These guys are good. They're using the money to buy something, have it shipped to a buyer somewhere, and presto, the money is laundered."

"Wow, simple but effective. They probably have a company set up to receive the wire transfers."

"It's very slick. They use dirty money to buy a product, ship to an overseas buyer, and collect the money in a clean transaction. Why hasn't anyone figured this out?"

"They need a willing seller and buyer."

"Yes, but they can overpay for the goods and sell them at a discount."

"True. It'd be hard for someone to turn down a good price."

"We need to find out what this company is about."

"I'll check around."

"We have to be discreet."

"I can—"

"I'm going to speak to Pembroke. We can trust him, or at least I think we can."

"Good idea. I'll see what our embassy in Peru has on the export company."

"No, don't. It's too risky, they could be dirty."

"Don't take it the wrong way, but you're acting paranoid."

"It's not paranoia, it's reality; drug money has compromised some of the best of us."

He nodded. "Okay, okay. You're right."

I opened my laptop, putting *what does Peru export?* into the search bar. Their top export was slag, the stony waste separated from metals when they were smelted.

"What the heck does somebody use that for?"

Bradley said, "They use it in furnaces to make high-grade cement."

"Copper is the next biggest, then gold."

"There's a lot of illegal gold mining in Peru. It's a real problem. They're destroying the environment down there."

"I saw something on a news program about that a while ago."

"It's a mess."

"I didn't know Peru supplied so much fish; it's the second largest supplier behind China."

"Fish would be a good product to launder money with. After a short time, no evidence is left."

"You think it could involve seafood?"

"I'm just throwing out ideas."

"That's a good one. We need to see if this Santos Exporting Company has any refrigerated warehouses or trucks."

"They could just be playing a middleman role, taking the money from the cartel for the buys, and arranging the sells without touching the goods."

"Can it get more complicated?"

Bradley chuckled. "These cartels are not only violent, they're sophisticated."

"The wall keeps getting taller. Keep your eyes on this place. I'm going to see Pembroke."

Chapter Twenty-Six

Pembroke came out of his corner office to greet me. "Frank, it's good to see you." He gripped my hand firmly and said, "Come on back to my office."

"I'm sorry I couldn't give you advance notice."

"No need to apologize. We're grateful to have your help."

He closed his office door. I took a seat in front of his desk.

Pembroke eased into his chair. "What's going on? I hope you have some good news. It's been one of those days."

"I need some help."

"Okay. Let's see how we can get that for you."

I explained the situation, ending with, "I need intelligence from someone on the ground, and it can't be someone working for or with the DEA."

Pembroke steepled his fingers. "They'd be the natural agency to work with on something like this in Peru."

"Appearances can be deceiving."

Pembroke raised his eyebrows, and I said, "You're going to have to trust me on this, sir."

"I see. Well, Treasury doesn't have many assets inside Peru. One or two in Lima, but they're monitoring the central bank there and are strictly financial types. I was hoping to use some of the money we'd confiscate from this and the Wall Street investigation to fund positions like this. After your cut, the agency gets to keep whatever we seize, and the Adams operation presents the largest possible seizure in history. I'm anxious to have you start on it."

"I understand, but what about another agency? Can we use someone from, say, Homeland Security?"

"Unfortunately, Romney, the man you met, told me they're overwhelmed at the moment. With everything going on with China, Russia, and Iran, they're stretched thin. I think our best bet is with the CIA. They always have a couple of undercover assets in most countries."

"Spies?"

"I'm not sure how they characterize their agents. However, that's not important."

"You'll reach out to them?"

"Yes. I'll get back to you immediately."

MARY ANN WAS in the car when I called her. "Where are you going?"

"To the book club, it's at Miranda's."

"A good excuse to drink wine?"

She laughed. "Yes, but we do discuss the book. What are you doing? How's the case going?"

"We tracked the cash to an export outfit in Peru. Now we need someone on the ground to help figure out what the connection is."

She hesitated before saying, "Don't tell me you're going to Peru."

"No, no—"

"You said you'd be home in a couple of days."

"I know, but things ramped up."

"You're not going to Peru, right?"

"No, I'm not. Pembroke is reaching out to his contacts to see what assets we have on the ground down there."

"Good. You had me worried for a second."

"I don't want to talk when you're driving."

"It's okay."

"I'm meeting Bradley for a bite to eat in a bit."

"What's he like?"

"He's a good kid. Not really a kid, I think he's thirty-six."

"That's a man, Frank."

"Yeah, he's smart, and frankly, he's wasting his talent with the Feds. He could be making a ton of money with a tech company."

"Why doesn't he leave?"

"Taking care of his father. But the poor man doesn't even recognize him anymore."

"That's so sad."

"Shoot me if I get to that point."

"Stop that. Look, I'm in front of Miranda's. Have a good night."

"Don't drink too much, it's not good for your MS."

PEMBROKE'S SECRETARY CALLED ME, her boss wanted to talk.

I hustled into a conference room and dialed his office.

Pembroke got right to the point. "I'm afraid we've hit a dead end."

"How so?"

"I've made calls to every agency, even those I knew would say no, but I can't get any help on the ground in Peru."

"What about the CIA?"

"Apparently, the Peruvian government, who is friendly,

raised fuel prices a couple of days ago and severe protests broke out. The opposition party, Shining Path, is taking advantage and aligning itself with the communists to challenge the government. I don't know if you know it or not, but there has been an ongoing armed conflict between the government and Shining Path that started back in 1980 but quieted down the last couple of years. But this current upheaval is making it probable things will heat up. The timing couldn't be worse."

"A major distraction like this plays right into the cartel's hands. Nobody will be focused on what they're doing, and the cartel will be spreading money around to buy protection."

"That's unfortunate. But we must work with what we have."

"What does the CIA have? Manpower-wise down there?"

"I'm afraid their hands are full and they have no one to spare."

"Damn."

"I'm sorry."

"And there's nothing else we can do?"

"I'm afraid not. I shook every tree I could. Believe me, after chasing you for two years, the last thing I wanted to do was to disappoint you."

"I know you tried. Let me think this over."

BACK ON THE SURVEILLANCE FLOOR, I collapsed into a chair. Was this the end of the line? A political uprising was going to prevent me from trying to take down the bastards who killed Steve and Jimmy?

The cartel was going to benefit, justice would be denied, and I'd be stuck chasing suits in New York City.

I revisited the conversation: Pembroke had said we had to work with what we had, but we had nothing. Just Bradley and me sitting in a Washington, D.C. office watching the bad guys. What good was surveillance if you couldn't act upon it?

There was a knock on the door. Bradley said, "Frank?"

"Come in."

"Is everything all right?"

I wagged my head. "No. We hit a wall. Pembroke can't get us anybody on the ground. The government down there is dealing with an insurgency, and even the CIA can't spare us anything."

"I saw some breaking news on that and thought the distraction might be good for us."

"It could've, but we have no one needing cover."

"Damn, and all we need is just to connect a few dots. We were getting so close."

"I know. I wish I could go down there myself."

"Why can't you?"

"What do you mean?"

"Why not go to Peru yourself. You've investigated a million crimes. You can get the information we're looking for and get out without anybody knowing."

"What, I'm just going to show up? I'd need cover, some reason for being there."

"You speak Spanish. So, what about a retiree checking out cheap countries to live in?"

"Maybe that would fly in Lima, but this place is so remote, an American would be a red flag."

"You could be an investor looking over possible places to make investments in."

"Invest in what?"

"They're big into fishing, maybe a seafood processing plant."

"It'd have to be near the port. These guys are operating in the Amazon jungle."

"A botanist."

We looked at each other and laughed at his suggestion.

Bradley said, "What about posing as a conservationist? There's a lot of uproar over protecting the rainforest. You can be an emissary from an American organization working to conserve the Amazon rainforest."

"That's actually a pretty good idea."

"Or maybe a journalist looking into what's going on with the rainforest."

"I still can't just show up. I'd need an introduction, someone to show me around."

"We can get cover from one of the scores of climate change agencies the Feds created. It'll be easy."

"Easy? Everything is easy until you have to do it yourself."

"I know, I'm just talking about the cover part. If you want, instead of you, I'd love to go. Get me out of here for a couple of days."

"It's too dangerous. Did you forget the threat the cartel made?"

Part Three

Pucallpa, Peru

Chapter Twenty-Seven

Outside the window lay a wide expanse of jungle. A brown, meandering ribbon of water, leading to a mountainous area, split the green swath.

The pilot squawked over the loudspeaker. I pitched forward as the plane rapidly descended.

The green canopy closed in, and so did fear. I braced my feet against the legs of the seat as the plane bounced off the dirt runway. A plume of dust rushed by the window as the aircraft skidded onto the landing strip.

I held my breath as the plane fishtailed. It slowed and came to a halt. The pilot came into the tiny cabin. "Rico is on the way."

He popped open the door and dropped the stairs. I put on glasses and the ballcap Jimmy had gotten me years ago for Father's Day and grabbed my duffel bag. "Thanks for the ride."

"I'll see you back here in three days." He looked at his watch. "Around the same time."

Surveying the area outside the door, I hesitated. What the hell was I doing here? Not only was it in the middle of nowhere, but I was also alone. Maybe I should've taken Bradley.

Stepping down the stairs, my heart sped up. It wasn't the heat, but the warnings from Derrick and Mary Ann bouncing around in my head.

The distant sound of an aircraft caught my attention. Someone else was using the runway. My shoulders relaxed until I realized it could be a cartel plane.

I headed to a tin-roofed building with a rusty sign reading Aviacion. Its window and door were open. Pawing the beard that I'd grown, I was sure the hotel didn't have air-conditioning.

Pulling out my phone, I checked for service. There were five bars. The Starlink satellite service they set up was working. I pecked out a text to Mary Ann to let her know I had landed.

A mud-splashed Volkswagen Beetle pulled up. A man in a tan hunter's shirt got out. He tipped his baseball cap to me. It had to be Rico.

I hustled over to him. "Hola."

Rico stuck out his hand. "Luca?"

I took his hand. "Si, soy yo."

"You speak Spanish?"

"Yes, that's part of the reason they sent me."

"Lucky you." He smiled. "You look a little white. How was the ride in?"

Rico had a chin cleft so deep it looked like a coin slot. "A little bumpy, but I've been on worse."

"Oh yeah? Where? In Nam?"

"No, my number never got called. How about you?"

He hiked a thumb toward his car. "Did two tours, the second in special ops."

"You must have seen a lot."

Rico nodded and opened the driver's door. I threw my

bag in the rear seat and got in. He eyed me. "So, you're supposed to be some kind of envoy from a global warming group?"

"We're a new offshoot of Go Conscious Earth. Our focus is on the Congo Basin in Africa."

"Conscious Earth? If the planet could talk it'd tell you it's in a natural warming cycle."

"Look, whether or not we can do anything about it getting hotter, people need to know what the implications of destroying the Amazon rainforest are."

He swerved, avoiding a pothole. "It's about economics. People here need to feed their families. They aren't worried about what's going to happen in thirty years."

"We understand, and that's why I'm here, to see what we can do."

"Whatever. They asked me to hook you up and I did. You're going to meet this guy, Eduardo Villarosa. He's in Pucallpa."

"What's he like?"

"The closest thing this region has to an environmentalist."

"Anything else on him?"

"Villarosa had gone after one of the gangs that are mining illegally and barely escaped getting executed."

"What's he do for a living?"

"He's a gold consolidator."

"A what?"

"He buys small lots of gold that miners get. They're little bits that smelters and such don't want to deal with, and they're generally mined illegally. There's a whole bunch of them who eke out a living doing it."

"Interesting. How far do we have to go?"

"We'll be there in five minutes. I'll drop you at his place, and then I'm done."

"And if I need anything?"

"Call the States, my man. The agency is going nuts about

the communists getting a foothold here. So, I've got more on my plate than I can handle."

Rico was with the CIA. "Does the embassy have anyone out here?"

"No. You're in the jungle. They only sent me here because Shining Path originated here, and there's a lot of sympathy for them around these parts."

He turned off the dirt road onto a poorly paved street that was shared by motorbikes and pedestrians.

"Sounds like a tough situation."

He shrugged. "Look, keep your head down and do whatever you're here to do."

"I will."

"And then get the hell out as fast as possible. Life is cheap down here. It doesn't get any more dangerous than this place."

The number of hut-like buildings increased. A motorbike with three passengers on it flew by.

Rico said, "We're in Pucallpa. This is where everybody living out here comes to for supplies and to do business."

"Is there a bank?"

"Bank? This is the middle of nowhere. The last bank left a long time ago. The poor bastards kept getting robbed by the commies."

We drove past a burned-out car, stopping in front of a shack whose windows and door were barred. Squares of white paint covered graffiti.

Rico shut the engine. "We're here."

My heart sped up. Was it too late to go back?

Rico hopped out. "Come on, this is it."

I stepped out of the car. The only thing I knew about this place was that it was dangerous. Extremely dangerous.

Chapter Twenty-Eight

"Un minuto!"

The door opened a crack and a brown, leathery skinned man peeked out before unhooking the chain.

"Rico, entra."

We stepped inside. There was one room divided into three spaces by colorful curtains. A table and mismatched chairs sat in the middle.

Rico said, "This is Frank, the American I told you about. He's from an American conservation organization."

He smiled, exposing a gap in his teeth. "Senor, it is very nice to meet you."

I shook his callused hand, saying, "Same here. I appreciate your time and willingness to meet me."

"No, no, senor, we appreciate you coming here. We need help or we're going to lose the rainforest."

Rico said, "I've got to run, or I'll be late."

Before I could say anything, Rico darted out of the small house.

Villarosa said, "Sit. I will get you a drink. You have to try pisco sour, it's a special Peruvian drink."

"Does it have alcohol?"

"Yes. No good?"

"I don't think I should, you know, the traveling . . ."

"Of course, I'll get you an Inca Kola."

I never drank soda. "Sounds good."

He set a glass of bright yellow liquid down. I was expecting a brown, Coke-like beverage. I tried some. It tasted like bubblegum mixed with lemon.

"You like?"

"Yes. It's good, different."

"It's number one in Peru."

I nodded and took a tiny sip. "Thanks. So, tell me what is going on with the Peruvian rainforest."

"It's being destroyed. I don't know if anyone, even America, can stop the deforestation. But the environment and our people are being poisoned."

"Who is doing what?"

"Most of new damage is from illegal mining."

"Gold mining?"

"Mostly." He lowered his voice. "I don't want to get in trouble by talking too much."

"You can tell me; I won't say anything."

He stared at his hands but said nothing.

I said, "You can trust me. I came all the way here to help. Anything you say is confidential."

"Okay."

"You were telling me about the gold mining."

"Yes. We have legitimate mines in Peru, and it's an important industry here, but the illegal mines, they're run by criminal gangs, and they don't care what mess they create. They just move on to another place and destroy that as well."

"That's terrible."

"I will take you, you will see. What once was green is now

mud, and there are toxic pools everywhere. The river runs brown and has a lot of mercury in the water.

"How long has the illegal mining been going on?"

"A long time. We don't have many jobs here, so when people can't find work, many try to dig up gold to feed their families. But it's gotten very bad the last couple of years. The price of gold went up, and everyone thought it was the easy way to make money."

"People are making money doing this?"

He wagged his head. "Not the workers. They get paid pennies, and it's killing our way of life. The fish are dying, and our crops don't grow because of the poison. And there is too much violence. The gangs are bad people, and they threaten anyone who stands in their way."

"What have the Peruvian authorities done about all this?"

Villarosa scoffed. "They send in troops for a couple of days. But nothing changes. The miners go deeper into the forest and wait. There's too much money involved, too much corruption."

"Just like the drug problem."

"Yes, it is the same."

"Do you have ideas on what needs to happen to stop this?"

He slapped his hand on the table. "What needs to happen is for corruption to end!"

I nodded. "That would solve problems around the world."

"Yes, senor. It would."

"Besides that, what practical things can be done? Maybe we can help."

"We need police in the mining areas, every day, not just for show. And more jobs so people would not have to mine to take care of their families. If there were other ways to make a living, maybe they wouldn't destroy the place where they live."

"That would make a good start."

"I want to take you there. You might see it for yourself, so you can see and tell Americans how bad it is."

"Sure, my organization wants an accurate picture of the situation, so we can decide how best to help."

"We can go in a little while. I must open my shop for afternoon business. Then we go."

"Now?"

"Si, why not?"

"I can see you are passionate about protecting your land."

"It's not only our land." Villarosa patted his chest. "The Amazon is the world's lungs. What goes on here affects everyone."

Chapter Twenty-Nine

"How long have you been there?"

"Oh, forever. I took over when they killed my father."

"He was murdered?"

"Yes. Before Reyes took over, different gangs would steal, and it was violent, even worse than now."

I wanted to ask who Reyes was, but there were men lined up in front of his shop.

Villarosa said, "Buenos dias, buenos dias."

He unlocked a gate, then a metal door. I followed him into a small, dark room. My eyes were adjusting as he closed the door behind us.

He reached for a cord, and an overhead light brightened the space. A gray safe dominated the room, which had two tables, and a rack filled with bottles.

Villarosa unlocked a metal plate over a shelf on the front wall. Light streamed through the bars behind it as he swung it open.

The man at the head of the line set a cloth pouch on the counter, pushing it forward. Villarosa reached through the opening. "Where did you get this?"

"I was sifting by the water."

"Where?"

"I don't know exactly. My friend took me there."

"You got this from the Madre Dios?"

"No, no. Not there. We were in the north working at a real mine."

Villarosa opened the bag, staring at the lumps of gold. "These didn't come from a legal mine."

"They did! I worked ten days to make this much."

"These are crudely amalgamated."

I craned my neck to see. The little chunks looked like worthless rocks.

"You have to believe me." The miner raised his hands. The skin on his billy-club fingers was cracked and dirty. "I busted my ass to get it."

Everything I'd read said mining was hard work and dangerous. In addition to the bandits and wildlife threats, miners used mercury to get fine slivers of gold to bond to each other. You got the gold, but your nervous system and health paid a price.

Villarosa, who must have seen too many men whose motor skills were impaired, pulled on gloves. He poured the contents of the bag into a small bowl. He used an eye dropper and put white vinegar on the pile.

I didn't know what he was looking for.

He drained the vinegar and put the nuggets on a scale. It must have been gold.

"How much have I got? At least a quarter of an ounce, no?"

"Barely an eighth."

"No, no. Check again, check again."

"It's an eighth. I'll give you two hundred US."

"Can you do better? I have five mouths to feed."

"Two hundred is all I can pay."

"Okay."

Villarosa paid the man and gave him back the pouch. The

next one in line stepped to the window as a motorbike pulled up. The driver had an AK-47 hanging off his shoulder. His passenger got off the bike and set his helmet on the seat.

The man at the window stepped aside for the new arrival. The passenger pulled a bag out of each pocket of his leather jacket and walked up to the window.

"Buenos dias, Eduardo."

"Buenos dias."

He shoved the bags through the opening. "Don Pedro sends his regards."

Villarosa emptied both pouches into the weighing bowl. "An ounce and a quarter."

Those in line whispered in amazement.

"How much?"

Villarosa picked up a small calculator and punched the keys. "Twelve hundred and eighty."

"Make it thirteen hundred and we've got a deal."

Villarosa nodded. He counted out the bills.

Would the men who worked like dogs to get the gold see more than twenty dollars of it?

Villarosa slid the money under the bars. "Send my well wishes to the Don."

As the man pocketed the money, Villarosa sent a text. He told the men in line to wait and closed the metal plate over the window.

Villarosa headed to the safe. I whispered, "Who is Don Pedro?"

"He runs several mining operations, all of them illegal. Don Pedro has scores of poor laborers who break their backs for him, but they barely make enough to survive."

Villarosa opened the metal plate and processed the next three men in line. As the next miner dug out his pouch of raw gold, a motorbike pulled up. Two men hopped off, brandishing AK-47s.

The miners in line scattered. Villarosa swung the metal plate shut as the men began firing.

I hit the floor. Villarosa said, "No, come with me."

Villarosa headed out of the back of the building. I followed him, catching a glimpse of an open-air Jeep skidding to a stop.

Shots rang out as the men in the Jeep fought it out with the bandits. I ducked behind a rubber tree as Villarosa pressed himself onto the floor of the forest.

The firefight ended after two minutes. I peeked around the tree, then at Villarosa, who lifted his head. I strained to make out what the voices were saying.

He put his head down. Someone was walking toward the woods. "Eduardo! Get out here!"

Villarosa asked, "Jacinto?"

"Si. Come out, we got them."

Villarosa put a finger to his lips. I hugged the tree as he scrambled to his feet. "You came just in time. A minute later and they would've killed us."

"I will tell Reyes. We need to put the word out; you screw with our people, and we'll hunt you and your family down."

"People are desperate. I'd rather they give me somebody to protect me."

Jacinto shook his head. "Not going to happen." He extended his AK-47 and smiled. "All you need is one of these."

"No. No more guns."

"Why? You killed before."

They walked toward the building. "It was a mistake."

"It was either them or you. That's how it works."

Villarosa held the back door open and followed Jacinto inside. Ten minutes later, they emerged. Jacinto jumped into the Jeep, and it drove off. Villarosa walked toward the forest. "Luca, my friend, it's okay. Come out."

"What the hell was that?"

"Bandits. If you run, they don't kill you. They just want the money."

"Who were the guys in the Jeep?"

"They're Ramon Reyes's men. They came at the right moment. I texted for money to buy more gold, and they came just in time."

"Who is Reyes?"

"He buys the gold I collect from the miners. I gave him what I bought, and he gave me money to buy more."

"They must trust you."

"They do, I've never stolen from them. That's why they never killed me and keep me safe."

"I wouldn't exactly say you're safe after that."

He shrugged. "Come on, enough for today. Now we go. I will show you how Peru's land is being cleared, mined, and left in unusable condition."

Chapter Thirty

I followed Villarosa to an old, mud-caked motorbike parked on the side of the building. He unlocked two heavy chains, securing them around a tree.

He swung his leg over and started up the motorcycle. A plume of blue smoke belched out of the exhaust.

Villarosa nodded for me to get on. There were no helmets. I said, "How long a ride is it?"

"Thirty minutes."

Would the ancient motorbike make it that far? Climbing on behind Villarosa, I wrapped my hands on the rusty frame of the motorcycle.

We lurched forward and I tightened my grip. We rode through town. The hard-packed street turned into a desolate dirt road. We bounced along as the greenery thickened.

Twenty minutes went by before Villarosa slowed. He turned onto another path, and we plunged into the jungle. The narrow road was rutted and puddle filled.

Water splashed my legs as we moved to the side to let a pair of motorcycles by. "How much more?"

"Five minutes."

I loosened my grip and nearly slid off the seat when the motorbike fishtailed. Between the thick humid air and the smell, we could have been driving inside a greenhouse.

Thick drops of water began pelting us. My shirt got soaked as the rain intensified. Villarosa slowed again. He cut to the right, onto a ribbon of a path and drove uphill.

I buried my face in Villarosa's back as branches smacked my arms and legs. The rain lessened as we crested the hill.

Villarosa slowed to a halt. "We stop here."

I got off, staring at the brown gulch below us. As Villarosa walked the bike into the tree line, I pumped my hands, trying to stimulate blood flow.

I pointed to a vast expanse of churned earth, splattered with dead pools of water. "What is all this?"

"An abandoned mine. They left it a year ago and moved deeper into the forest."

"Looks like they dropped a bunch of bombs here."

He nodded. "Follow me, we're going to go down and around to where they're mining now."

"Okay."

Sticking behind him, we followed a poorly defined footpath down an incline. When it flattened, the forest floor got mushy. Swampy pools of water were off to the side.

Villarosa said, "Stay away from any water. We don't want to run into a caiman."

"What's that?"

"A crocodile."

I stiffened and walked as closely behind him as possible. We left the marshy area behind and the ground hardened.

As we walked to an area where the sunlight broke through, the rich aroma of the jungle morphed into an acrid smell.

"What is that smell?"

"Chemicals. Don't touch the dirt around here."

My nose tingled. I pulled my wet T-shirt over my nose.

Body odor was preferable to the rancid smell. Taking the bend in the path brought a large pool of water, slicked over with oil, into view.

We hit the bottom of the trail and circled around a large crater. Littering the area were rusty pieces of machinery and a dozen empty fuel drums that had sunk into the mud.

"How long will it take Mother Nature to put it back the way it was?"

"Without help, it would take over a hundred years."

"Really?"

"Yes, the water is toxic. You see any birds here?"

I looked at the sky. I hadn't noticed the lack of bird chatter. "No."

"There's nothing here, not even bugs. No lizards, animals, nothing but chemicals."

"That's terrible."

He pointed to a patch of gravel leading to a dirt road. "We're going to follow that, but we have to stay to the side. If anybody comes along, we must duck into the forest."

"Lead the way."

We stayed close to the tree line. Straining my ears, I heard the hum of a motor running. Villarosa turned and put a finger to his lips. "We're getting close."

He slowed and pointed. Through the gaps in foliage, I could see the forest floor had been stripped, replaced with a muddy expanse dotted with machinery. The sun baked two dozen men hard at work.

We inched closer and the motors got louder. I pulled my T-shirt back over my nose. Diesel fumes were irritating the back of my throat. The motors were powering pumps, drawing water from a wide stream.

Two sets of hoses, each manned by shirtless workers, were spraying powerful jets of water at the edge of the pit. I whispered, "What are they doing?"

"They're loosening the soil to find gold locked in the sediment." He pointed to a ramp-like device where barebacked workers were massaging the dirt loosened by the hoses. "They're separating the rock from the sediment."

Four men were waist-deep in water thickened with mud. I couldn't imagine being in that sludge.

I nudged Villarosa. An armed guard came into view, an AK-47 slung over his shoulder. He looked in our direction before turning around. He circled around a handful of blue plastic barrels before moving out of sight.

I whispered, "What are the blue drums for?"

"There's mercury in them. When they use it, all the tiny pieces of gold come together to make a small chunk. That's the only way they can sell it."

I stiffened. A voice shouted over the drone of the machinery, "Julio, ven aqui!"

I scanned the area, elbowing Villarosa; a second guard was pointing in our direction. The first one ran to his associate. They both started to jog in our direction.

Stepping back the way we'd come, I said, "Let's get out of here."

"Not that way, come with me."

I followed Villarosa as he crouched under a leafy branch, and we disappeared into the jungle. It grew darker the deeper we went. Here and there, slices of sunlight made their way through the thick canopy.

I kept my hands on either side of my face, but my legs were getting scratched left and right. A bright opening shined about a football field away.

"What's up ahead?"

Villarosa said, "Another old mine."

We came to the clearing and stepped into the sun. I said, "Geez, this is crazy."

Felled trees lined the outskirts of a muddy expanse the size of Central Park. Destruction spread as far as the eye could see. I didn't know much about environmental crimes, but this had to rank as one of the worst.

"There are many, many more like this. Take some pictures."

I used my phone and snapped away. "Okay. I took enough. Let's get out of here."

He pointed. "We can go around that way, and we'll end up close to where we left the motorbike."

It took us twenty minutes to get back. Villarosa rolled the motorcycle out of the woods. He mounted and fired it up. I threw my leg over the seat and a barrage of shots rang out.

"Get moving!"

Villarosa peeled out. A shot ricocheted off the bike's frame and Villarosa lost control.

The bike slid. We fell off. The guards started shooting. Bullets hit the path as we crawled into the woods.

The riflemen ran up. I held my breath as we hid behind a giant anthill. The shooters took a couple of steps into the woods before giving up and turning around.

As the tension in my jaw released, my cell phone rang. I dug into my pocket as the guards shouted and entered the woods.

Swiping away the call from Mary Ann, I pressed myself into the muddy hill.

Their footsteps closed in. Praying the Hail Mary, one of them shouted in Spanish,

"On your feet!"

I looked up. An AK-47 was pointed at my head. I raised my hands and struggled to my knees. "Please, please don't hurt us."

Chapter Thirty-One

Villarosa said, "We're just exploring. My friend is visiting Peru."

The guard standing over me poked my shoulder with his gun. "You're an American?"

"Si, senor."

"Why did you come here? And don't lie, or I'll shoot you."

"I just wanted to see the area."

"You speak Spanish?"

"Si, my mama was Mexican."

"And you come to Peru? To the Amazon?"

"I, uh, I was always interested in the rainforests, it's an incredible—"

Villarosa cut in, "A friend of a friend said—"

Oomph! A guard jammed the butt of his AK-47 into Villarosa's stomach. Villarosa doubled over.

He moved to me next. "Now, what are you doing out here?"

"Nothing, really. Just checking the place out. We don't have anything like this in America."

"Give me your phone."

After handing it over, the armed man said, "Unlock it."

I did as he asked.

The guard scrolled through. He showed the screen to his associate and turned it toward me.

"Why are you taking pictures of the mine?"

"I wanted to show my wife what we saw, that's all."

"Who sent you here?"

"Nobody. We just took a ride and—"

"Stop lying or I'll shoot both of you and leave you to rot!"

I said, "We're telling the truth. I swear."

The taller guard said, "You want to take them to Cabrerra?"

His associate said, "We should just shoot them here."

"Please, please let us go. I have a daughter and wife."

He raised his gun. "Shut up or I'll blow your head off."

Villarosa said, "Easy, he's an American. If anything happens to him, they're going to send the military all over this place."

"They won't find you or him. We'll feed your asses to the caimans." The guards laughed.

I shuddered.

The two men huddled, talking for a couple of minutes. The shorter of them said, "Start walking, we're gonna let Cabrerra deal with you. He'll decide what to do."

Villarosa said, "You don't want to do that."

"Don't tell me what to do!"

"He'll get mad that you didn't deal with us."

The guards exchanged glances.

Villarosa said, "Tell him you caught us. Tell him you shot us and dumped us in one of the pools from an old mine."

Why was he giving them ideas on how to dispose of us?

The tall guard pointed his gun at him and smiled. "Good idea."

"Hold on," Villarosa said. He dug into his pocket and came up with a small leather pouch. "Take this."

"What is it?"

"A gold nugget. It's half an ounce. Take it and let us go."

The guard took the pouch and loosened its drawstrings. He

pulled out a craggy, round ball of gold. He held it so his partner could see, then put it back in the pouch.

"We're still going to take you to Cabrerra, but thanks for the gift."

I wanted to wipe the smile off his face.

Villarosa said, "If you let us go, I'll get you another one."

"Where are you going to get that from?"

"I work with many miners in Pucallpa as a middleman."

They looked at each other. The tall one raised the pouch. "We want two more of these, one for each of you."

"Two more? That's a lot of money."

"Or we kill you now and keep this one."

"Okay, okay. I can have it in three days. You come by my place, on El Prado, near the corner of Jiron Lima."

"If you're screwing with me, we'll hunt you down and kill you."

"No, no. I'm telling the truth. You come, and I will give you two more. It's all I have, it's my entire life's savings."

He looked at his partner, who nodded.

"You got lucky today. And don't screw it up. Make sure you have the gold. We'll be there in three days."

"If I'm not there, my daughter, she is about to have a baby. Tell me your names and I will have her give you the gold."

"I'm Cesar and he's Ramon."

"And your family names?"

"That's enough. Now get the hell out of here and make sure you have that gold for us or you're dead, and so is your daughter."

"I'll have it, don't worry."

We walked away. I looked over my shoulder. The armed men were examining the gold nugget. I said, "Was what you gave them real?"

"Yes. I always keep one with me in case I need to bribe someone."

"If it wasn't for that, we'd have been in trouble."

"Dead is more like it."

"But they're going to come back. What are you going to do? Give them more?"

"No way. I couldn't afford to if I wanted to. I'm going to tell Reyes. He'll get a message to them, and it will be over."

"They'll listen to him?"

"If they want to stay alive they will."

"I guess you don't mess with Reyes."

"He is connected to some nasty people."

"The cartels?"

He nodded.

"He buys the gold you collect for the cartels?"

"I'm pretty sure."

"What do they do with it?"

"I don't know. Maybe they keep it in a vault somewhere. Maybe they trade it for weapons with the Russians or Chinese."

I thought of the export company. "Holy shit."

"What? What's the matter?"

I couldn't tell him and said, "I can't believe we got out of there alive!"

"It was a close call. I have to admit, I thought they were going to shoot us."

"Me too. I was praying like crazy."

It was a close call, but I couldn't think about that. I was rolling around what I figured was the key to the cartel money-laundering operation.

Chapter Thirty-Two

I sent her a text that I'd call back in ten and hopped into the shower. My legs and arms look like they had hosted a chicken fight. I dressed quickly and made the call.

"Hey, Mary Ann."

"Hi, Frank. Eww. That beard has to go."

"It will. As soon as I get home, I'll shave."

"What happened to your arm?"

"It's nothing, just got scratched up from a bush when I took a walk."

"Be careful, Frank. Keep it clean and make sure it doesn't get infected."

"It'll be fine. How's Jessie?"

"She's doing good. Trying to finalize her classes for next semester."

"I hope she changes her mind about majoring in criminal justice."

"She may, but everything that happened has turned her into a mini-you."

I laughed. "Isn't that's supposed to be a good thing?"

"Not the stubbornness part."

"Stubborn? Me? I call it persistent. Anyway, what have you been doing?"

"Not too much, been trying to get Connie out of the house."

"How is she doing?"

"Not good. Everything reminds her of Jimmy, and then she starts crying."

"That's too bad. It's going to take a long time to dull the pain she's feeling."

"I know. I feel so bad for her. I don't know why her sister doesn't come and stay with her for a while."

"Maybe she's busy, or Connie said not to come. You don't know what kind of relationship they have."

"I know, but she lost her son, after losing her husband. I'd go and stay in a hotel just to be around if I had a sister."

"You're special, Mary Ann."

"Yeah, so special my husband took off for Peru."

"Oh, come on now. You know I had to do something about all this."

She stayed silent.

"Anyway, I'll be back in a day or so, don't worry."

"Hurry up, I miss you."

"I miss you too. I'll call you tomorrow."

A blue feeling descended on me. Calling her for comfort had backfired. I shoved aside the conversation and opened my laptop. Using my phone as a hot spot, I searched for information on Ramon Reyes and the Santos Exporting Company, where the cash had gone.

Looking out the window, I took a sip of my Pilsen Callao. The beer was good. The label said it was made by a subsidiary of Anheuser-Busch. I stuck a fork into my dwindling dish of causa, the Peruvian version of potato salad. Contemplating whether to order another serving, two men came into the bar and grill.

They had deep tans, but I knew they weren't locals. The pair moved like Americans. They walked up to the bar and ordered in a combination of Spanish and English. They were Americans.

I finished my dish. Nursing my beer, I eavesdropped on them. Did I just hear them say Biscayne Bay?

I fished a paper bill out of my pocket and left it on the table. It was a twenty-dollar bill. The snack and beer had amounted to just five US dollars.

Approaching the men, I said, "Excuse me, I couldn't help notice you were from the States."

The beefier one elbowed his friend and stuck his hand out. "Hey, what do you know? Another gringo."

I took his hand and used an alias. "My name is Larry. I'm from Southwest Florida."

He shook my hand. "Nice to meet you, Larry. I'm Matt, and this is Eric."

"Where are you guys from?"

"We're also from the great state of Florida. But on the other coast, in Miami."

"What are the odds of meeting here?"

"It's crazy. Let me get you a drink. What do you like?"

"I've had enough for the middle of the day."

"Are you sure, Larry?"

"Yes, thanks anyway."

Matt lowered his voice but was still too loud. "So, what are you doing in this shithole of a place?"

"I'm with an environmental organization out of Washington, D.C."

He exchanged a glance with Eric. "Doing what?"

"Keeping an eye on what's going on with the illegal mining and rainforest. It's a real tragedy."

"Good luck with that. Look, I hate to cut off a fellow American, but we have some important business to discuss before we have a meeting."

"Sure. Good luck to you."

"Yeah, you too."

Red flags were waving. My body odor was as bad as the next guy's, but that wasn't why they were ditching me. Were they involved in unlawful mining and the damage it caused? I stepped outside and tried to figure out in what capacity they might be connected.

A bodega was across the street. I dodged a stream of motorbikes to get to the other side. I bought two liter-sized bottles of water and left the store.

As I let a family of three perched on a motorcycle go by, a silver Land Rover came around a corner. It pulled up in front of the bar and grill I'd just eaten in.

The front passenger door opened, and a slab of granite got out. The bodyguard surveyed the area before opening the rear door. A man in a straw fedora and light blue polo shirt stepped out. I'd seen him before.

The hired gun opened the door for his boss, and they disappeared inside. I stood there for a minute trying to identify the man and then made a beeline to the eatery.

Instead of going in, I sauntered by the window and looked inside. The man in the hat had his back to the window. But he was talking to the two Americans who'd brushed me off. Who was this guy?

I circled around the block and peeked into the window again. The face of the man in the fedora was visible. But I still couldn't place where I'd seen him. Was I confusing some of his features with a mixture of people?

Chapter Thirty-Three

His gold tooth showed when he smiled. "No, not to a mine. I want to show you what this does to our people. Come on."

He started the motorbike. My inner thighs hurt as I got on the seat.

We rode for fifteen minutes, arriving in a town smaller than Pucallpa. The buildings and homes were in better condition.

"Where are we?"

He shouted over the engine noise. "Nueva Pucallpa!"

"Where are we going?"

He pointed to a large red cross that reminded me of a pharmacy.

Villarosa parked in front of a building whose sign read *Nueva Pucallpa Clinica*. A line of people snaked outside the door. We got off the bike and he said, "You see these people? Almost all of them are sick from mercury."

I followed him as he approached the line waiting to get into the clinic. "Buenos dias." A handful of people returned the greeting. Villarosa walked up to a mother holding a child on her hip. "How is your baby?"

"Very sick. She is not developing. The doctors blame mercury poisoning."

"I'm sorry to hear. And you, sir, why are you here?"

The man's voice trembled. "My nerves are damaged."

He held out his arm, and his hand shook. He was no older than forty. My stomach turned.

"Is this your son?"

"No."

Villarosa asked the younger man, "Are you here for yourself?"

He looked at the ground and whispered, "Yes, I can't get my wife pregnant, and we want to have a family."

Villarosa patted his shoulder. "I hope they can help you."

"Me too."

Villarosa turned to me. "Mercury destroys reproductive systems."

It was painful to see so many people affected by the release of mercury into the water, soil, and air. Pulling Villarosa aside, I lowered my voice and said, "I've seen enough. Let's go."

He pointed to a large white house perched on the side of a mountain. "You see that?"

"Yes. Who lives there?"

"That's Ramon Reyes's house. He lives in luxury while the people he helps poison suffer."

Didn't the drugs he sold do enough damage?

"Can we take a ride and see it?"

WALKING TOWARD MY HOTEL, my stomach growled. It'd been a long day, and though my mind was reeling, I was dragging. I needed to eat and surveyed the storefronts on the main drag. On the corner was El Bar y Parilla Cruz. I'd get something from yet another bar and grill.

Spanish music was playing, and it got louder when I opened the door. It took a couple of seconds for my eyes to adjust. The seedy bar was dark. I hesitated before stepping inside.

The air was heavy, smelling of cigarettes, booze, and body odor. A dozen men were bellied up to the stool-less bar and every table was full. Turning to leave, I did a double take.

Near the back of the room, Rico, the CIA operative, was at a table along the wall. I took a step toward him, when I realized the man he was sitting with looked familiar.

Then it came to me. Sneaking another look at the man, I confirmed it. Spinning on my heel, I turned around and hit the door.

Once outside, I crossed the street. Standing in the shadows, I kept my eyes on the bar's door.

Every time it opened, I crouched behind a stand of parked motorbikes. After waiting forty minutes, Rico stepped out. My knee cracked as I ducked down. Right after Rico hit the sidewalk, Reyes followed. I stiffened. The man connected to the cartels was talking to Rico. They stepped to the side of the building.

Phone in hand, I zeroed in on them and hit record.

Reyes looked around and dug into his pocket. He held out a thick wad of bills. Rico took the money and fanned the bills. My stomach dropped. The CIA agent was on the cartel payroll.

The pain in my knee intensified. I shifted my weight and lost my balance. Trying to steady myself, I reached for the seat of a motorbike.

The bike pitched to the side, knocking into the motorcycle next to it. Trying to prevent it from falling, I fell on my ass and watched the domino-like effect of the line of bikes crashing to the ground.

I scrambled to my feet as the chain reaction ended. Rico was beelining toward me. I shoved my phone in my pocket and said, "Hey, Rico, is that you?"

"What are you doing here?"

"Just got something to eat. What are you up to?"

His eyes narrowed. "The streets around here are dangerous. A man can get hurt out here."

"Just tripped, that's all." I snickered. "Who knows, maybe my new limit is one beer."

"It's easy to make mistakes when you don't know the lay of the land. You're leaving tomorrow, right?"

How did he know? "Yes."

Rico pointed a finger at me. "You be careful now. People around here don't like anyone, especially Americans, sticking their noses where they shouldn't be."

He turned on his heel and walked away.

I trudged back to the hotel. If the CIA was infected, what chance did we have? The swamp of corruption had spread everywhere.

Every half a block, I looked over my shoulder. No one seemed to be following, but I was out of my element, and a CIA operative was involved.

The hallway of the dumpy hotel was empty. I jogged to my room and slammed the door shut. Dragging a rickety chair over, I positioned it on its back legs and forced the top under the doorknob. I pulled the curtains closed and shut the light.

Sitting on the floor, on the far side of the bed, I took my phone out to call Mary Ann. The home-screen picture of Jimmy, Steve, and Jessie stared at me.

Keeping my eyes on the sliver of light under the door, I called Mary Ann. It was an hour later than it was here. "Hi, Frank."

"Hey, how are you?"

"I'm excited you're coming home. What time are you leaving?"

"Around ten in the morning. I should be home about five your time."

"I can't wait. How is it going?"

"I wish I could say better, but it's—" Two patches of dark broke up the yellow line of light under the door. Someone was standing in front of it.

"Frank?"

I lowered my voice. "Hold on."

"What's the matter? Why are you whispering?

Whoever it was tried the doorknob and left.

"I wasn't whispering."

"You certainly were."

"It's probably the connection or something."

"Maybe. So, how is it going? Did you do what you needed to?"

"Mostly, but we'll talk about everything when I get home. How is Jessie?"

We chatted until another pair of feet paused by the door.

"Hey, I just remembered I must make a call. I'll see you tomorrow."

After hanging up, I thought about changing rooms or finding another place to stay. But they were watching me and would know where I'd gone.

Pulling the pillows off the bed, I tried to make myself comfortable on the floor, as far from the door as possible. It was going to be a long night, but I was heading home and would catch up on sleep in my own bed.

I played the video I'd taken of Rico and Reyes several times. There was no doubt, Rico had been given a bunch of cash. He was dirty. Frowning, I shook my head. The drug cartels were getting an assist from an agent of the US government.

Did the corruption extend higher up the CIA chain of command? Were other agencies also involved? It was no wonder efforts to stem the tidal wave of drugs entering the country had failed.

Chapter Thirty-Four

A man on a motorbike came buzzing down the street. He slowed, pulling up a couple of car lengths away. He swung his leg off the seat. There was a bulge on his hip; he was carrying a pistol. Leaning against his bike, the man lit a cigarette. He took his phone out and made a quick call.

I moved a couple of steps away and checked the sky for the arrival of my ride home. The tension-filled minutes passed, and I relaxed a bit. Unless he was going to shoot me as I walked to plane, this guy was only here to make sure I left.

A speck in the sky grew larger. A minute later I could see it was my plane. It wobbled as it descended to the ground. A plume of dust kicked up as its wheels hit. My heart rate sped up. I was going to get out of this armpit of a place.

The aircraft came to a stop. The pilot got out as I approached.

"Hey, it's going to be twenty minutes or so." He waved a credit card. "We have to refuel."

"Can I wait on board?"

"There's no air-conditioning."

"I'm from Southwest Florida, I can handle it."

"Be my guest."

I looked over my shoulder. The man hadn't moved; he was still leaning on the motorbike.

It was hot on the plane. I alternated between sitting near a window to keep an eye on the man and standing by the open door to catch what little breeze there was.

Refueling finished, the pilot boarded and pulled up the stairs. I'd make it out of Peru alive.

It was more than a five-hour flight. Once the excitement of survival passed, my mind drifted back to the case. The trip had been dangerous, and I had nothing more than smoke-like wisps of a trail to pursue.

Having bunked down on the floor with my eyes on the door most of the night, I was beat. Closing my eyes, I traced through the entire trip. There was no way Mary Ann could find out some of the things that had happened.

Trying to figure out Rico's role in the mess I'd waded into, I bounced into and out of a sleepy state. I jerked awake. The identity of the man in the bar talking to the Americans came into focus. Was he the guy who ran Santos Exportadora?

I dug into my duffel, pulling out the laptop. Flipping it open, I realized the aircraft didn't have Wi-Fi.

Part Four

Naples, Florida

Chapter Thirty-Five

Before I could get out of the Uber, Mary Ann had swung open the front door to our house. Her red-carpet smile boosted my energy. She threw her arms around my neck. "I'm so glad you're home."

I squeezed her. "Me too."

"That beard has to go; it's scratching my face."

"Don't worry, it'll be gone in five."

Walking into the house, I said, "Ah, the air-conditioning feels so good."

"You'll be turning it up in an hour." She smiled and said, "How was the flight back?"

She didn't have to know about the bumpy ride. "Not too bad."

I put my duffel bag down as she said, "So, how it'd go? You get any solid leads?"

"Not really, things are a lot messier than I thought."

"How so?"

"We went from chasing the cash from drug sales in the States to illegal gold mining and—"

"Gold mining?"

"It could be. The only thing I'm sure of is that it's convoluted."

"Convoluted? How?"

"I should have said complicated."

"It means the same thing."

"It does? I thought convoluted was, you know, all mixed up, which this is."

"How was your contact? Did he take you around?"

"No. I was on my own. He was dealing with an insurgency."

"What kind?"

"The communists are trying to make a comeback and are stirring trouble. The CIA is worried they're going to team up with the cartels."

"Sounds chaotic."

"It's dangerous."

As soon as it tumbled out of my mouth, I knew it was a mistake.

"It was dangerous there?"

"Nothing I couldn't handle."

She put her hands on her hips. "And what did you have to handle?"

I loved her, but it wasn't easy being married to a former detective. "It was no big deal."

She made a face. She didn't believe me. "You never should have gone down there."

"I had to go."

"That's right, you're the only one who can save the world."

"It's not like that."

"Then what is it?"

"Did anybody shut down the dealers? No. Did anyone get the guys who killed Jimmy? No. I can't just look the other way, Mary Ann. This is too close to home."

"I know." She smiled. "You're a good man, Frank. Just don't go overboard with this. No more crazy trips."

I put my arms around her. "Don't worry, I'm not going anywhere."

"I don't want anything to happen to you. We put our time in, now it's time to enjoy life a little."

I let her go. "I know. Did you do any more research on a trip?"

"Oh, you're going to like it. I can't wait to show you."

"Sounds great. I'm starving. I ate a bag of pretzels so stale they must have been on the plane since the Wright brothers invented flying."

She laughed. "I picked up fillet mignon from Whole Foods. I'll put the grill on."

"Sounds good. I'm going to jump in the shower."

The water felt good. The water pressure in Peru was terrible. Letting the stream pelt my face, my thoughts went to the man in the bar with the Americans.

Checking the company's website as soon as I got off the plane, confirmed the owner of the export company was the same man who'd met with the Americans.

What was the meeting about? Was the export outfit a front for the cartel? And if it was, what did the Americans have to do with it?

Finished with my shower and shave, I put on shorts and a T-shirt from the sheriff's department. Picking up my phone, I made a call.

I pawed my cheek; it was as smooth as a baby's ass. "Bradley?"

"Hey, Frank. Are you Stateside?"

"Yes. I got in a little while ago."

"I can't wait to find out where we're at with the case."

"Trust me, I wanted to call you, but it was too risky. This is a hell of a lot bigger than we thought."

"I'm not surprised. Tell me."

"I'll call you tomorrow and give you the blow-by-blow, but right now I wanted to see what you might be able to find out about a company I think might be central to the case."

"In Peru?"

"Yes. Santos Empresa Exportadora."

"What do you want to know about them?"

"As much as you can, but in particular, can you find out what they ship to the United States and to who?"

"I have good contacts with customs and the census department."

"But we have to keep the circle small, as tight as possible. I ran into a couple of things in Peru that stunned me."

"Like what?"

"How about the CIA contact?"

"What about him?"

"I think he's on the cartel's payroll."

"Jesus. Are you kidding me?"

"I wish I was. That's why I'm concerned about who knows what."

"No problem. With my security clearance, I can get what I need on my own."

Mary Ann was seasoning the steak when I came into the kitchen. She looked up and said, "You're wearing that? What, do you think you're back on the force?"

"It's just a shirt."

She tilted her head. "How long are we married, Frank?"

"Twenty-two years. Did I pass the test?"

"Plus, we were partners for more than a year, and you want to tell me it's just a shirt?"

"It is."

"I put it at the bottom of your drawer. So, what's going on? Are you trying to signal you're going back to work?"

"No. No way. As soon as this case is over, I'm back on the sidelines."

"All this drugs and money. Face it, Frank, you can't fix it."

"I've learned if you face a problem, you can fix it. Maybe I won't solve everything, but I'll make a dent."

She shook her head and picked up the plate of meat. "Just remember, you're not the savior."

Chapter Thirty-Six

The Nespresso machine spit out the last bits of coffee, and I took my cup out to the lanai. Naples was as green as the jungle in Peru, just manicured. Was I too soft or civilized to live in a country without everyday conveniences?

My cell vibrated. "Good morning, Bradley."

"Hey, Frank. How do you feel? Suffering from jet lag?"

"Pretty good, actually. What do you have?"

"I dug into the Santos Exporting Company."

"Already? It's only eight in the morning."

"I jumped on it last night. After what I found, it wasn't easy not calling you at two in the morning."

I jumped out of my seat. "What did you find?"

"They send a couple of products, mostly fruits, like grapes, to the United States, but the majority of what they ship is gold."

"So, there's the connection."

"I know, right? But here's the thing, I went back two years and looked over the census and customs data. And guess what?"

"What?"

"Their gold volume, dollar wise, is up three hundred

percent. Now, that's got to be adjusted for the currency. Peruvian has been devalued and the price of gold has gone up, but—"

"Who are they shipping the gold to?"

"A couple of refiners."

"Anything stand out?"

"In what way?"

"On the companies receiving the gold."

"They ship significant tonnage on a regular basis to two refiners in the Miami area. One is Miami Pure Refiners, and the other is Noble Metals."

Miami was only two hours away. "We need to check them out."

"I've compiled at dossier on both of them."

Dossier? Between going to Peru and this, it felt like a spy operation. "Send them over."

"They're on the way. I also put together some interesting macro data on Peru's gold trade."

"Thanks, Bradley."

"What else do you need me to do?"

"I've got a couple of ideas but give me some time to read what you put together."

"Certainly. Let me know."

"Thanks, again. I'll fill you in on the trip in a bit."

I chugged the rest of my coffee and checked my phone. His email had come in. I made another cup and took it and my laptop into the den.

Bradley had attached three documents: one for each company, and a report on Peru's gold trade with the United States.

Clicking on the summary report, I made a mental note to check on where else Peru was shipping gold.

Bradley was a godsend. He included a bar chart showing Peruvian exports to the United States were a billion dollars in

2023. That was up from $300 million in 2022 and $200 million in 2021.

I sat back. Was the meteoric rise due to illegal mining? Maybe a new mine had opened, or possibly they ramped up production at an existing operation. I jotted down a note to check, then opened another tab.

Searching for new gold mines in Peru didn't generate any results. There was mention of a mine that had changed hands and a line touting Barrick Gold, another operator, and their future expansion plans. But nothing new. I rephrased the search and tried again. It still came up empty.

It wasn't scientific, but the only explanations that made sense were a dramatic increase in the productivity of the existing mines, or the extra gold had to be coming from illegal mines.

My mind's eye brought up the scarred areas Villarosa had taken me to. I had no idea how much gold came out of these makeshift operations. I Googled how many illegal mines were in Peru.

Staring at the number ninety, I tried to do the math. Picking up a pen, I divided the 700-million-dollar increase by seventy. It worked out to over seven million dollars' worth of gold per mine in a year.

That made sense. The mines required machinery, chemicals, and a lot of labor. It also fit with the high number of mines. Why would you destroy the environment you live in if you couldn't make a lot of money doing so?

The cartels were involved, either in protecting the illegal mines from the authorities or operating them outright. It was another stream of dirty money for the powerful criminal enterprises.

I grabbed my phone and made a call. "Mr. Pembroke, please."

"Who may I say is calling?"

"Frank Luca."

After a brief wait, the Treasury official answered. "Frank. How was your trip home?"

"Good."

"Was the trip fruitful? Did you make any progress down there?"

"Yes, it's why I'm calling."

"What's on your mind?"

"What kind of protections does the United States have to prevent illegally mined gold from getting into the country?"

"We consider TCOs a national security threat."

"TCOs?"

"Transnational Criminal Organizations."

There was no end to a bureaucracy's love for acronyms. "Oh right. You were saying?"

"The potential to cleanse illegally mined precious metals and diamonds is a threat to the financial system, the stability of partner countries where the mining takes place, as well as the environmental disaster these operations leave behind."

"How do we defend against the gold getting into the States?"

"Several laws have been passed to prevent that. Customs requires documentation as to the origination of the gold. They've recently ramped up oversight on shipments of jewelry as they found several shipments that were mis-declared."

"Documentation can be easily faked."

"True, but I'm told they're taking closer looks at these things."

"I wonder if enough is being done."

"Gold is heavy. Smuggling large quantities is not as easy as say diamonds, or cash. A million dollars' worth of gold weighs about fifty pounds."

"It's still doable."

"And then you have to sell it to someone, on an ongoing

basis. Or store it somewhere and keep it guarded. It's too difficult."

"Storing it makes no sense. Why risk transporting it to the States if all you're going to do is sit on it?"

"I agree. Unless they have a solid contact in the jewelry business, it'd be tough to launder."

"Okay. You've been helpful. I'll be in touch. I have a line I'm going to pursue."

I hung up. Pembroke was one of the few people I trusted in the nation's capital. But he was in Washington, out of touch and holding positions that were outdated, like too many in D.C.

If he was right, I had a big fat zero on my hands. What would I tell the families about my vow to get justice for Jimmy and Frankie? I wouldn't have egg on my face, I'd have an omelet dripping off me.

I sat back. Was there something here, or was this a waste of time? Were my instincts dulled by Father Time? Inhaling deeply, I grabbed the mouse and clicked on the report Bradley had compiled on Noble Metals.

Chapter Thirty-Seven

The Miami-based refiner, Noble Metals, had been in business for thirty years. They were a privately held company whose facility was a mile from the airport.

The tiniest of vibrations ran along the base of my skull when I read that the refinery had expanded two years ago. The enlargement was estimated to have doubled Noble's capacity.

The increase mirrored the rise in Peru's gold exports to the United States over the last couple of years. Synchronicity occurred, but until proven otherwise, coincidences were evidence.

The company was a partnership owned by two brothers, John and Cesar Medina. They'd inherited the outfit from their father when he died six years ago.

I popped their home addresses into Zillow. Both siblings lived on Star Island. According to the listings, they both paid over six million for their houses, and, curiously, both transactions closed a year ago.

I'd dig deeper, but the Medina brothers seemed to be living large.

I ran down the list of employees Bradley had included.

There were three hundred of them. But the records from the IRS didn't provide a clue.

Noble's top ten clients were impressive. Along with three jewelry firms, several financial firms were listed. But two names jumped off the page: the United States Bullion Depository, better known as Fort Knox, and the Federal Reserve Bank of New York.

I wasn't up on the whole financial thing, but weren't they both run by the Treasury Department? I went to Google. The AI-generated response confirmed both the bank and the depository were under the Treasury Department's jurisdiction.

Reading that the New York bank had the world's largest stockpile of gold and that most of it was held for foreign governments, the idea that someone, maybe even Pembroke, was involved in some kind of scheme crept into my mind.

I pushed the thought away, replacing it with a vision of the vault that was five floors below the bank's Manhattan building. Had anyone tried to steal the two hundred billion dollars' worth of gold like they did in the Netflix series set in Spain?

The Fort Knox website said it held half of the gold the United States government owned and was under the US Mint, another arm of the Treasury Department.

Noble was selling gold to two high-profile units of the Treasury Department. Did all refiners do that?

I clicked on the document complied on Miami Pure Refiners. The company was another family operation, stretching back to the 1950s. It was run by a sister and brother, Faye and Jim Farber.

Their refinery was in Hialeah and behind a concrete wall. The company's offices were in the tony district of Brickell. Miami Pure's client list didn't offer any clarification like Noble's.

I went to their website and clicked on a button reading What We Do. A picture of what looked like raw chunks of metal, and another of gleaming bars of gold framed a paragraph that read,, *Miami Pure Refiners processes mined, raw precious metals and scrap and purifies them. We remove impurities and other metals using chemical processes, electrolysis, and melting to separate the various elements. We then refine it to the desired purity level, usually defined in carats or fineness. The resulting precious metal is then cast into bars or used to make coins, jewelry, and other products.*

It was something I never thought about. It was hard to envision the shiny gold bars pictured coming out of the muddy waters being worked in the Amazon rainforest.

But one thing was clear, after the gold was refined into bars, it was impossible to trace. There was no way to know whether the bullion came from a legitimate mine in Alaska or California or from an illegal operation in the Peruvian rainforest. Gold was untraceable.

Clicking on Meet the Management brought me to a page with photos of the executive team and their bios. Those pictured looked clean-cut, but so had Bernie Madoff.

I went back to reading the report Bradley had put together. Both companies had stayed out of trouble with the law, but Miami Pure Refiners had been fined two times in the last ten years by OHSA for safety violations. It may have put their employees in jeopardy, but I discounted the failure to adhere to the rules.

Closing the tab out, I navigated to Noble Metals' website. It was better designed than their competitor's. A tab marked Analytical Services caught my eye. The page it led to described five different services they offered, including fire assaying to determine how pure a lot of gold or a piece of jewelry was.

I clicked on Meet Our Team. Pictures of the Medina brothers in hard hats framed a banner at the top of the page. The look didn't jibe with the owners' Star Island mansions. I scrolled down. The chief financial officer was a woman with a bright smile. Though she had the Medina last name, any charge of nepotism was mitigated by her Harvard degree.

In the bio of the head of quality control was a bold-faced link referencing them winning an award as the refiner of the year. I followed the link to a picture-packed page that led with an owner holding a silver dish representing the award.

I scanned the pictures of the ceremony and did a double take. A man in a group shot grabbed my attention.

Zooming in on him, my mouth dropped open. "Holy shit! I can't believe it!"

Mary Ann poked her head in the room. "Frank? What's the matter?"

"Nothing. I have to check something out."

She raised her eyebrows, and I said, "Just give me five. I need to make a call."

Mary Ann shook her head and walked away.

I scrambled to my feet, closed the door, and punched a number into my cell.

Chapter Thirty-Eight

"Look, I think I've got something."

"You do? What?"

"Remember I told you I ran into a couple of Americans in a bar in Peru?"

"Yes. What about them?"

"I'm almost certain one of them works for one of the refiners you did the report on."

"Really? Which one?"

"Noble Metals. And they were meeting with the owner of Santos Exporting Company."

"What do you think this means?"

"I have an idea, but I'm not sure at this point."

"It could be legitimate. They may have a normal business relationship with—"

"And it doesn't rain in Florida in the summer."

"What?"

"How can we identify someone from a picture on their website?"

"There's a couple of ways. At worst, I can get the motor vehicle records for everyone listed as an employee and check the driver's license photos against the web picture. It won't be too bad as the Americans were male, right?"

"Yes. How long is it going to take?"

"I'll get on it now."

"Okay, and when you identify him, find out what his role is at Noble."

I paused before making a second call. It was a delicate matter, and trusting anyone could not only put the investigation in jeopardy, but it could also put my life at risk. Someone could be tapping my phone.

Getting up, I went into the kitchen. "Mary Ann, let me use your phone for a second."

"Why?"

"Somebody is dodging my calls. They might answer if I call from yours."

She handed it off. "Go ahead."

I took the phone into the den and slowly punched the numbers for the Treasury Department. Waiting for George Pembroke to get on the line, I debated how to approach the delicate subject.

Pembroke's voice startled me. "Hello, Frank."

"Hi, Mr. Pembroke."

"How is the case progressing?"

"I wanted to talk to you about something. It's highly confidential."

"What's on your mind?"

"Is the line secure?"

"You're getting me concerned, Frank."

"It's an extremely sensitive subject."

"Can it wait a day?"

"I guess so."

"Good. I'm flying into Miami tomorrow for a meeting with the Ecuadorian Minister of Finance. I realize you just returned, but can you make the drive over?"

"That'll be perfect. Where would you like to meet?"

"I'm sure you know the Fontainebleau Miami Beach hotel. How about noon? We'll grab some lunch and talk."

"Sounds good, but I want to make sure we can speak privately."

"We can talk in my room, say eleven thirty?"

"Thanks. Have a good flight down."

I went back into the kitchen and handed Mary Ann her phone. "You feel like taking a ride to Miami tomorrow?"

"Tomorrow? Why?"

"Pembroke is flying in, and I have to tell him about the CIA operative on the take. We can make a day of it or stay over if you want."

"I'm not doing any of the driving on Alligator Alley."

"What? You never drive it anyway."

"Oh, I forgot, the Youth Haven event is tomorrow. I can't go."

<hr>

MY AVERSION to paying for valet parking had me walking three blocks to the Fontainebleau Hotel. My eyes widened as I approached. If the place were any swankier, it'd need its own red carpet.

A pair of gloved doormen smiled and pulled open the doors. A rush of cold air smelling of jasmine enveloped me. The optics of a government official staying here were poor at best.

The staff was top-notch; within a minute of advising the front desk I was here to meet Pembroke, a manicured young man in a blue suit escorted me to the tenth floor. A lumberjack standing outside the Treasury official's door checked my identification and let me in.

The suite offered sweeping views of the Atlantic Ocean.

Seated on a gray couch, Pembroke was on the phone. As he ended his call, he waved me over.

He stood, offering his hand. "Frank, nice to see you."

"Same here. This is a nice hotel."

"One of my favorites. You'll like the food. They have a wonderful lobster salad."

I barely resisted commenting on a so-called public servant staying here on the taxpayer's dime. "That sounds good."

"So, before we go down for lunch, what did you want to discuss?"

"As I mentioned, it's a highly sensitive matter."

He nodded somberly.

I said, "There's no easy way to say this, but it's about the agent you put me in contact with in Peru."

"The CIA operative?"

"Yes, Rico Fortuna."

"What about him?"

"I'm afraid he's compromised."

Pembroke crossed his legs. "And what makes you believe this?"

"I saw him accept a bribe from the cartel."

"Are you certain?"

"Yes. Look at this video." I stood. "I uploaded a copy to the cloud in case something happens to me."

"Excuse me, but that sounds paranoid."

Shrugging, I showed him the film I'd taken.

Pembroke pawed his chin. "Perhaps he is conducting an undercover operation."

"I doubt it. He realized I witnessed the bribe and told me to watch my back."

"He threatened you?"

"That's how I took it. And I was followed back to my room, and someone was outside my door. I was even followed to the airport the following morning."

"You could have been tailed the entire time you were in-country as a safety measure."

"I wish I had been, I could have used help with an encounter at one of the illegal gold mines."

Pembroke didn't comment on the close call. Was he aware of it? The Treasury's Department of Intelligence worked with the CIA and the FBI and had access to all the government's secrets and operations.

"I'm not sure what you expect me to do with this accusation."

"I wanted you to be aware of it and possibly inform your CIA counterpart."

"Something like this might have been misconstrued. There could be several explanations for it."

"After observing him, I believe otherwise. But sure, it could be an undercover operation."

Pembroke reached into his pocket and came out with a cell phone. "Excuse me, I must take this."

He retreated to the bedroom and closed the door.

Rolling around whether to ask for having Rico questioned about the payment, Pembroke came out of the bedroom.

"I'm sorry, but I'm going to have to cancel the lunch. Something came up that requires my attention."

Was this the political way to brush someone off? I scrambled to my feet and extended my hand. "Sure. I understand, no worries."

After releasing my hand, Pembroke pecked at his phone, turned his back, and walked away. I left with more questions than I'd come with.

Stepping into the sunshine, I scanned the beach. It was busy. I checked the sky. The only thing in the cloudless sky was an incoming plane. I paused, thinking *why not*, and hustled to my car.

Chapter Thirty-Nine

I drove past the security gatehouse and followed the signs to the executive and marketing offices of Noble Metals. Miami was a flashy town, but there were more than the usual number of high-end cars parked by this entrance. Maybe it was normal for the decision-makers working with precious metals.

The burritos I'd bought from a food truck were repeating. It wasn't the ritzy lunch I'd pictured overlooking the Atlantic Ocean.

I wasn't sure what I was trying to accomplish, but since Pembroke canceled, I had two hours or so to play with before heading back to the other coast.

Bradley had identified the man in the picture as Eric Barrio. He was the head of the refiner's buying department. According to the Department of Homeland Security, Barrio had traveled to Peru and Colombia ten times over the last year.

Barrio was the man I'd seen in the Peruvian bar and grill. When I'd brought up the environmental damage illegal mining was doing, he and his companion cut me off quicker than a New York driver.

Either Noble Metals was doing business with a mine in

Peru or wanted to. There was no other explanation for traveling so often to South America. The only question was whether the mines were illegal or not.

If they were breaking the law by importing gold from illegitimate mines, they'd need documentation to cover their tracks. It wouldn't be difficult for the Peruvians to issue fake paperwork, but our forensics people would be able to determine if it was a charade.

Weighing whether to try and get customs to audit the paperwork on Noble Metals' imports, a white Mercedes convertible drove into the lot.

I squinted. The man behind the wheel was Eric Barrio.

As he closed the top, I instinctively got out of the car. Slinging my jacket over my shoulder, I walked toward the building. Would being clean-shaven, capless, and without the wide-framed glasses I'd worn in Peru be enough?

I timed my approach to the entrance to coincide with Barrio's.

In Florida it was normal to greet a stranger. "Good afternoon."

Barrio replied, "Good afternoon."

A step ahead of him, I looked over my shoulder. "Do you know if you need an appointment to see someone here?"

"It depends on whom you're seeing."

"I wanted to talk to an Eric Barrio."

He stopped in his tracks. "What about?"

"I represent a couple of gold mines in South America, and we're looking to diversify away from the Indian market."

"Where down south?"

"Our main supply comes out of Colombia, but we've just opened another one in Peru. The new supply is what we're looking to sell in the United States."

He nodded slowly.

I added, "To break into the market, we're willing to be flexible on the pricing."

Barrio looked me over. "You look familiar. Have we met?"

"No, we haven't, but a lot of people think I look like George Clooney."

He nodded slowly. "That must be it. What's your name?"

I used an alias. "Burt Freeman. And you are?"

"How did you know about our company and Eric Barrio?"

"A contact of ours in Peru. I think the name was Villa-something. He's an aggregator."

"Villarosa?"

"Yes, that's who I think it was."

He smiled and stuck his hand out. "I'm Eric Barrio."

"Oh my God, that's crazy."

"Maybe it means something."

"I hope so. I've got a lot of pressure from my boss to find this new stream a home."

"Come in. I've got a couple of minutes I can spare. If the pricing is sharp, we might be able to take it off your hands."

Barrio pulled out a plastic card and put it up to a pad on the side of the door. He punched a handful of numbers in, and the door clicked open.

"You must have a lot of security here."

"We do, especially in the processing and storage areas."

A perky woman behind the reception desk smiled as we passed by.

Barrio turned into an office smaller than I'd pictured. "Here we are."

He slid behind a desk loaded with molten chunks. He snatched a sticky note off the desk phone and crumpled it up.

"This is a huge complex. I saw you have other offices."

"We do. They built them a couple of years ago. We were cramped in here,"

"Where do you get all the gold to keep this place going?"

"We've been in business a long time and have contracts with many suppliers."

"Nice."

"So, how can we help you, Mr. Freeman?"

"Burt, call me Burt."

"Burt it is. What is on your mind?"

"Like I said, we're expanding and looking for a home for the production out of a new project in Peru."

"Who is we?"

"Oh, Omega International."

He tilted his head. "I don't know that name."

"We believe in keeping a low profile."

"Where are you importing from?"

"Well, we haven't done much of anything into the States. We supply significant tonnage to India for jewelry production."

"We sell there as well."

"It's a big market, but management is concerned with having all our eggs in one basket. If something goes wrong over there, we're screwed. I mean, with the price of gold these days, I'm surprised they still buy so much jewelry in India."

"It's a cultural thing."

"I know, but at some point, putting food on the table trumps adorning yourself."

"Have you been to Peru?"

"Not yet, I've been to Colombia a bunch of times. How about you?"

"I'm there all the time to keep an eye on things. I'm heading back down in two days."

"How long are you staying?"

"A week."

"Is it like Colombia?"

"Peru has many more illegal mines."

"How they get the gold doesn't matter, as long as they get it. We've dealt with, let's say, all kinds of producers in Colombia."

"Importing into the United States is very different than getting around customs in India."

"We're aware of the rules and what documents are required to pass muster with US Customs."

"We'd need to see a sample set of documentation to consider going forward."

"Don't worry, paperwork is not going to be an issue."

"Provided that's the case, it comes down to price and what capacity we have."

"We're prepared to discount the unrefined market rate by twenty percent."

His eyes widened. "That's aggressive."

"We need to be in the short term. We'd guarantee the reduction for six months."

"If you can stretch that to a full year, it'd be an easier sell to our owners."

"A year? I don't know, I'd have to check with headquarters, but we'd probably be able to tack on a month or two."

"Why don't you check into it and get back to me?"

"I will." I stood and stuck my hand out. "Thanks for seeing me without an appointment. I got to be honest, I came here on a lark. I didn't expect to see anyone."

"My pleasure."

"I'll reach out to management as soon as I can and get back to you no later than tomorrow."

Chapter Forty

Mind racing, I jumped in my car and drove for ten minutes. Right before getting onto Route 828, I pulled over. I had my suspicions about Pembroke, so I called Romney French. Since he was with Homeland Security, it made perfect sense and would give me cover if Pembroke questioned it.

French was cordial, agreeing to go along with the plan I'd cobbled together.

Speeding along Alligator Alley, I replayed the meeting with Barrio. It had been risky to approach him, but it seemed to have worked. He didn't say anything overt, but I was sure the refinery was working with illegal mines.

They were all about making money, and all Barrio cared about was the discount along with the need for the paperwork to line up. A blue feeling washed over me; it was another example of selling your ethics.

After hitting Naples in an hour, I'd call Barrio. He struck me as someone who wouldn't waste time checking into me until we had a deal, but I couldn't take the chance. I needed to tell him someone had made an arrangement to buy the new supply of raw gold, and I had nothing to sell Noble Metals.

My cell rang, it was Bradley.

"Hey, Bradley."

"Hi, Frank. Can you talk?"

"Sure. I'm driving back from Miami."

Refraining from telling him about Pembroke blowing me off, I filled him in on the visit to Noble Metals.

"Wow. I can't believe you went there. He didn't recognize you?"

"No. The entire time in was in Peru, I had a beard, wore fake glasses, and Jimmy's hat."

"Jimmy?"

"My neighbor's kid, the one who was murdered."

"Right. Plus, he saw you out of context."

"It sure was. So, what did you call about?"

"It's nothing. It doesn't compare with what you just did."

"Tell me."

"I wanted to let you know the woman driver was arrested today."

"What woman driver?"

"Carioca, the one we followed over the border."

"She went right back to it?"

"Yes, and she was moving three times what she did when we followed her."

"She was arrested once before, wasn't she?"

"Yes."

"Three strikes."

"No. She was charged for the first offense, and since we never charged her when we followed her across the border, this makes it the second violation."

"We can still file charges against her for the crossing. We have the video evidence."

"I guess so."

"We can. Send me the video of the new violation. I've got to think this over."

Hamster-wheel mind going full tilt made the ride go by quickly. I pulled into my driveway and called Barrio. When I told him the new supply of gold had already been committed, he said to keep them in mind in the future.

Mary Ann wasn't home. I changed and took my laptop out to the lanai. I clicked on Bradley's email. There were two attachments. I clicked on the video one.

The screen filled with footage of the border crossing. The image narrowed in on a white Honda. It was a coupe that looked like a Civic. The smugglers might have believed small cars wouldn't attract attention, but a male guard pulled it out of a long line of vehicles looking to cross into Mexico.

A pair of officers converged on the car, and the driver got out. I recognized her immediately. Shoulders slumped, she trudged behind the guard as if the ground was covered in glue. The Toyota was driven through the Vacis machine and directed to a covered area where the car would be physically searched.

Bradley had also sent images of the x-rays taken. Two dark gray areas filled both rear quarter panels.

Customs searched the compartments, seizing twenty million in cash.

I sent an email to Bradley asking him to check with the DEA. It'd be interesting to see if cartel communications contained any chatter about the seizure and arrest.

Mulling over the idea I'd come up with, possibilities emerged. If it worked, it'd provide leverage I might be able to use somewhere. With so many moving parts in this case, it was impossible to predict when it might prove critical.

PUTTING the finishing touches on an email to Pembroke, I noticed Mary Ann through the sliders. I hit send and went inside.

"Hey, how was it?"

"Good. They raised so much money it was incredible. Someone paid five thousand for two Taylor Swift tickets."

"That's crazy."

She asked, "How was lunch?"

"I never got to eat at the Fontainebleau. Something came up and Pembroke had to deal with it."

"Oh, what did he say about the CIA agent?"

"Not much. I'm hoping it's nothing more than Pembroke is sick of hearing bad news."

"It could be that. I mean, who would want to get into a tussle with the CIA?"

Shrugging, I said, "You feel like going out for pizza or something?"

"I'm not really hungry, but if you want to go, I'll get a salad."

"Yeah, let's go. We can try that new place, Trulli Pasta and Pizza, on Trail Boulevard."

"Okay."

"Why don't we hang by the pool for a while?"

"I need to stop by Connie's, she called me twice."

"What's going on?"

"She's had a couple of rough days. Clearing out some of Jimmy's stuff isn't the easiest thing to do."

Slamming my hand on the table, I said, "She should never have had to deal with this crap."

"Take it easy, Frank."

"Take it easy? I'm running all over trying to get justice for Jimmy and Stevie."

"That was your call, Frank, and you know it. Nobody asked you to do anything."

"I couldn't just sit on the beach while we're being attacked."

"Don't be so dramatic."

"Dramatic? Didn't you just say you couldn't hang with me because you had to go to Connie's?"

"I'm not the enemy, Frank, and you're not here to save the world."

Chapter Forty-One

"Good afternoon, Mr. Pembroke."

"Hello, Frank."

"What can I do for you, sir?"

"There are two things I wanted to update you on. First off, I spoke to Romney. He said you contacted him about an audit."

"Uh, yes. I figured there was no need to get you involved, since he's with Homeland Security."

He paused before saying, "Customs have agreed to cooperate. I'll send you the information on your contact, and you can take it from there."

"That's great, sir. Thank you."

"In the future, make sure you come to me."

"Yes, sir."

"Now, that Anna Carioca. She is in custody, and we've provided the prosecutor with the evidence to charge her with the initial violation. She's being arraigned tomorrow. Given the number of arrests and the flight risk she poses, they're confident she will not be granted bail."

It felt like a year had passed since we'd let her cross into

Mexico at the start of all this. "How long do we have until she's brought to trial?"

"I don't know, but federal courts are bogged down, so it's unlikely to be soon. However, I wouldn't let too much time pass."

"Where is Carioca being held?"

"Right now, at a detention facility in Brownsville, Texas, but she's going to be moved to San Antonio in the morning."

"Who is in charge of interviewing her?"

"I don't have that information, but I'll make sure the file is forwarded to you."

"That would be perfect."

"Let's hope you're able to do something with this. I want to move on to the Adams operation."

"I'm giving it my best shot, sir."

"That's all I can ask. We'll talk soon."

"Thank you, sir."

Pembroke had a Dr. Jekyll and Mr. Hyde personality. Leaders were supposed to be steady Eddies, resisting the day-to-day winds, but Pembroke bucked the trend. I hoped he didn't play poker.

Looking over the menu, I said, "You know the pasta here is supposed to be great."

"I thought you were getting pizza."

"I'm wavering. The pasta is from Italy. They use different wheat there. It's not the same we get. That's why they eat so much of it and never gain weight."

Mary Ann smiled. "You don't have to justify what you want to order."

"I'm not justifying anything, it's true."

"I know, don't you remember that guide we had in Rome?

He said he ate pasta every night of the week. Monday was pasta and beans, Tuesday was with vegetables, Wednesday was marinara, and so on."

We both laughed. I said, "And he was skinny."

"Maybe the wheat has something to do with it, but it's portion control if you ask me."

The server came over. Mary Ann ordered a salad, and I asked for the pappardelle Bolognese.

I said, "So how was Connie?"

Mary Ann said, "She needs to get away or something. Maybe I'll take her to Marco Island for the day. We'll go to the beach or something."

"Go tomorrow."

"Are you sure? Didn't you want to start looking at new tiles for the pool?"

"It can wait. I'm going to be heading back to Miami tomorrow anyway."

"Again? You just got back from there."

"I think I'm onto something, and I'm working with customs on something."

"Customs? On drugs being smuggled in?"

I lowered my voice. "No, we're looking at some of the gold coming in."

"From Peru?"

"Yes, but from illegal mines run by the cartels."

"You better not go back to Peru, Frank."

It was time to talk to Paul Casella, the lead on the Carioca case. According to the official file, Casella was a seasoned investigator who'd spent most of his career dealing with drug cases.

I called the number Pembroke provided. A raspy voice answered, "Casella."

"Hello, Mr. Casella, my name is Frank Luca. I'm on special assignment with the DEA and the Treasury Department and wanted to talk to you about Anna Carioca."

"Okay, Mr. Luca. What's on your mind?"

"When you interviewed her, did she reveal anyone up the chain?"

I heard him suck on a cigarette. "No, they never do."

"Well, she might if we apply pressure."

"The mules would rather do five behind bars than rat on the cartel."

"I understand, but we're going to charge her with two counts, each carrying five years."

Casella said, "I don't know if that'll do it."

"We're also going to charge her with laundering. She moved more than a hundred thousand twice within a year, and that carries a ten-year prison sentence. She could be looking at twenty years in prison. I think Carioca will talk when she is staring at what might be a lifetime behind bars."

"That would normally seal things, but the cartels have done a good job of scaring the hell out of people."

"I know, they threaten to kill the families of anyone who spills on them."

"Exactly."

"Do me a favor and talk to her and let me know."

"I will."

"I'm looking for a name or two, but nothing low level. I don't want the guy she dealt with; I want his boss."

"I'll press her and see what she provides, Mr. Luca. But don't get your hopes up."

Chapter Forty-Two

"JD?"

He smiled. "That's me." We shook and he hiked his thumb. "Hop in."

"Thanks for doing this."

"No problem. If we had the manpower, we'd do more field audits."

"How often do you get out?"

"Once every two months. Are you from New York?"

"Yes. I thought I lost my accent."

He chuckled. "Think again. My parents came down when I was ten, so I lost mine."

"You're basically a native."

"I know. I can't believe how Southern Florida has grown. It's unbelievable."

"Yeah, the secret is out."

He nodded. "So, tell me what's driving this audit of Noble Metals?"

I selectively filled him in.

He said, "You went to Peru?"

"Yes. It was something to see. All the illegal mining has destroyed an area more than ten times bigger than Miami."

"Really?"

"Yes. The rainforest is really being impacted."

"I've always wanted to check out the Amazon. Did you see the movie *Anaconda*?"

"No. What's it about?"

"Oh, you have to see it. This crazy hunter takes a film crew hostage. He wants to catch the biggest snake in the world."

It sounded like Hollywood drivel, and I had zero interest in watching it.

He said, "Here we are."

As he turned into a driveway, I sank into my seat. Though Barrio was supposed to be in South America, you could never be sure. I pointed out, "That entrance is for the marketing and executive offices. Go around the building, you'll see the other door."

A pair of armored trucks rumbled into the parking lot as JD held his badge up for the camera. I caught a whiff of diesel as the door buzzed open. We stepped inside. JD announced, "We're with US Customs."

The receptionist was flustered. "Uh, hold on. I'll get my manager."

"Tell him we're here to audit your import records."

A woman in a dark pants suit came out. "Hello, gentlemen. I'm Evelyn Rose, the office manager. How I can I help you?"

JD explained we needed to see six months' worth of records covering their imports from Peru. The lady showed us into a small conference room.

Ten minutes went by, and the door swung open. The manager and a young man with an armful of folders came in. "Here's the first batch of files. Is there something specific you're looking for? We might be able to make it easier for you."

JD replied, "That's fine, we'll go through them on our own."

We went through the batch and the others they brought in. We pulled the invoice and certificate of origins from each file and made copies. The paperwork covered four suppliers: Pan American Silver, Internacional Gold, Precious Internacional, and Casa de Gold.

The largest supplier for the batch of files was Pan American Silver. JD separated their files and randomly chose five of them. JD asked for documentation showing the payment for the raw gold detailed in the shipping paperwork.

The manager came back in with copies of the wires sent by Noble Metals. JD took them and said, "These files don't have copies of the FinCen form 105."

Her face dropped at the mention of the anti-money-laundering declaration. "Really? I'm not sure where they keep them."

"The regulations require them to be produced upon request if they're not with the entry documents."

"I'll check with the traffic department. They handle the clearance paperwork."

"Thank you." He handed her his card. "Send them to me. No later than tomorrow."

"We will."

"Okay, that's it. We're done."

Once we got back in his Bronco, I said, "What do you think?"

"Outside of the FinCen 105, the paperwork looks to be in order, but fake documentation is a common ploy to cover tracks. We'll trace the wires, see who received the funds and go from there."

"I can get the Treasury Department to trace the wires."

"Be my guest."

"Are you going to check the files they sent to customs to see if the FinCen documents were with the clearance papers?"

"Everything is electronic. We hardly request hard docs on a shipment these days."

"So, they never filed a FinCen?"

"Probably not. They know the penalties for a misdeclaration are up to a half-million-dollar fine and a ten-year prison sentence."

As soon as I hopped in my car, I took photos of the wire transfers, making sure the transaction details and transaction data were clear. I sent them to Bradley and called him to be sure he understood the urgency.

Alligator Alley was empty, and I moved along at eighty miles an hour. It felt like we were on the edge of a breakthrough.

THE SUN WAS ABOUT to peek over the treetops as Mary Ann and I were in the middle of our morning walk. My phone rang. We had an informal policy of not touching our phones when getting a dose of exercise.

I pulled it out. It was Bradley. "Uh, I have to get this. We're—"

She didn't make a face, proving again she was the better person. "Go ahead, Frank."

"Bradley, what's up?"

"We traced the wires, all five of them."

"And?"

"Not one of them went to Pan American Silver."

I stopped in my tracks. "Who got the money?"

"They went to three different Colombian banks, but the beneficiary was an outfit named Pan Am Enterprises, not Pan American Silver, like the paperwork said."

"Jesus."

"And here's the best part. I checked them out but can't find anything on them."

Mary Ann was a block ahead.

"These bastards are laughing at us."

"What do you want to do? Go after Noble Metals?"

"Not yet. We can't spook them any more than they are already."

"This means the gold is probably being sourced from illegal mines."

"That's what it looks like. I wonder how many cartels are laundering money like this."

"You put it together, Frank. That was great work."

"It doesn't mean a thing yet, so don't celebrate."

"We'll get there."

"I have to think about our next step. I'll call you later."

Pocketing my cell phone, I jogged and caught up with Mary Ann.

"Did you save the world?"

"Come on, this is important."

"I'm only kidding, Frank. What happened?"

"The cartel is buying raw gold that comes out of illegal mines and shipping it to the refiner I went to in Miami."

"You went to a refinery?"

"I went with customs to check their paperwork."

"Oh. I'm confused about what's going on?"

"I could be off on one or two things, but they're buying the raw gold with the cash from the drugs they sell in the States. Then they sell the gold to Noble Metals, which refines the gold, making bars out of it, and it's clean as a whistle; you can't trace where it came from."

"Oh my God. That's actually a pretty smart way to launder money."

"It is, and you want to hear something crazy?"

"Go ahead."

"The United States government is buying a lot of it."

"What? How can that be?"

"It's true. Noble sells refined gold bars to the government, and some of the illegally mined gold is sitting in Fort Knox and the Federal Reserve."

"Talk about embarrassing."

"Right? Not only is it coming from illegal mines that are destroying the rainforest, but they're helping to cleanse the drug money that paid for it."

"You can't make something like that up. It's disgusting, so corrupt."

"You see why I'm trying to shut this crap down? It's making the cartels stronger and stronger. They're buying political power, right here, in the States."

"I don't know about that."

"They sure are. This kind of money we're talking about is hard to pass up. It's corrupting far too many law enforcement officers, including the DEA."

"I hope you're not saying that out loud. People will think you're crazy."

"Crazy? Then tell me how the Fisherman got out of the country? As soon as we were onto him, he disappeared into the wind."

Chapter Forty-Three

After Casella said hello, he started coughing. I waited but the fit continued. In between hacks, he said, "I, I, I'll call you back."

Wondering if smokers realized the coughing was a sign, a bad one, my phone lit up. It was him.

"Hi, are you okay?"

"Yeah, I swallowed the wrong way."

Whatever you want to tell yourself, buddy. "Oh. What's going on?"

"Well, I had an interesting talk with Anna Carioca today."

"I like interesting. Is she ready to trade information?"

"Uh, interesting wasn't the best word to use. She doesn't want to reveal her superiors."

"Did you tell her she was looking at a minimum of ten years if she's lucky?"

"Of course. They know if they talk they're as good as dead."

"She's that confident she'll survive ten years in prison?"

"Carioca made a reference that the lawyers representing the people she worked for would get her a better deal."

"Is she aware this case involves some of highest officials at the Treasury Department?"

"I never mentioned names but said money laundering was a priority of the federal government."

"Is it worth taking another run at her?"

"Honestly, I think you're wasting your time. She's scared out of her mind."

"She have any children?"

"None that we're aware of."

As I was considering what to do, Casella said, "Look, I've been down here my entire career. I've prosecuted a stadium full of these kinds of people. Take it from me, you're wasting your time. You should move on."

"I don't know . . ."

"Carioca will go to prison, for how long will be determined by the judge. But we'll press them not to allow her to serve her sentences concurrently."

"Give me a day to think this one over."

Chapter Forty-Four

I clicked on the link he provided and granted permission for my laptop to allow use of audio and its camera. A window popped open. It was a video feed of me.

My neck looked flabby, making me look older than I cared to admit. I'd read that changing the angle of the camera could shave years off.

Fiddling with the angle, another window opened. It was Bradley. "Hey, Frank. I see you got on. Is everything working all right?"

Instead of asking if there was a filter to make me appear younger, I said, "Yes. Thanks."

"Good. Casella should be signing on any minute now. I'm going to mute myself and shut my camera. If you need me, send a text."

"Thanks again."

A chime sounded and Casella's face filled another video box stream. "Hello, Frank. I'm here with Anna Carioca and her attorney, Benito Juarez."

We exchanged greetings, and Carioca's attorney said, "You requested the meeting, so it's your show, Mr. Luca."

Carioca appeared smaller than she had in the border videos. As she picked at a fingernail, I said, "Thank you for hearing me out. Now, the charges against Ms. Carioca are as serious as they get. We're certain we'll obtain convictions on all three counts."

The lawyer said, "We're going to mount a vigorous defense and believe at least one of the charges will be dropped before the trial begins."

"You're free to challenge the charges, but we're confident they'll stand."

"I beg to differ, but I'll save our arguments for motions we'll submit to the judge."

"Mr. Juarez, forgive me for being blunt, but bravado is not going to help Ms. Carioca. We have irrefutable evidence your client engaged in money laundering, breaking several statutes. What will help Ms. Carioca is agreeing to provide information on who directed her to commit the offenses."

"Without admitting to any of the infractions, Ms. Carioca doesn't want to cooperate with those that put her in here."

"She'll get a minimum of ten years."

"If, *if* she's convicted."

"Ms. Carioca, do you honestly believe you'd survive ten years in a maximum-security prison?"

She looked at her lawyer, whispering, "I guess so."

I said, "Ma'am, excuse me, but physically speaking, you're a little nothing. How would you defend yourself against some of the most violent people on earth?"

"We'd petition the court."

"Mr. Juarez, rest assured the highest levels of the United States government are determined to end the scheme your client engaged in. They'll lean as hard as they can to ensure she does hard time."

Carioca slumped in her chair.

Juarez patted her arm and said, "Hypothetically, if a similarly situated person were to cooperate, what would you offer them?"

"If she provides concrete information on upper-level members of the cartel she worked for, we'd get her into the federal witness protection program. That way, she'll be safe from the people she informs us about."

"The charges would be dropped?"

"Yes. Provided she cooperates fully."

"Would someone have to testify?"

"Possibly, but that remains to be seen."

Juarez leaned into Carioca, whispering in her ear. Carioca shook her head and whispered back.

Juarez turned to the camera. "We'd need the protection extended to her mother and sister."

"Where are they located?"

Carioca said, "They live in Texas."

"Provide their contact details. If you give us what we need, we'll get a protection order covering all three."

"Allow me to confer with my client."

"Of course."

Juarez muted the video meeting and huddled with Carioca. The body language told me she was going to cut a deal. Her attorney shook his head and patted her shoulder. He took the mute off.

"Okay. We're willing to cooperate if the charges are dropped and protective custody for Ms. Carioca, her mother, and her sister is assured."

"You have my word, counselor, as long as she identifies the men who manage La Familia's cartel operations in the state of Florida. We don't want low-level players. We need a player with direct report and responsibilities to the Mexican cartel leaders. Do you have that information?"

Carioca nodded.

"Okay. Tell us who they are and what they do, and you have yourself a deal."

Carioca started talking. She gave us two names: Javier White and Ernesto Carmen. I questioned her about relationships, and she provided what sounded like incriminating information.

I had enough to work with and ended the Google meeting by saying, "Thank you. We'll vet the information you provided and be in touch. In the meantime, we'll instruct the prison authorities to keep Ms. Carioca separated and safe from the general population."

I closed out the dialog box and called Bradley.

"Wow, Frank. That was good. You were just tough enough and she cracked."

"We'll see if the information she provides is any good."

"I didn't know you obtained permission to offer an immunity and protection deal for her. That really clinched it."

"Well, I don't have it yet. I didn't want to broaden the number of people knowing what I was doing."

"That's probably a good idea, but do you think you'll get it?"

"You know the old saying, rather than ask for permission, ask for forgiveness."

"Yeah, and the bottom line is we got the names. So if they don't get her into witness protection, it doesn't matter."

"It matters to me. I gave my word."

"Oh, sure. I understand, of course."

"All right, now we need as much intel on Javier White and Ernesto Carmen as we can get."

"If they're as important as Carioca made them out to be, the DEA would know about them."

"We can't involve the DEA."

"You're worried about a leak?"

"Yes. We just don't have enough cards to play to have these two guys tipped off."

"I could check and see what we may have on any cross-agency investigations."

"Do it, but make sure you don't leave fingerprints. Act like the only people we can trust are each other."

"No problem. What else can we do?"

"I have an old contact who might be able to help with this. I'll see what he says."

Chapter Forty-Five

"Federal Bureau of Investigations. How may I assist you?"

"Special Agent Haines, please."

"Who may I say is calling?"

"Frank Luca."

After a brief hold, Haines answered, "Frank, how the hell are you?"

"Doing good. And you?"

"Same old, same old. How is Mary Ann doing?"

"She's good. Her health is good, and she's busier than when she was working."

"That's great. So, how's retirement treating you?"

"It's okay, but I got a little bored, and you may have heard about the drug killings we had down here."

"Yeah, I heard that was La Familia."

"It was. And I've been on a special mission with the Treasury Department."

"Really? You're back in action?"

"It's complicated, but, and I don't say this lightly, the killer was tipped off by the DEA, and I was close to the boy. I just felt like I had to do something, you know?"

"Absolutely, I get it. Sometimes making it personal is what's needed."

It was hard to believe I'd misread this man when we first met. I snickered. "Well, Mary Ann would say I'm obsessed with bringing these punks to justice. The truth is, she's right."

"How can I help you with it?"

"I'm looking for information on two men: Javier White and an Ernesto Carmen. Both of these cretins work for the La Familia cartel."

"What do you have so far?"

"We've got someone, a mule who moves cash for the cartel, in custody, and she's talking. We're putting her and two family members into protective custody."

"You're looking for confirmation on what's she's providing?"

"That and anything else you might have."

"Let me check into them and I'll get back to you."

"It's got to be super discreet. I can't have these guys disappearing into the wind."

"My clearances are a notch below the highest. I'll do it myself and include a bunch of other queries to make it look broadly based if anybody looks into it."

"I really appreciate it."

"No problem, Frank. I've got an hour or so before a meeting. Let me see what I can dig up."

"I owe you."

"Don't thank me yet."

Hanging up, I thought about what Haines had said about making it personal. It was true and something I tried to avoid doing when I was working homicides. It was all about focusing on the killer.

The problem with this case was there were so many bad guys. There was no doubt about wanting to get the Fisherman, but he wasn't alone. This one had drug dealers, money launderers, illegal miners destroying the rainforest, and corrupt law enforcement officers and politicians.

Instead of focusing on one person, I was fighting a multi-headed beast. Something like this required an army.

In my old life, once a killer was behind bars, justice was had. In this case, if I was somehow able to nail the Fisherman and a money launderer or two, the cartel would still be operating. I had to rethink what a win was, or it would eat me alive.

NEWLY RENOVATED, The Turtle Club was packed. My buddy still tended bar, and he'd made sure our table was beachfront.

It was impossible not recalling it was the place where I'd met a woman named Kayla. She was in from Chicago, and, at the time, Mary Ann and I were only partners on the job.

We hit it off and I thought Kayla was something special. Then, on our first official date, I collapsed in a La Playa bathroom. It was bladder cancer. They made me a new bladder and I recovered. It was a nightmare, but it led to Mary Ann and me becoming a couple.

Mary Ann and I were looking over the menu when a woman came up to our table. Mary Ann introduced her to me. The two of them took classes at a fitness club.

As they chatted, my phone buzzed. It was the customs agent I had visited Noble Metals with. Telling Mary Ann I was going to the boy's room, I hustled off the patio and answered while walking through the dining room.

"Hey, JD, how are you?"

"Good. You have a minute?"

Pushing through the entrance of the restaurant, I said, "Sure. What's up?"

"We checked into Noble Metals suppliers, and they all appear to be shell companies. All four of them were created within weeks of the first shipments under their names, and the owner of all of them is listed as Rosario Castro."

"The same guy is behind all their suppliers?"

"That's what we uncovered. I'm betting if we look further, we'll find a lot more companies were created to avoid attracting attention."

"Do we know anything about this Castro guy?"

"Not yet. We'll lean on Noble Metals and see what we can dig up."

"Hold off on that until I have a chance to see who Rosario Castro is. He's got to be a front for someone, and I have an idea who is behind all this."

"Okay, let me know."

"I'll get back to you."

I disconnected the call and put another one through to my FBI buddy, Haines.

He picked up, saying, "You know, Frank, most people from New York City have at least a tiny bit of patience."

Scoffing, I said, "No, this is something different, something new."

"What is it?"

"I have another name for you, Rosario Castro. Can you investigate him? He's behind a couple of shell companies shipping raw gold out of Peru to a refiner in Miami."

"Is he related to the other two you asked me to check on?"

"Not directly, but this case is a Hydra."

"All right. I'm not done, but I found a couple of interesting cases involving the men you asked me to check into."

"What did you find?"

"Let me call you back when I'm finished."

There was that word again: interesting. The last time I heard it my spirits rose and then crashed when Casella said Carioca wouldn't cooperate. Now Haines had invoked it when referring to the men Carioca identified.

It couldn't be anything but good for the case. Could it? Carioca needed a deal, or she'd be away for a minimum of a decade. She couldn't be lying. It didn't make sense to try and fool us. But, then again, she wasn't sitting behind bars because she was smart.

The wild card was the cartel. Cemeteries were filled with evidence of their ruthlessness when seeking revenge.

Instead of putting my phone away, I made a call.

"Dad?"

"Yes, honey."

"Is everything all right?"

"Yes, just wanted to say hello."

"Oh, I'm working."

"Sorry, just wanted to see how you were."

"Everything is good. I'll call you later."

I ducked into the bathroom before heading out to the Turtle Club's deck. Mary Ann was looking at her phone. She picked her head up and wagged it.

As I pulled the chair out, she said, "You called Jessica?"

"Yeah, just wanted to check in."

"You know she's working."

"I forgot."

She raised her eyebrows. "What's going on, Frank?"

"Nothing. Can't I call my daughter?"

"She told both of us her boss doesn't want her getting personal calls."

I picked up the menu. "I'm probably getting the fish sandwich. What are you getting?"

Chapter Forty-Six

Taking it and an iced coffee out to the lanai, where Mary Ann was reading, I settled into a chaise lounge. Ten minutes later, I snapped the book shut. I was turning pages, not reading.

Mary Ann said, "What's the matter? I thought you liked Churchill."

I put the book down and grabbed my cold coffee. "I do."

"You have to learn to relax. And the coffee isn't helping."

A drop of condensation from the glass plunked onto my shirt. "I'm okay, just waiting on an important call from Haines."

"So? Read or relax until he calls. Being wound up about it isn't going to make him call any faster."

My phone buzzed. I waved it at her. "See? It worked. Haines is calling."

I hustled inside and answered. "What do you have?"

"You get straight to it, don't you?"

"Sorry, just a little anxious with this one. I'm afraid these bastards are going to disappear on me."

"I'm just busting your chops, Frank."

"I know, sorry I'm keyed up."

"I get it, so, here's what I pulled out of the files. Javier White doesn't have a record, but ten years ago, Ernesto Carmen was arrested for possession. He received a suspended sentence."

"Yeah, that much I know."

"I figured. Okay, there are two active investigations, and White and Carmen are mentioned in both. One is an FBI probe into the La Familia presence in the country. The agency estimates there are at least three thousand members of the cartel operating in the States. We've identified over twenty-five hundred members thus far. Once that is accomplished, we're planning to launch countermeasures."

"Why are they waiting until figuring out who everyone is? These guys are getting more embedded in the country every day."

"I don't make the rules, but they probably want to establish how big the threat is before applying resources."

I respected Haines, but he was talking like a politician. It was the same thing that happened when any institution was questioned; they'd circle the wagons to protect themselves. Maybe it was baked into our genes.

"Just great, kids are dying while the bureaucrats take meetings."

"Come on, Frank, you know better than that. This drug problem wasn't created overnight, and it's going to take a long time to cripple the cartels."

"The longer we wait, the more entrenched and powerful they become on our turf. They get any stronger, we'll turn into a third world country where most of the politicians and law enforcement agencies are on the take."

"As far as I'm concerned, that's a wild exaggeration and an insult to the brothers and sisters I work with."

"Am I the only one who thinks this needs to be dealt with urgently?"

"Believe me, narcotics trafficking is a top priority, especially as it threatens our national security."

"Well, why isn't anyone acting like it is?"

"Frank, I'm trying to help you, really, I am, but attacking the agency is making it difficult."

"I have the highest regard for you and I'm sorry you're offended, but it's the way I see it. I wouldn't have come out of retirement if I believed there was a credible process to deal with the drug problem."

"Look, out of respect and considering kids you knew died, I'll give you what I have on White and Carmen, but that's the end of it."

Through clenched teeth I said, "What do you have?"

"Javier White owns a small accounting practice in Punta Gorda, which is where he lives. He was born in Mexico, married an American woman, and became a citizen ten years ago. We believe he launders money for La Familia, using a couple of his clients who have cash businesses. It's believed his brother, Tonino, who is a member of the La Familia cartel and operates out of Sonora, was the connection."

Making notes as fast as I could, I asked, "He have any kids?"

"Three daughters under ten years of age."

"And Ernesto Carmen?"

"He's running the cocaine pipeline from the Carolinas down to Florida. He's listed as the owner of a trucking firm called Galactic Freight. They're moving appliances for a bunch of different retailers."

"That's convenient."

"Nobody said these people were stupid."

"I assume he's moving drugs inside his trucks with legitimate deliveries."

"That's what an informant told us."

"A near perfect cover. What about his personal life?"

"He's married with five kids."

"Five?"

"You heard that right. Carmen lives in Port Charlotte, and

the trucking company is in North Port. He also has a mistress he visits at least twice a week. The woman, named Estelle Blicker, lives in South Venice."

"Not surprised. Who do White and Carmen report to? Someone in the States?"

"We don't know for sure, but it appears whoever it is, is in Mexico."

"Have we tapped their communications?"

"Yes, but they've produced nothing to date. The members of La Familia are as diligent a group as we've encountered. They're highly disciplined."

That fit with the cultlike status the DEA analyst told me about when I first got to Washington. I'd built a career out of knowing that, sooner or later, everybody makes a mistake or takes a shortcut. Was La Familia a different animal altogether?

"Nobody is unbeatable."

"And Rosario Castro is a member of La Familia. He was born in Mexico and moves around South America. His last known address was in Colombia. He's a known launderer."

"That makes sense."

"That's all I have."

"Okay, thanks, I appreciate it."

"No problem. Look, Frank, you're a great cop, but you're going to have to keep your emotions out of things if you want to make a difference."

I mumbled thanks, hung up, and left the den. Reaching into the fridge for a bottle of water, Mary Ann came in from the lanai.

"Who were you arguing with?"

"It wasn't a fight."

"Don't tell me that. I came in to use the bathroom and you were shouting."

"I wasn't shouting, just a little excited."

"You're going to give yourself a stroke or something if you keep this up."

"I'm fine."

"You tell me all the time to be careful of stress. You know, it applies to you as well."

"Take it easy, Mary Ann. It was just a phone call that got a little heated."

She shook her head and made for the master bedroom.

I said, "I'm going for walk."

Putting my sneakers on, I tried to focus on what Haines found out about White and Carmen. What Carioca had said looked to be true. What was I going to do next?

Chapter Forty-Seven

The other option was to wait and watch them. The FBI and DEA appeared to have an operation focusing on La Familia, but joining them was not something I'd consider. There was just too much money floating around to be sure no one would feed info to the bad guys.

Creating a separate investigation would create pushback, but Pembroke promised he'd back me in anything I proposed. I couldn't do something like this alone. What I needed was manpower. People I could trust. Bradley was one. Would Derrick join the effort?

Thinking about my ex-partner, my phone vibrated. I half expected it to be Derrick. It was Paul Casella, the lead investigator on the Carioca case.

"Hey, Paul, how are you?"

"Not good."

My shoulders tightened. "What's the matter?"

"They've kidnapped Carioca's sister."

"What? Who?"

"We have to assume it's La Familia."

"Damn it! When did this happen?"

"Last night."

I said, "They're putting pressure on her to stop her from testifying."

"There's no doubt about it. Her lawyer, Juarez, left a message for me a few minutes ago."

"She's going to back out of the deal."

"They're warning her; if she cooperates, her sister and mother will probably be murdered."

"We should have put them in protective custody from day one."

Casella said, "We had no reason to. Carioca told us she would do the time."

"As soon as she agreed on the video call, we should've picked up her family."

"That would be highly unusual. And we had no authorization."

"The cartel got to her."

"How? Nobody knew about the offer but us."

"It was Juarez. He either volunteered the information, or La Familia got to him as well."

"You think so?"

"It has to be."

"Frank, do you want me to talk to Juarez?"

"What do you think he's going to say? Let me think this through. I was counting on Carioca's testimony."

"I have to admit, I was surprised she agreed to talk in the first place. The cartels have just about shut down everyone."

"Well, I hope she realizes she is going away for a long time."

"I'm going to hold off on the charges. Let me know what, if anything, you want to do with Juarez."

Hanging up, I banged the desk with my fist. The smell of defeat was in the air.

My plan was swirling down the drain. The cartel had

kidnapped Carioca's sister. Snatching people off the street in Mexico was a tactic criminals used all too frequently.

Only this kidnapping didn't happen in Mexico but in Texas. If there were any doubts about there being any limits on what the cartel would do to protect themselves, they evaporated.

I grabbed my phone and made a call. "Jessie, it's Dad."

"Hi, Dad. How are you?"

"Good. And you? What are you doing?"

"I just left the gym. I took two resistance classes. They were tough, but it felt good to work out."

"That's sounds like it was fun."

"It was."

"Where are you going now?"

"I'm walking to my car. I'm going home to shower."

"Be careful."

"Uh, hold on, Dad. Hey, what are you doing? No! Stop! Don't—"

I shot out of my chair. "Jessie! What's going on?"

The line went dead.

I ran out of the den. "Mary Ann! Mary Ann!"

"What's the matter?"

"Something happened to Jessie!"

"What?"

"I was talking to her, and I think somebody kidnapped her or something."

"Kidnapped? Who? Why are you saying that?"

"I was on the phone with her and . . . We have to call 911 and report it."

"Tell me what happened!"

My cell buzzed. It was Jessie's number. "Hello?"

"Sorry, Dad. They were about to tow my car, and I got there just before they hooked it up."

"Oh, thank God you're okay."

"Of course I'm okay. Why are you so worried?"

I couldn't tell her the cartel was a possible threat. "You were shouting, and then the phone got disconnected, and you know—"

"You shouldn't worry so much, Dad. I can take care of myself."

I didn't want to tell her what every parent does–just wait until you have kids of your own. "I know you can, it's just . . . anyway, forget it. Is your car okay?"

"Yes. They were like two seconds away from hooking it up."

"A close call. You have to watch where you park."

"There was no sign saying you couldn't."

"You would've beat it in court, but that takes time."

"I'm about to drive home, so I'll call you guys later."

"Okay, get home safely."

Mary Ann had a lottery winner smile on.

I shrugged. "I guess I panicked a little."

She snickered. "A little?"

"Like you've never overreacted?"

She pecked my cheek. "I'm just playing around."

I wrapped my arm around her waist. "You want to really play around?"

She smiled. "We'll see. I have to go by Connie's now."

"Can't she wait?"

She rolled away from me. "Don't they say anticipation is the best foreplay?"

"You're killing me."

She picked up her pocketbook and headed for the door. "I'll see you in an hour or two."

"I don't know if I can wait that long. I may have to come to Connie's and drag you back."

She wiggled her hips and left.

I retreated to the den knowing I had something to look forward to. Sitting in my chair, I closed my eyes. Carioca had folded on us. What could be done without Carioca's support?

Ideas came in and I pushed them out. Using my subconscious was something I was learning to do. At times, I would try not to actively solve a problem but observe possible solutions. It wouldn't fly at the academy, but it worked every now and then.

The thought of dropping the charges against Carioca came into my head. We could follow her. No, there was no upside. The cartel would wonder what was going on.

Carioca hadn't given us what we wanted, but she did tell us about Javier White and Ernesto Carmen. My larger plan to get the Fisherman hinged on Carmen. And White could give us information on the laundering. But without Carioca, how could I get them?

Once the cartel knew Carioca was no longer a threat, they'd release her sister. What if we waited a week after her release before taking Carioca and her family into custody? Would Carioca cooperate then?

As an idea floated in, my eyes sprung open. It was bold and dangerous. Innocent people could be killed. It was a complicated plan, but it could work.

Chapter Forty-Eight

It was still unclear why Pembroke had reacted in the Fontainebleau Hotel when I told him Rico, the CIA operative, was corrupt. Was it a lack of stomach in going toe to toe with the CIA, genuine disappointment in the agency, or something sinister? Keeping the operation under wraps would also be challenging for someone at the top of the command structure.

Until the Rico incident, he'd been as accommodating as one could imagine. Pembroke was the reason I had a shot at getting the Fisherman and putting a dent in the cartel's money laundering.

The other option would be hard to swallow, asking Haines for help. Suffering a large dose of humiliation over what I had said to him would hurt. The flip side was Haines would go out of his way to be sure there were no leaks to show me I was wrong.

Instead of calling the FBI office, I dialed Haines's cell number. "Frank? Is everything okay?"

"Yes. I'm calling about something sensitive and thought your cell was a better option."

"Frank, the FBI has its problems, like any organization, but corruption isn't widespread."

"I know, and first off, I wanted to say I'm sorry for what I said. I was out of line and, uh, let my frustration speak for me."

"Apology accepted. Now, tell me what's going on."

"I need your help. I realize it's asking a lot, but I need four teams, with vehicles, and we have to move quickly."

"What's the operation?"

I detailed the plan I'd concocted, and Haines jumped on board.

After thanking him, I hung up and made a call to Casella.

The lead on the Carioca case answered on the first ring. "Paul Casella."

"Hey, Paul, it's Frank Luca."

"Hi. What's up?"

"I want to talk to Carioca's lawyer, Juarez."

"I don't think you're going to change anybody's mind."

"I just want to talk to him."

"You want me to set up a Zoom?"

"Yes, please. I want the focus of the call to be trying to get him to influence Carioca to cooperate."

"You're wasting your time, buddy."

"Maybe, but I owe it to the boys who lost their lives to give it another shot."

Casella seemed to be a solid man, but there was no reason to take more chances than were necessary.

"I think you're wasting your time, but okay, we'll give it a go."

"Thanks. I've got to report on where we're at, so can you get it set up as soon as possible?"

"Sure thing. If Juarez is available, we'll do it in an hour or so. I'll let you know."

"That would be perfect."

THE ZOOM MEETING was set for four o'clock my time. I wasn't superstitious, but the timing was a good omen.

Mary Ann was on the lanai. I popped my head out of the slider. "I have to be back for a call at four. How about we go for a nice lunch at Nosh on the Bay?"

"For lunch?"

"Why not? It's a beautiful day, and we can sit outside."

She checked her watch. "Okay. Give me twenty minutes. I want to hop in the shower."

"Take your time."

She came into the house as my phone pinged. It was a text from Haines: *Everything is set. We have four teams ready to roll.*

I told him I'd call him around five.

I parked under the Naples Bay Resort, and we emerged by the marina.

Mary Ann said, "I like the way white looks."

"I don't know, when the buildings were all different colors, it felt like Portofino or something, like we were on vacation."

"How would you know? You've never been to the Italian Rivera."

"Well, how about we go there? You've been so good with me on this case and all."

"You going somewhere?"

"Maybe, but that's not why I am saying that."

She rolled her eyes. "I can put up with a lot if you want to make up for it with traveling."

I pointed to a big yacht. "As long as you don't want one of those."

"No way. But when we're in Portofino, we can take a day cruise on one."

"That's a deal."

We were shown to an outdoor table. Mary Ann said, "This is nice. We should be doing things like this all the time."

She was right. But not until this case was over. "Portofino and fancy lunches, you're getting to be high maintenance."

"Never. That's one of the things I'm proud of. We were lucky to get more money than we ever thought we'd have, but we really didn't change our lifestyle."

"There's no reason to. I mean, what's better than having escarole and beans for dinner?"

Sharing four small plates was the perfect lunch. They were delicious, making me want more. But the clock was ticking.

Mary Ann reached for my hand as we walked back to the car. My mind was on the Juarez call, but I dropped a few hints to remind Mary Ann that too many days had passed since we'd been intimate.

When we came home, I retreated to the den and called Bradley. Circling my desk, I told him my plan.

He said, "Wow. It sounds amazing."

"I'm going to need you to work your magic. I want to see what's going on real time."

"I'll get assets in position and provide the links."

"Thanks. Hey, I'm sorry this is so last minute but I—"

"I understand; you wanted to keep the circle small."

"It's coming together quickly. I've got to get on the Juarez call now."

I leaned forward and clicked to join the Zoom call. Paul Casella was talking to Juarez. He said, "Good, Frank has joined the call."

"Hello, gentlemen. Before we get started, I just wanted to thank you, Mr. Juarez, for agreeing to talk on such a short notice."

"No problem. I'm curious why you requested the meeting."

"To be honest, I wanted to see if you could convince Ms. Carioca to reconsider her refusal to honor the plea agreement."

"I've spoken to her at length, and she is firm in her position."

"And that's because her sister was kidnapped?"

"She's concerned about the repercussions of any testimony she'd have to give about the activities of Javier White and Ernesto Carmen."

"There's been a development that would relegate Ms. Carioca to a supporting role."

"What development?"

"Both Mr. Carmen and Mr. White are cooperating with a joint DEA and FBI investigation."

Juarez hesitated before saying, "Define cooperation for me."

"They're talking, providing specifics about the activities of the La Familia cartel. Your client's function would be one of collaboration, to support their testimony."

Juarez narrowed his eyes. "If you're sure she wouldn't be the one providing bedrock evidence, I can speak with her again."

"I'm positive. I've been privy to the transcripts of conversations our guys have had with Mr. Carmen and Mr. White. It's powerful and detailed."

"All right, I'll speak with her."

"Don't wait too long. Things are moving very quickly on this case. I wouldn't want her to miss the opportunity."

"I'll visit her tomorrow morning."

"That works. Let me know. Have a good day, gentlemen."

I left the video meeting and grabbed my phone. Before I could complete dialing, Casella called. I swiped it away, texting that I'd speak to him later. He responded, *What the hell is going on?*

Haines answered on the first ring. I said, "Everything is set. Get your guys rolling."

"Will do."

"Tell them I'm on my way."

Chapter Forty-Nine

Parked in the rear of a Walmart parking lot, I watched two dark-blue vans pull in. I hopped out of my car. The rear doors of the second vehicle opened. I climbed inside and we lurched ahead.

A man with headphones pulled down around his neck extended his hand. "Tom Mortar." We shook and he introduced me to a woman sitting at a console. "This is Special Agent Dorothy Main." He pointed to the driver's seat. "And Vic Belair is behind the wheel."

I said, "It's good to be with everyone. This is an important mission, and I appreciate being allowed to tag along."

"Our pleasure." He motioned to a place on a bench running along the van's side. "That headset is for you."

I sat and grabbed the headphones hanging from a hook. "What's the ETA?"

"Seven minutes."

A few minutes later the van slowed and turned onto a residential street. Mortar said, "Okay, we're approaching the target."

Darkness was closing in quickly, and the streetlights in

Carmen's Candler Park neighborhood were already on. The street was quiet, and no one was outside any of the neighboring homes.

The lead van pulled in front of the Carmen house. We came to a stop a driveway away. Looking through the windshield, I saw two agents jump out of the lead vehicle.

Backs of their windbreakers emblazoned with FBI, they approached the front door. I leaned forward.

A blaze of yellow outlined the agents when the door opened, but they blocked out whoever had answered the bell. The agent to the left bent down. It had to be one of Carmen's five children.

A minute later a woman came to the door. Mortar said, "We've got confirmation it's Carmen's wife. They're going inside."

The agents stepped into the house and the door closed. I exhaled and asked Mortar, "What is she saying? Is she going along?"

He pulled the headset off one ear. "They told her she and the children are in danger and must leave now. She wanted to call her husband, but they convinced her the cartel was monitoring their calls."

"So, they're agreeing?"

He stuck a finger in the air and nodded. "She's getting the kids organized to leave."

Five long minutes later the door opened. An agent led the way. Mrs. Carmen held two of her children's hands and the three other kids followed like ducklings.

The rear doors of the lead van opened. The agents helped the Carmen family get in.

Mortar flashed a thumbs-up and spoke into his headset, "The groceries are on board."

I pumped a fist. "Nice going! How long until they are at the safe house?"

"Twenty-five minutes or so."

"Perfect. Now we wait for part two."

"We'll get in position while they're being dropped off."

My cell vibrated. It was Haines.

"Hang on, this could be something."

I answered the phone and Haines said, "Carmen just got off the phone with Charro Esperanza, who we know to be an enforcer for the La Familia cartel."

"There you go. What did he say?"

"He told him a meeting was called and Carmen was expected to be there."

Carioca's lawyer, Juarez, had told the cartel what I said about Carmen and White cooperating. "Did Carmen say he was going?"

"Yes."

"How did it sound? Normal?"

"Yes, it was low-key. Esperanza is no dummy."

"Where are they meeting?"

"At the Boulevard Industrial Park in Opa-locka."

"They're probably planning to torture him."

Haines said, "Either that or kill him outright. I Googled the place, and if there is such a thing as a perfect location for murder, this is it."

"What time are they meeting?"

"Ten o'clock tonight."

"Okay. Let me know what happens with White."

We parked the van across the street from Galactic Freight's parking lot. Trucks were backed into six of the ten loading docks. They were doing a decent volume of legitimate business to cover the drug-running Carmen was engaged in.

Mortar said, "We can't take a chance, we have to put on our body armor."

I took one off a hook and strapped the vest on. Picking up a pair of binoculars, I focused in on a white Escalade parked by the trucking company's offices. The plate number confirmed it was Ernesto Carmen's vehicle.

A text pinged. It was a video. I watched it. Out of the corner of my eye I saw a tractor trailer backing out of a bay. It drove toward the exit.

I said, "That truck is hauling one of those containers that go on a ship."

Mortar looked and said, "Yeah, that's MSC, Mediterranean Shipping Company."

"Oh, I thought it might have been from South America."

"They're a global company. They even have cruise ships."

"How do you know so much about them?"

"We took a cruise a couple of years ago on one of their ships, and I read up on them."

"Do they have service to South America?"

"Yes. I remember that. Why are you asking?"

"I'm hoping the cartel isn't getting bold. They could be moving large quantities of drugs into the States in one of them."

"Customs would catch them."

"Don't be so sure of that. They only check about one percent of the cargo coming in."

"I thought it was around twenty percent."

"It's not. Hold on, that looks like Carmen coming out of the door."

Mortar used his binoculars. "That's him. He's getting in his car."

I said, "Okay, it's showtime. We've got to be careful. Assume Carmen is armed, and heavily at that."

The taillights of Carmen's car lit up. He backed out of his space.

Mortar said, "Okay, it's game time."

Chapter Fifty

We slowed as we approached the traffic light at the corner. Carmen beeped his horn as the yellow light turned to red. We came to a stop.

My heartbeat sped up. I looked at Mortar, saying, "Ready?"

He nodded. "Let's do it."

Mortar opened the rear doors and he and I got out. Carmen's head was down. He was looking at his phone. We approached, holding our badges up as he lifted his head.

"Open the door and put your hands on the steering wheel!"

He complied.

"Get out!"

"I didn't do anything."

"Get out!"

He swung his legs out the door and stood.

"Where is your phone?"

He stuck his chin toward the car.

"Turn around."

I patted him down. "He's clean."

Mortar put a hand on his shoulder. "Come with us."

"I can't leave my car in the middle of the street."

"We'll take care of it"

"But it's still running."

I said, "Get in the van."

His eyes narrowed.

"If you want to see your family again, get in the van. Now!"

"Don't threaten me, man."

"It's not a threat, it's your new reality. Now, get in the van."

Nostrils flaring, Carmen trudged to the van. We got inside and he said, "Where are we going?"

I said, "That depends on you."

"What do you want?"

"Look at this." I showed him my phone and played the video.

His eyes widened. "Where the fuck are they?"

"They're in a safe location."

"You kidnapped my family?"

"No, we rescued them."

He took a deep breath but said nothing.

"We know La Familia is coming for you and your family."

"That's bullshit."

"Oh yeah? The meeting tonight? You'll be slaughtered if you go."

"I don't know what you're talking about."

"The cartel believes you turned on them. You have two choices. You can get back in your car and go back to your empty home. If you insist, we'll bring your family back, but you'll all be dead within a day."

He closed his eyes. "Or?"

"You can help us."

"I'm no rat."

"What matters is that the cartel thinks you are."

"How the hell could they believe that?"

"What counts is they do. If you want to risk it, you're free to leave and see if you can convince them."

"You're bullshitting."

"Look, three different agencies are monitoring La Familia. We've got several wiretaps going, and we picked up chatter on a leak. Then we heard them talking about how they were going to shut it down. Your name and two others were mentioned. When we heard the call you got from Esperanza, we sprang into action to save your family."

He shook his head. "No, no. This is crazy. I didn't betray anybody."

"Like I said, it doesn't matter, but if you want to take a chance, go ahead. Just let us know what you want us to do with your family."

"I want to talk to my wife."

"I'm not going to allow you to speak with her, but I can do a live video to prove she is safe."

"Why can't I talk to my wife?"

"Because you're not in control, we are. If you want to see them, I'll place a call."

He nodded.

I sent a text and muted my phone. My cell vibrated. I held the screen out so Carmen could see it. The youngest child was sitting in his wife's lap, and the other four kids were watching TV.

I ended the video call and said, "Now, are you going to cooperate?"

"I want a lawyer."

"If you insist, our offer of protective custody for you and your family goes away"—I snapped my fingers—"just like that."

"You can't do that. I got my rights."

"Sorry, but you have no right to protective custody. All we're saying is, if you cooperate, you and your family will go into the witness protection program."

"This is bullshit. You guys are screwing with me. You cops are all the same."

"You should be thanking us for saving your family. If we weren't conducting surveillance, you and your children would be—"

"I need time to think this whole thing over."

"You don't have time; the cartel is coming for you."

He put his head in his hands. "I don't get it, man. This is fucked up. I didn't do anything."

"What you did do was distribute drugs. We know it and so do you. Distribution, on this scale, will get you decades behind bars, and I'm going to go after every single one of your assets: the house your family lives in, your cars, your bank—"

"Okay, okay! I'll do it, but you got to guarantee my kids are going to be safe."

"You tell us everything you know, and you and your family will get new identities and be safely relocated."

WE BROUGHT Ernesto Carmen to a safe house. It was close to the stadium the Dolphins called home. He'd be moved the next morning, but I needed something from him before he was interrogated by the DEA and FBI.

After we ate pizzas, the three agents began playing cards. I motioned for Carmen to follow me into the back bedroom.

I closed the door behind me and said, "Sit."

Carmen sat on the bed. "What now? What do you want?"

"I'm looking for specific information, and if you give it to me now, I'll make sure you get a chance to talk to your wife."

"You will?"

"Yes, but just for five minutes."

"What about my kids? They've got to be scared."

"If you help me, I'll let you say a quick hello."

"I need to see them and tell them it's going to be all right. I don't want them scared."

"That's going to be up to you. And it's going to start with you telling me who runs the drug-dealing network in Southwest Florida for La Familia."

"There's a lot of people involved."

"Who are the main players?"

He hung his head.

I squeezed his shoulder. "Everything is going to be better for you if you talk. You'll be out of this racket and given a fresh start in life with your family."

He frowned.

"Who runs Southwest Florida for them?"

"Farro Acuna, they call him Cherdo."

Cherdo was pork in Spanish, but the name didn't register. "Where does he operate out of?"

"Fort Myers."

"Where specifically?"

"There's a car wash right by Sam's Club. I think the name is Crystal Clear."

A procession of cars provided a convenient cover for handing off drugs.

"Is that where Acuna distributes from?"

"Yeah, there's a building where they do stuff like detailing, and they transfer merchandise inside there."

Merchandise? These thugs were like politicians, renaming things for legitimacy.

"What territory is Acuna responsible for?"

"I'm pretty sure from Sarasota down to Naples."

"What do you know about an Emmanuel Ruiz?"

"I don't know him."

"You don't know Manny Ruiz?"

"No."

"What about the Fisherman?"

"That doesn't ring a bell."

"Are you sure?"

"Yeah, I don't know who that is. Why? Is he important?"

"Manny Ruiz, aka the Fisherman, ran all the dealers in Lee and Collier County."

"Hey, I don't know all these guys. All I knew was everybody was happy about how it was going. There was a lot of growth. It kept getting bigger and bigger."

"Tell me about Acuna."

"What do you want to know about Cherdo?"

"Everything you know about him."

Chapter Fifty-One

In 2003, he was released four years early, having been a so-called model prisoner. When he got out, Acuna went to work for his father, who owned the car wash. He inherited it eight years later when his father passed in 2011.

I wanted more information on Acuna but was afraid to call any of my Lee County Sheriff's Office contacts, fearing he would be tipped off.

Acuna lived in Cape Coral with his second wife, Marta, and his twenty-three-year-old son, Ferdinand. Their house was a modest Key West styled home valued at seven hundred thousand.

I checked into his forty-year-old wife, Marta. She didn't have a criminal record, but, curiously, there were nine properties in her name. According to Lee County's tax records, the homes were acquired starting in 2018. The cumulative value of the real estate she owned was fifteen million dollars. None of them encumbered by a mortgage.

Like his father, Ferdinand had a record. Because he was a minor, the record was sealed on one of the charges. I rooted around the date of the incident, finding the arrest of two individuals at the Crystal Clear Car Wash on the same day. Like father, like son; the arrests were made for dealing marijuana.

What was available in the records was another arrest. This one had Acuna's son, Ferdinand, being picked up two years ago in a drug raid in Lehigh Acres. His statement said he was just visiting a friend and playing video games.

He was represented by a high-powered law firm and the charges were pled down. Ferdinand didn't serve a day behind bars and was given probation for three years.

There were no properties held in the son's name, but his birth record listed Joan Flannery Acuna as the mother. Acuna and his first wife had divorced a year after Acuna Sr. had gone to jail.

An idea hit me. Leaning back in my chair, I considered how to move it forward. After a minute, I made a call to check on a record. As the information was read to me, I smiled.

THE TV WAS on when I came into the house. I tiptoed into the family room. Mary Ann was asleep on the couch. I picked up the remote and shut the boob tube off.

Mary Ann woke up groaning. She muttered, "What time is it?"

"A little after eleven. Are you all right?"

She grabbed her phone off the cocktail table. "It's a quarter to twelve. Where were you?"

"We were tailing somebody in Fort Myers."

She put her head down and closed her eyes. "I'm worried you're going to get hurt."

"Don't be worried. I'm careful."

"I want this to be over."

"Me too. We're close to getting justice for Jimmy and Steve. Let's go to bed."

She winced. "My right cheek is killing me."

It was her MS flaring up. "When did this start?"

"Last week, when you were in Miami."

"You didn't say anything?"

"You were busy."

"Did you call the doctor?"

"No."

"Why not? You know we have stay on top of this."

"It's not too bad."

"You just said it was killing you."

She shrugged.

My not being around was the reason she wasn't feeling good. She was worrying about me, and that caused stress. Doctors had warned us stress was a trigger for MS.

I got her two extra-strength Tylenols. Handing her a glass of water, I said, "We're going to call the doctor in the morning."

She took the glass but didn't say anything. She was hurting more than she let on.

When she finished taking the pills, I said, "Let me help you get to bed."

Neither of us fell asleep for a long time. She was hurting, and I was ping-ponging between her health, my guilt, and what I was supposed to be doing tomorrow.

We made a doctor's appointment for one p.m. It was barely enough time to run back and forth to Fort Myers. I rinsed my coffee mug and put it in the dishwasher.

"I'll see you later."

"Aren't you coming to the doctor with me?"

"Definitely. I just have to take care of something first."

"Where are you going?"

I pecked her cheek. "By the airport."

Traffic on the interstate wasn't too bad. Taking the exit after the airport, I turned onto Daniels Parkway and headed west. I hit Route 41 and took it north.

Passing the flight training center, the signage for Sam's Club came into view. I turned left just after the discount retailer and made another right. I slowed as my destination came into view.

There were three cars in the lane leading to Crystal Clear Car Wash. I pulled around them and parked alongside a building in the rear of the property. A red and blue sign listed the vehicle detailing services offered.

A heavily tattooed man in ripped jeans came toward me. "You got an appointment?"

"Yeah, but I need to talk to Farro first."

"He's busy."

I turned and headed toward the corridor customers used to see their car getting washed. "Me and Cherdo go way back."

Someone was paying for his wash. I toyed with air fresheners until the cashier was free. I approached the lady in a housecoat behind the counter and said, "Hi."

She offered a quarter of a smile. "You got a ticket?"

"I need to see Farro."

"He ain't here."

I flashed my agency credentials and whispered, "Tell him it's about his ex-wife."

"Did she get hurt or something?"

"Sorry, ma'am, I need to talk to Mr. Acuna."

The cashier studied me before getting off her stool. She lumbered toward a door just off the merchandise area. The cashier knocked, whispered something, and went inside. A long minute passed until she emerged.

She pointed to the door. "He said to go on in."

"Thank you, ma'am."

I opened the door. Acuna's office was adorned with soccer posters and a giant photo of Miami's star player, Lionel Messi.

White haired, Acuna was standing behind a metal desk. "What happened to Joannie? Is she okay?"

"You can sit down, she's all right."

Potbellied, Acuna eased himself into a chair. "So what happened?"

I sat in one of the chairs in front of his desk. "Nothing. I'm actually here about your son."

Acuna shot out of chair. "What the fuck is going on here?"

Chapter Fifty-Two

"Sit down, Mr. Acuna, and we'll talk this through."

"What's going on with Ferdy?"

"Your son is fine. For the moment."

"What is that supposed to mean?"

"That if you cooperate, he'll be okay."

"Mister, I don't know who you are or what you're talking about."

I leaned forward. "I'm a special agent for the Treasury Department, Homeland Security, and the DEA. I know all about you and La Familia."

Acuna slid his hand off the desk.

"If you're reaching for a weapon, buddy, you'd be making the biggest mistake of your life."

He put his hands on the desk.

I said, "I'm not here about anything you or your son did."

He picked up his phone. "I'm calling my lawyer. This is—"

"Put it down. We can work this out between us."

"I already pay plenty. But I'm always willing to, uh, tip someone to make a problem go away."

There was a knock on the door.

Acuna said, "What?"

"Are you okay, boss?"

"Yeah, get back to work!"

He looked at me. "Now, how much you want?"

"It's not money I'm after."

"Yeah, that's what they all say."

Lowering my voice, I said, "I want you to help me get one of the dealers you work with."

He smiled and shook his head. "You guys are something else."

"I'm dead serious, Cherdo. You're going to help me get the Fisherman."

He blinked. "I don't know who you're talking about."

"This is going to go a hell of a lot faster if your stop the bullshit. You know Manny Ruiz, and you're going to help bring him back to the States."

He cleared his throat. "Even if I knew him, why would I do something like that?"

I couldn't suppress a smile. "Because if you don't, your son is going back to prison."

"Stop the bullshit already. You can't threaten me with crap like that."

"Oh, it's not a threat, Mr. Acuna, it's a promise. I'll get your son's parole revoked."

"You can't just do something like that out of nowhere. My lawyers will fight it."

"It's not out of nowhere, he violated the terms of his probation."

"He did not."

I cued up a video on my phone and hit play. "Here is your son coming out of the Sandbar on Cleveland Avenue. Take note of the time stamp: it's 12:37 a.m. If I recall, he's got to be home by eleven."

"What kind of game are you playing?"

"Oh, trust me, Mr. Acuna, this is no game. I'm as serious as cancer. You don't help me, and I promise you, your boy will go back to jail."

"We'll fight that."

"If you want to risk it and see if a judge will look past the violation, be my guest. But I can tell you, it's not going to fly, especially when we tell His Honor about you and La Familia."

"I don't know what you're talking about. I don't even know what La Familia is."

I switched to Spanish. "Vamos, Cherdo. Hemos estado escuchando, sabemos lo que estás haciendo por Ernesto Carmen y los demás."

The color drained from his face when I mentioned the wire taps and his boss, Ernesto Carmen.

"You got this all wrong, mister. I'm not mixed up with anybody. I left that life a long time ago."

"You don't know me, but I know all about you. For example, the properties you put in your wife's name. And I can tell you two things you can take to your grave; one is if you don't cooperate, your son is going back to prison—"

"You can't—"

I put up a palm. "Shut up and listen to me. Like I said, I'll get his probation revoked, there's no doubt at all. The other thing is, if you help get the Fisherman out of Mexico, this thing you got going on out of your detailing place will remain between the two of us."

"How do I know I can trust you?"

"You don't know. But I was with the Collier County Sheriff's Office for a long time. You can check with your contacts."

He nodded slowly.

Standing, I said, "I've got to report the curfew violation within forty-eight hours. You've got until tomorrow, this time."

After giving him my cell number, I told him we could meet in a neutral location and left.

I navigated back to Route 75 and headed south. Five minutes later traffic began slowing to a crawl. I had under an hour to make it home. I got off the Corkscrew Road exit and took Oaks Parkway onto Imperial. It was slow going but better than the interstate.

Coming in from the garage, I called out, "I'm home!"

Mary Ann was in my recliner. "Good. How did it go?"

"Good. How do you feel?"

"A little better."

That meant she was still hurting. "Did you eat anything?"

"I don't feel like it."

"You have to have something. I can make something before we go."

"Maybe I'll have a protein bar."

"I'll get it."

I took one out of the pantry, opened the wrapper, and handed it to her. "Eat the whole thing."

"I'll have it in the car."

THE DOCTOR SWEPT into the exam room. "Sorry to keep you waiting."

Mary Ann said, "That's okay."

It wasn't. Why did doctors get away with making patients wait so long?

"How are you feeling, Mary Ann?"

"Not the best the last couple of days."

She examined her, saying, "How are your stress levels?"

"Okay."

I'd been admonished for jumping in before, but I had to say, "It's been stressful, two of our neighbors' boys have died recently."

"That's terrible. Were you close to them?"

Mary Ann nodded.

"I know it's difficult, but you have to manage the grief as best you can."

"I have been. In fact, I'm doing good, helping one of our neighbors who's a widow, and as upsetting as it is, I don't get down about it at all."

"Are you doing the exercises? Swimming?"

"Yes, every day."

"Has anything else changed?"

She shrugged.

"What is it?"

"Well, Frank has been away a lot. He took on a special assignment."

And there it was. I wanted to crawl out of the room.

Chapter Fifty-Three

The ocean-blue and white-colored Margaritaville Beach Resort in Fort Myers fit the bill.

Mary Ann and I had watched the sun dip into the Gulf of Mexico on the resort's Sunset Terrace. It was hours earlier than when she and I had come, and today, as the clock hit noon, the beach and pool areas were getting busy, but the deck was sparsely occupied.

Surveying the area, I chose one of the blue Adirondack chairs lining a wall providing a wide-angle view.

A steady breeze and shade had me wishing I'd worn a T-shirt under my dress shirt.

Wearing a straw fedora hat, Acuna ambled onto the football-field-sized terrace. I stood, waving my arm. He nodded and approached.

Dark circles under his armpits marred the yellow shirt he wore. He said, "This place is huge. Feels kind of commercial."

"Part of the new Fort Myers. There's so much building going on, we probably won't recognize Fort Myers Beach in five years."

"I don't know if that's a good thing."

"It's debatable, but you have to admit, most of the buildings and houses needed serious updating."

"Back in the day, I used to come down here as a kid. Life was simpler back then."

I stuffed the lecture I wanted to give him that there were less drugs and crime then and that he was part of the problem. Instead, I said, "Much as I enjoy reminiscing, we need to get down to business."

He frowned. "I'm taking a big risk here. You go back on your word and . . . I'm done."

A stream of boisterous teenagers flowed onto the deck. They headed to the thatch-roofed Tiki Bar.

"You have my word. I'm only after one guy. Nothing has been said to anyone about you. And it won't, but you have to know you and the rest of your gang have been on the radar a long time."

"Whose radar? The DEA? What can you tell me about it?"

"You've done nothing to earn my help." I took my sunglasses off. "Now, are you going to cooperate?"

"Okay, all right already. Look, I've thought about it, but I don't know how to get Manny to the States."

"I've got a couple of ideas. From what I know, you guys travel around a fair amount."

"We do, but there are a few guys like me, you know, a little older, who don't like to run around as much."

"But you've already been to Mexico five times this year."

He scanned the area. "The bosses, they, uh, insist on doing business face-to-face. You know, they're old school."

La Familia was disciplined. Doing things in person, in places they controlled, limited the chances law enforcement would learn their plans.

"Do you see Manny Ruiz when you're there?"

Acuna nodded. "Oh yeah, just about every time I'm there. The organization insists you meet with everyone who reports to you. They want you to spend time, build relationships. I mean, that's why they call it La Familia. We have a culture."

Yeah, a culture of killing. "I've heard it operates like a cult."

"I wouldn't say that, but they got rules, and frankly, they're anal about them."

I was tempted to ask what the rule was on killing and on destroying lives with their drugs. "Is it true they don't allow any members to do drugs?"

"Yes, if you're caught using, you're out, or, you know, worse."

"When is the next meeting?"

"A week from now."

"What do you do when the business part of the get-togethers is done?"

"A little bit of socializing, and then there's always a big party, you know, a barbecue, and a lot of guys, they ride ATVs or horses on the ranch. Sometimes a couple of the newer guys will do some sightseeing."

Narco tourism? "How close are you to Manny Ruiz?"

"Look, I learned a long time ago how to get along with everybody."

To survive a long stint in prison, you had to. "I'm asking about Ruiz specifically."

"We get along fine. He knows the biz and would've got a lot further, but the kid's got a bad temper, and he's not good with delegating."

The cartel was using corporate tactics to manage their illegal activities. "Delegating? What are you going to tell me next—La Familia has a human resources department?"

"It's run like any other business. We have thousands of associates."

I refrained from taking the butt of my pistol and smashing his knee with it. "Let's focus on getting Ruiz, or your son will be spending Christmas as a guest of the State of Florida."

Acuna's face reddened.

I said, "Can you get Ruiz to spend time alone with you?"

"I'm pretty sure, why?"

"What about getting him to take a trip to another town or to the coast, maybe a day or two at the beach, or someplace else?"

"I don't know. It might be difficult not having someone tag along."

"It's got to be just the two of you."

"Okay. But I don't know how to get him—"

"Tell him you're going to buy a small ranch to use when you're retired. Tell him you want him to see it. You think he'll go for that?"

"Probably. Besides, if I ask him to do something, since I'm his boss, he's got to do it. It's the way we work."

"Good. Find an area around two hundred miles away from the La Familia ranch. A desirable place, so he's not suspicious."

Chapter Fifty-Four

JD, the customs agent working the Noble Metals part of the case, called. "Frank, it's JD. How are you doing?"

"Pretty good, what's going on?"

"I've been monitoring all clearance filings made by Noble Metals."

When people had information you wanted, they made you squeeze it out of them. "And what did you find?"

"There's a container load of gold coming from Callao, Peru. It's on the water."

"Are you sure?"

"Their customs broker filed the clearance documents, and guess what?"

"Just tell me."

"The seller, according to the filing, is located at the same address as two of the bogus companies they've used before."

"How do you know all this?"

"Importers are required to disclose the seller, and Noble's broker declared it using an MID code."

"What's an MID?"

"An identifier for the supplier."

"You said it's on the water. Where is the container now?"

"It's due in Miami in three days."

"Doesn't Noble usually pay the supplier after they receive the gold?"

"That's right, they assay the gold to check the quality before remitting payment."

"We have to stop it. I don't want the cartel getting any more money than they already have."

"They've received a release for the shipment."

"How can that be? It hasn't arrived yet?"

"That's the way it's done. I can get the release rescinded and request hard documents. If they turn out to be bogus, it'll be fraud, and we can seize the load."

"How long does that take?"

"It should be fast. The customs broker they use to clear the shipment has the paperwork."

"Do you think they'll tell Noble there's a problem?"

"They shouldn't right away. We request hard papers every now and then, to keep importers honest."

Was the government that ignorant? JD was helping, and I forced myself not to criticize the policy of checking every now and then.

"Okay, thanks, let me know when you get the documents."

IT WAS on and off the brake as I crawled along Alligator Alley. Traffic was screwing with my plans. I wanted to talk to a few people to see if I could get an angle on how to apply pressure on Barrio, the salesman for Noble Metals.

Once I had the background, my plan was to wear a wire. I'd make an offer and get Barrio to knowingly agree to buy raw gold from an illegal mine connected to a cartel. With the recording, I'd force him to cooperate. It was risky. Other than the one time I'd met him, I hadn't laid enough down to be sure he believed who I purported to be.

I patted my side. The Glock was reassuring, but there was hundreds of millions at stake. Who knew what kind of fire-power these people had?

Paying a toll still rankled me, but I jumped onto the express lanes to avoid a backup and motored my way to Coconut Grove. Twenty minutes later, I weaved my way toward the water. Mary Barrio lived in the Residences at Ritz Carlton.

I'd never been inside one and was curious to see what they looked like. Mary Barrio lived in a three-bedroom unit on the nineteenth floor. A two-bedroom, on the tenth floor, was listed for over three million dollars. How much was this one worth?

The front desk greeted me like royalty. After calling Mrs. Barrio, he directed me to a bank of elevators.

Mary Barrio opened the door a second after I rang the bell. Marine-like posture countered the wide smile she offered. We shook hands and I followed her in.

Key Biscayne Bay shimmered in the distance. "You have some great views."

"It's what attracted us. It took some time getting used to living in a high-rise, but we adjusted."

"How long have you been here?"

"We bought it about two years ago."

After the run-up in prices. "Thanks again for seeing me."

"I'm not surprised Eric is in trouble."

I hadn't said much more than we were investigating Noble Metals. "Did you mention anything to your husband?"

"No. I haven't spoken to him in more than a week."

"I understand you're separated. How long have you been married?"

"We've been together for fourteen years, married for twelve of them."

"May I ask what caused you to separate?"

"Eric is no longer the man I fell in love with. He completely changed."

"In what way?"

"It really started when he got the promotion and started traveling. I know it's not easy to be on the road all the time, but he started drinking, and, I don't know, he was touchy. He'd get into dark moods, and I'd ask him what was going on and he just wouldn't open up. It's not like I didn't try, but after a year, I gave up and told him I wanted a divorce."

"Did he do anything more than drinking?"

"One time I was doing laundry and found a little plastic bag of white powder in his jeans. I knew it was cocaine, and when I confronted Eric, he said it was a one-time thing and that he didn't like it and so forth."

"Did you believe him?"

"No. But there were no signs I could tell that he was using drugs, but he was drinking, and heavily."

"Do you think the job changed him?"

"Definitely. I mean the money was nice, otherwise we couldn't have afforded this place. But what's money if you're not happy? I mean, look at Hollywood."

The Dalai Lama couldn't have come up with a better analogy.

"Did he travel to South America often?"

"Yes. And almost every time, he'd drink himself to sleep when he came home."

"Did he ever tell you what he did when he went to Peru or Colombia?"

"I asked him, but he would tell me I wouldn't understand. I said to try me, and all he said, one time, was he was dealing with difficult, dangerous people. I tried to get him to expand on it, but he'd shut down."

"Did Eric ever do anything shady?"

"No, he'd never been in trouble the whole time I knew him."

"But yet, you assume he's in trouble now."

She shrugged. "Well, I knew by his drinking, he was trying to get away from something, and then you called. It didn't take much to put it together. So, tell me, what did he do?"

The lady was on her way to a psychiatry degree. "I'm sorry, but I can't talk about an open investigation."

"So, this is a one-way street?"

I stood. "I appreciate you taking the time to see me."

IT WAS NICE PARKING UNDERGROUND; the interior of my car was still cool. Circling to the exit, I thought over what Mrs. Barrio had said.

I exited into the sunshine and put my sunglasses on. Before the first stoplight, I decided to change the tactic I'd use with Eric Barrio.

Chapter Fifty-Five

Watching the boats go by as I waited for Barrio to arrive, I reviewed the phone call I had made to him before driving to Miami. The buyer for Noble Metals was hesitant when I asked to meet but came around when I said it would be worth his time.

The Rusty Pelican was perched on pilings overlooking Biscayne Bay. It had a great view of the Brickell area of Miami. As I was thinking we needed more waterfront dining options in Naples, Barrio pulled out a chair.

I stood, extending my hand. "This place has amazing views."

"There are better ones further down Key Biscayne, but it's another twenty minutes away."

A server came by. I ordered a glass of the house wine and Barrio asked for a tequila.

I said, "How is business?"

"Good." He smiled, adding, "But it could always be better."

"If you're not growing, you're dying."

"Truth, man. But it's not easy to keep doing more and more each year. There's a lot of pressure."

"Well, either you increase the volume or get better margins on what you're doing."

"Our margins are good, but management says it can always be improved."

The server set his drink down. Barrio downed the shot of tequila and asked for another one before she put my wine glass down.

I took a tiny sip and winced. "This wine is terrible."

"You ordered the house garbage. Get a bottle of something good. You only live once."

"That's all right, my stomach has been acting up."

"Stress is bad for your belly, man."

"Mine is usually cast-iron, but the last couple of weeks . . ."

His second drink came. Barrio tapped the shot glass before knocking it back. He moved his forefinger over the rim of the empty glass. "So, what did you want to tell me?"

"You want another drink?"

"Sure, why not?"

I flagged down the server and put the order in. Leaning over, I lowered my voice. "Look, I know you're under a lot of pressure to produce."

"And you're going to make it easy for me?"

"That depends on how you look at things."

"What is that supposed to mean?"

"Short term it might be rough, but in the long run, you're way better off."

"Man, you like talking in riddles, don't you?"

A server swooped in and set down his tequila.

Barrio dragged the shot glass closer, and I quietly said, "I don't represent gold suppliers, and my name isn't Burt Freeman."

"What? What the hell are you talking about?"

"My name is Frank Luca, and I'm a federal law enforcement agent."

He blinked before growling, "You motherfucker."

"Take it easy."

He knocked back the drink and jumped to his feet. "See you around."

"Sit down or you'll be sorry."

He hissed, "What do you want?"

"I know you're laundering money for the cartel."

"No, that's bullshit."

"It's not, and you know it. I saw you in that bar and grill in Peru."

He shook his head. "You sleazebag."

I leaned in. "First off, if anyone is a sleazebag, it's the drug dealers you're helping, and secondly, I'm your only lifeline. You cooperate with me, and you'll be fine."

He wagged his head. "I can't believe this. I need another drink."

I ordered another for him and said, "You tell me everything you know, and nothing will happen to you."

He pinched the bridge of his nose. "This is bad, man. I can't believe it."

"It's not as bad as you think. You help us and we help you."

"Yeah? What about my fucking bills? Who's going to pay them when I get fired?"

"You'll get another job."

"Not making the same money."

"The money is dirty, that's why you made so much. If you were honest with yourself, you'd admit it."

"What's going to happen to the company if I help you? I mean, the people I work with, a lot of them are regular people, they're good people who did nothing wrong."

"If they weren't involved, they have nothing to worry about."

The drink came and Barrio chugged it down. "Everyone will blame me, man. No, I can't do that."

"The alternative is a lot worse. If you don't cooperate, you'll go to jail, and the company and whoever engaged in the laundering is going to pay a price commensurate with what they did. I hate to say it, but you have no real options here."

He exhaled. "I have to think about it. I can't even process all this. First my wife leaves me, and now this?"

"It's going to be okay."

"Yeah, right."

"I understand you're going through a rough patch."

"Rough patch? My whole world is crumbling."

I stood. "Look, think it over, and I'll call you in a day or so."

He shook his head. As I walked away, I heard him shout for another drink.

I burped as I opened the door to my car. As some of the hot air escaped, I surveyed the area; people were enjoying the sun, water, and sand. The only two not having fun were Barrio and me.

I was making progress, but handing out Get Out of Jail Free cards grated on me. It wasn't my normal modus operandi, but immunity was a powerful motivator.

Chapter Fifty-Six

"Noble Metal's broker uploaded the docs, and guess what?"

Here we go again, just like Derrick used to do. "What? Tell me."

"As phony as a politician."

I snickered. "That bad, huh?"

"Yep, the certificate of origin is bogus. The mine listed doesn't even exist. But they did file a FinCen."

"As a result of you calling them out."

"Exactly, but now we have proof of them falsifying a declaration."

"You're going to seize the shipment coming in?"

"Absolutely."

"Wouldn't it be better if you let them receive it and then swoop in after they have possession?"

"We could do that."

"It'd give us a couple days to think about how to do all this. I'm working on Barrio, the buyer for Noble."

"I'll get the seizure documents prepared; they need to be signed off. That way they'll be ready when the ship docks."

"Sounds good. And I'll stay on top of Barrio."

"Do you think you're going to be able to turn him?"

"That's the goal."

"I know, but do you think he'll bite?"

"Yes, I'm confident he'll cooperate. He has no choice."

"That'd be great. Let me know how it goes and if I can help."

Chapter Fifty-Seven

I hit the button, and the coffee for my second cup flowed. When I was on the job, it was days like this that made the struggle for justice worth it. Once Barrio began talking, we'd be on our way to shutting down one of the spigots of money the cartels had streaming.

Tying the belt around her robe, Mary Ann said, "Good morning."

"Morning."

I slipped a pod in the Nespresso machine, put her cup under, and hit brew.

"Thanks. I don't know if you remembered, but I can't walk this morning. I'm taking a yoga class with Connie."

"Yes, I know. I'm going for a walk as soon as I'm done. I've got a big day today."

"What's going on?"

"Barrio, the sales guy or buyer or whatever, is going to take the deal I offered."

"You have to go to Miami?"

"Maybe not today, but tomorrow for sure."

"I can't wait for this case to be over and done with."

"Hang in there. The finish line is in sight."

"I hope so."

"It is, don't worry. Soon, we'll be packing for Italy."

"That reminds me, I was on Trip Advisor, and I wanted to show you some of the itineraries they have. A couple look interesting."

"Sounds good. When you get back, we'll go over it."

I'd gone just three blocks before my T-shirt was peppered with sweat spots. I waved to a neighbor walking her bichon and checked my phone. No messages from Barrio.

Barrio was another person who'd succumbed to greed. He'd gotten the fancy Ritz Carlton apartment but had lost his wife and was on the verge of losing his freedom. Had he even considered the downside when he tucked his ethics under the bed?

Turning the corner onto our street, I scanned one of the lakes in our community for alligators. There weren't any. My phone vibrated. It had to be Barrio.

Pulling it out, I noticed it was 8:07 a.m. It wasn't Barrio but JD, the customs agent.

"Hey, JD. What's going on?"

"Hey, Frank. If you can believe it, they took me off the case."

"The Noble Metals one?"

"Yep. They're reassigning me to a team working on designer counterfeits coming in."

"Wait, hold on. I don't understand. What happened?"

"When I got in this morning, the chief wanted to see me, and he told me I was reassigned. I was surprised as well."

"Did he say why?"

"He said they needed help on a counterfeit ring they were onto."

"Oh, come on! They're going after designer bags instead of drugs?"

"I don't know."

"No wonder we have a national crisis on our hands. This is ridiculous."

"Take it easy, Frank. The guy taking over for me is a good guy."

"Who? Who took over the case?

"Jason Wiley."

"How long has he been with customs?"

"Not long, maybe a year or two, but he's good."

"I have to deal with a rookie?"

"Let me give you his direct number."

I stuck the newbie's contact in my phone and hung up.

Mary Ann was pulling out of the driveway when I got back to the house. I stripped off my T-shirt in the laundry room and called Barrio.

It rang five times before going to voice mail. Where the hell was he? I headed into the master bathroom to shower. I had to cool down in more ways than one.

As soon as I got dressed, I called Barrio. No answer. Again. I took a bagel out of the freezer and stuck it into the microwave. I stared at the carousel as it turned. This case was just like it, spinning in circles but going nowhere.

Since my wife wasn't home, I grabbed a jar of strawberry jelly and smothered the bagel. The good feeling vanished before I finished eating it.

After brushing my teeth, I called Barrio again. When it went to voice mail, I said, "This is Frank Luca. Call me back. If I don't hear from you, I'm going to have an arrest warrant issued for you."

Scrolling through my contacts, I found the new one JD had given me. I hit dial.

"This is Jason Wiley. Who's calling?"

"Frank Luca. I'm the special agent that worked with JD on the Noble Metals case."

"Oh, hi there. Good to meet you."

"I need to know where we are with the Noble Metals case."

"I was just about to get the file on that one."

I took a deep breath before saying, "Look, we don't know each other, and I realize this was just dropped in your lap, but you have to get up to speed immediately."

"I've got a desk full of other investigations. I can't just drop everything. I have—"

"Either you're going to help me, or I'll go it alone. I'll call you in a couple of hours. Read the file and let me know if you're in or not."

Pacing the house, I tried to make sense of not being able to get a hold of Barrio and the fact JD had been pulled from the Noble Metals case. Was there something larger going on behind the scenes? Was someone looking to derail the investigation?

I could be paranoid, but who could direct customs? They were a part of Homeland Security, and Romney French, the guy I'd met on day one, bragged about the reach of the agency's investigative unit. It was plausible, but why now? They could have stopped it earlier.

And Barrio. Why hadn't he returned my calls? I realized it could simply be he was stalling for time, not avoiding me. It was never easy admitting to a serious crime and turning against your coworkers.

It was human nature to avoid facing reality. But I'd given him a deadline. Did he think I'd go away?

I made a call.

"Good morning, Noble Metals. How can I help you?"

"Eric Barrio, please."

"I'm sorry, but Mr. Barrio isn't in."

"When is he expected?"

"I don't know, but I haven't seen him for two days."

A bad feeling came over me as I hung up. Had something happened to Barrio? Had the cartel gotten to him? Was he dead? Or had he run?

Chapter Fifty-Eight

"Mrs. Barrio? This is Frank Luca, we met at your apartment the other day."

"Yes, of course. What can I do for you?"

"Have you spoken to your husband?"

"Did something happen to Eric?"

"When was the last time you spoke to him?"

"Over a week ago. What's going on?"

"At this point, I'm not sure anything happened, but he hasn't returned my calls."

"I hope he didn't do anything stupid."

"What do you mean by that?"

"You know, he was in a dark place and . . . oh God, please, I hope not."

"You believe he may have taken his own life?"

"I don't know what to believe, but he hasn't been himself for a year now."

"Okay. Don't panic. Let me make some inquiries and I'll get back to you."

Suicide was never an answer to any problem. If Barrio was

feeling down, I hoped like hell he'd seek help. It was crazy to hope he had checked himself in somewhere to get assistance.

We had tools to track people. I made another call. "Bradley, it's Frank."

"Hey, how's it going?"

"It looks like Eric Barrio is either on the run or something has happened to him."

"Are you kidding me?"

"I wish I was. I left several messages for him. He hasn't been to work, and his wife hasn't heard from him."

"Uh-oh."

"I don't want to jump to conclusions, even if I'm an Olympian at it, but I'm afraid somebody got to him to silence him."

Bradley chuckled. "You think they'd go that far?"

"We're talking hundreds of millions of dollars. Yes, I think it is a real possibility he was killed. Or maybe he killed himself."

"I can get an order right away. I'll check his phone records. It's the quickest way to find out if he's alive and where he is."

"Go for it. If you have any problems getting it, let me know."

"I won't. I'll have it signed off now, and I've got inside contacts at the phone companies."

After hanging up, I called Noble Metals again. "Hi, I'm Frank Luca, I called earlier for Eric Barrio."

"Yes, I remember."

"Eric worked with another man, they traveled together. I can't recall his last name, but his first name was Matt."

"Sir, I think you should speak with the office manager, Evelyn Rose. Hold on, I'll pass you to her."

It was the woman we met when doing the audit. She answered, "This is Evelyn."

"Hello, Ms. Rose, this is Frank Luca. I was on the custom audit with JD."

"Hi, Mr. Luca. How can I help you?"

"I'm looking for Eric Barrio. Do you know where he might be?"

"I'm sorry, but he no longer works here."

"He quit?"

"No, not just Eric. The buyers and the entire traffic department were let go."

"Because of the audit?"

"Yes, considering the violations uncovered, the lawyers said we had to."

The attorneys were playing a common version of the blame game, assigning responsibility to lower-level staff to protect the owners and executives. I was sure the lawyers were high-powered and expensive.

I KEPT my eye on the clock. Once two hours had gone by, I made a call.

"Customs. This is Jason Wiley."

"Hi, Jason, it's Frank Luca. I'm the federal agent who was working on the Noble Metals case."

"Yeah, I know who you are. What's up?"

"Did you review the Noble file?"

"Not yet. Like I said, my desk is covered in cases—"

"They have a container about to dock. It's filled with gold from an illegal mine. JD was going to seize the container. Where are you with that?"

"I'll get to it. If you give me a chance."

"When? We can't let this one slip through the cracks."

"I'll take a look at where we're at and call you. What's your number again?"

Through clenched teeth I gave him my cell number and hung up.

My pulse thrummed in my ears. I jabbed my phone's keypad.

"Treasury Department."

"Mr. Pembroke. Tell him it's Special Agent Frank Luca."

"Hold on, Mr. Luca. I'll check if he's available."

Holding, I was getting the bad feeling that Pembroke would dodge the call.

"Hello, Frank. How are you?"

"To be honest, I'm not doing so good."

"What's the matter?"

I told him about JD being taken off the Noble Metals case.

"Well, I wouldn't get down about that. Agencies move staff frequently to address pressing needs."

"I understand, but this is a big case, and I'm afraid it's not going to be handled the way JD was doing it."

"Don't worry, customs has a deep bench."

I sat on the edge of my chair. "Well, it feels like they put a rookie on it, and according to him, he's swimming in cases and hasn't even read the file yet."

"One of the things I like about you, Frank, is you're impatient. You want things to happen quickly. The government moves slow, but I'm sure the agent handling the case will move it forward."

I had less confidence than he did. "We're talking major laundering by the cartels. Can't we get them to prioritize the case?"

"I'm aware of the seriousness, Frank. As for interfering in managing customs' day-to-day operations, it's a bad idea, and I don't believe the situation warrants an intervention."

"I hope you're right, sir."

"Do me a favor and give the new agent a chance to get up to speed."

"I will. I'll let you know how it unfolds."

Pembroke hung up without saying goodbye. I'd cut off my

share of calls earlier than intended and chalked it up as a mistake. But replaying our conservation, I settled on Pembroke being upset with me calling.

I respected him and needed him as an ally. I picked up my phone to apologize, when it rang.

"Hey, Bradley, can I call you back?"

"Uh, this is important."

"What's going on?"

"You're never going to believe this."

Chapter Fifty-Nine

"Stop the guessing games and tell me what the hell you have."

"Sorry. I was able to get Eric Barrio's phone records from Verizon."

"Does it look like he's alive?"

"Definitely, he's made several calls over the last two days."

"Where is he?"

"According to the cell tower data, it looks like he is in Weston, Florida."

"I want to know who he's been talking to. We'll find out where he's hiding."

"I figured you'd want that, so I got all that."

"You're the best, Bradley. I'm sorry I jumped on you, but I was upset with Pembroke. He refused to push customs on the Noble—"

"Frank, you're not going to believe this, it's crazy."

Here we go again. "What?"

"According to Barrio's cell records, he called Pembroke."

I bolted upright. "What? That can't be. Are you sure it was George Pembroke?"

"Yes. I checked the billing information for the phone

number. It's a cellular one billed to George Pembroke at the Treasury Department's Washington address."

"When was the call made?"

"Two days ago."

"That was the day I met with Barrio and told him he had to cooperate."

"That makes sense."

"No, this whole thing make no sense at all. Pembroke is the one who approved the mission in the first place."

"Well, I'm sure he didn't think it would end up where it did."

"Damn, you're right. Who thought this would lead to illegal gold ending up being bought by the US government?"

"What's in it for him?"

"Money, what else would it be?"

"How do you think he's involved?"

"He probably got Noble in as a supplier for the gold that Treasury buys. Maybe skims a piece of every shipment."

"We should root around, see if we can find Pembroke's money."

"We can try, but I'm sure he's got it buried in some tax haven like the Cayman Islands."

"Probably."

"Or maybe he's got gold bars stored in a couple of places. It's untraceable."

"What are we going to do?"

"I've got to really think this one over. We probably have just one shot at this."

"Okay. Let me know what I can do."

"You can be sure of that. And, hey, don't tell anyone what you discovered."

My stomach was clenching. I collapsed into a chair. What the hell was going on?

Going over my interactions with Pembroke swelled my concerns. Almost from day one, there were signs that I'd ignored. Where had the threatening phone call emanated from? And what about Rico, the dirty CIA agent? He brushed off evidence that he was corrupt. Pembroke chose Rico in an attempt to control my mission.

Then when I'd gotten back from Peru, I raised the concern gold was being used to launder drug money, but Pembroke discounted it.

Assuming he was a good guy because he had climbed to a top position in the Treasury Department was a mistake. A bad one. Was it too late?

It felt like I was on a raft that was drifting farther out to sea. It was time to paddle as quickly as possible and go back to the basics.

The State of Maryland's DMV listed an address for Pembroke in Annapolis. Checking it out, I found it was inside a gated community known as the Downs on the Severn. It was a luxury neighborhood with two marinas and a bunch of amenities.

Zillow claimed Pembroke's home was valued at three million dollars. That was an expensive home for a public servant to own. I checked into his wife, Patricia. She came from old money. Money so old it needed a walker.

It surprised me to discover both Pembroke's father and grandfather had been in politics. His grandfather rose to deputy chief of D.C.'s legislature. But Pembroke's father outdid him, running Maryland's Department of Budget and Management. It was the perfect position to create a scheme. Once again, like father, like son.

Checking the property records revealed there were three properties owned by Pembroke and his wife. But that was just Maryland. And it was clear Pembroke was a master of illusion.

His phony persona, combined with his knowledge of all things financial, guaranteed his wealth was masked better than New Orleans during Mardi Gras.

It was depressing, and doing something about it appeared impossible. I was essentially on my own, fighting what amounted to system-wide corruption. It was David and Goliath, except I didn't even have a slingshot.

Reviewing the players in the case, I assessed my allies, and an idea came to me. Not wanting to make the same mistake I made with Pembroke, I resorted to the fundamentals and investigated him beforehand.

Mary Ann came down the hall and into the kitchen. She looked at me. "What's wrong, Frank?"

She had incredible instincts, and it made me feel good. "What makes you say that?"

"You're sitting at the kitchen table. And the only time you do that is when you're eating."

The detective in her never left. "I need your opinion."

"Sure. What's going on?"

"I found out Pembroke is dirty."

"What? The man running the Treasury Department is corrupt?"

"Yes." I told her about the calls with Barrio, the buyer of illegal gold, and the fact customs seemed to be burying the case against Noble Metals.

"This is just unbelievable. You really stumbled upon something big here."

"I did. The problem is, I don't know what to do."

She reached for my hand. "You'll figure it out, you always do."

"But if I go after Pembroke, he'll retaliate, and he's got a lot of power. I can forget about the laundering case, but I don't want to jeopardize getting the bastard who killed Jimmy. The thing is, I just can't let go of the laundering part."

"I understand."

"Am I being greedy? Should I just focus on the killer, get the Fisherman and play it safe?"

"Getting the Fisherman is arguably the most important thing and the reason you got involved. Right?"

"It is. I have to get him."

"And when you do, are you going to be able to let the money laundering part and Pembroke go?"

I shrugged. "I guess so."

"Come on, Frank. We both know there's no way you would be able to. It'd gnaw at you. You'd be miserable."

"You're right, but I'd have to find a way to live with it. I don't want to bring any more stress into the house than I already have. It's not good for you."

"I'm okay. Don't worry about me. Take care of business."

I got up and wrapped my arms around her. "You're the best. I can't believe how lucky I am."

"You're right on that!"

"No, seriously, thanks for backing me up a thousand percent."

I told her about the man I was looking to call for help.

She said, "So, you're worried he and Pembroke might be in it together?"

"Yes."

"I think there's a small chance. But like you always say, the more people that know a secret, the more likely it won't stay a secret."

"That's true. If he's clean, this is my plan."

Chapter Sixty

I took my cell out of my pocket. The home screen picture of Jimmy, Steve, and Jessie stared at me. It was an easy decision.

"Homeland Security Investigative Bureau. How can I help you?"

I hesitated before saying, "Romney French, please. This is Special Agent Frank Luca calling."

"Hold on, sir."

Waiting on hold, it was hard not wondering if Romney, when he heard I was on the phone, had called or sent a text to Pembroke.

"Mr. Luca, how are you? It's been too long."

"Yes, it has. Is everything going okay with you?"

"That would depend on your definition of okay."

Was he trying to be funny, or was he alluding to something? "Anything I should know about?"

"Nothing in particular. What did you call about?"

I told him what I'd learned about the calls between Pembroke and Barrio.

He paused before saying, "That is concerning, but there

might be a plausible reason for them to talk. Maybe they're related, through marriage or something."

"Are you aware that the lead investigator on the Noble Metals case has been removed?"

"No. When did this happen?"

"A day or so ago. And the new agent is a rookie. I'm getting the feeling this is orchestrated."

"That is concerning on a number of levels. It may have been an oversight, but I should have been notified."

"I believe it was intentional, sir."

"I'm assuming you called for more than to notify me."

"Yes. I need your support."

"With Noble Metals?"

"In a roundabout way, yes. But now it's bigger than that, but I have an idea that could work."

"I'd like it hear it."

Reviewing Barrio's phone records, I zeroed in on a series of calls that pinged off certain cell towers. They were being handled in an area on the edge of the Everglades.

Pulling up a map, it became apparent Barrio was hiding out in either the towns of Weston or Southwest Ranches. I grabbed my phone.

"Hello."

"Mrs. Barrio, it's Detective, oops, Special Agent Frank Luca.."

"Yes. Hi."

"Have you heard from Eric?"

"No. What do you know?"

"He's in either Weston or Southern—"

"His mother used to live in Weston. He bought her a condo

there two years ago, but after she fell, he moved her closer to us."

"What is the address of the condo?"

"Oh, I have to look it up, but the community is called Lakeview."

"Thanks, I appreciate your help."

"Hold on a second."

She gave me the address.

"Thanks. Look, please don't tell your husband I called if you speak to him."

"I won't. Is he going to be arrested?"

"No. At this point he has information on a large-scope investigation, and we need his help."

"Good, I hope he helps. You know, Eric; I mean, he's changed, but deep down he's still a good person."

"By the way, do you know anyone named George Pembroke?"

"Pembroke? No, I don't think so."

Chapter Sixty-One

Mary Ann was on the phone. I said, "I'm going out for a while. I'll be back in a couple of hours."

She pulled the phone away from her ear. "Where?"

"Barrio is in Weston. I'm going to see him."

"By yourself?"

"Yes, he's greedy, not dangerous."

"Are you sure?'

"Yes, a thousand percent. He doesn't own a firearm."

"Be careful."

"I'll see you later."

"Good luck."

I'd been on Alligator Alley more times for this case than when Derrick and I searched and found an enormous amount of money hidden in another drug case. I slid into the eighty-miles-an-hour flow.

Weston was a tony town close to both Fort Lauderdale and Miami. The town center was manicured and immaculate.

I circled around and pulled into Lakeview. It wasn't gated. I drove past the unit I believed Barrio was hiding in and parked in a spot reserved for visitors.

The sun was strong, but the humidity was low. I approached Barrio's first-floor unit. A tropical breeze fanned the bird-of-paradise plants along the path to his door.

I rang the bell and then knocked. No one answered. Peeking inside a window, it didn't appear anyone was home. I'd go into town, grab an iced coffee, and come back.

Making a U-turn, I saw a man in a bathing suit with a towel slung over his shoulder. It was Barrio. I pulled back into the spot and watched him take the walkway to his condo.

I hustled after him. "Mr. Barrio!"

He turned around and his shoulders slumped.

"I just want to talk. I think you'll be interested in what I have to say."

"What can you say that's going to make me change my mind?"

"Trust me. Give me five minutes, and if you say no, I'm out of here."

The door to the upper condo opened and a blonde lady stepped out. "Eric, is everything all right?"

"Yes, Muriel. Everything is fine, just an old friend stopping by."

He turned to me. "Come on in, Frank."

As we stepped inside, the sun dipped behind a cloud, blocking the natural light. Barrio put the kitchen high hats on. The cabinetry was dark and dated. Two bottles of tequila, one with two fingers left, the other unopened, sat on the counter.

"Give me a second to get changed."

"Take your time."

Barrio disappeared into a room, and I peeked in a few drawers before going into the family room. Newspapers dated yesterday and today were on a glass cocktail table next to three empty beer cans. A pair of sliders offered a view of a lake.

Barrio said, "You want something to drink?"

"I'm okay."

He opened the fridge and took a beer out. He twisted the cap off and, after taking a long slug, said, "All right, what do you have to tell me that's so earth-shattering?"

"I understand you and many others were dismissed by Noble Metals."

"They're a bunch of bastards. They're covering their asses."

"They can try to hide behind lawyers, but it's not going to work."

He smiled. "You don't know who you're dealing with."

"Tell me."

"No, you tell me why you came out here."

"Who are you hiding from?"

"I'm not hiding from anybody. I needed to clear my head for a few days. Now, you going to tell me why you're here?"

"I know who you called."

He took another swig but said nothing.

"You called George Pembroke. Why?"

"We're old friends."

I scoffed. "You think he's going to protect you?"

"Protect me from what?"

"You participated in a conspiracy to import gold from illegal mines and broke a whole slew of laws, including money laundering. You're looking at a decade or more in prison."

He blinked and I continued, "If you think Pembroke is going to fix things like he did with the customs audit of Noble, you're dead wrong. He can pull a few strings to try to derail the investigation, but the jurisdiction for this doesn't sit with the Treasury. The case is moving forward and is about to ramp up."

Barrio opened a cabinet and pulled a shot glass out. He poured himself a drink, downed it, and emptied the remains of the bottle into the glass.

"What do you want from me? I'm not going to cooperate."

"You're going to jail, and you'll lose everything you own. Your beach house, this place, the Ritz apartment, anything you bought with dirty money. Whatever you have left will go to the lawyers trying to save your ass. Even if you get a lenient sentence, you're still going to prison, and you'll be broke when you get out."

"If that's the way it goes, I'll deal with it somehow."

"I don't get it, I'm offering you a way to avoid jail."

"They'll probably kill me if I talk."

With Barrio in hiding, he believed the threat was real. "You don't have to worry about that. We'll get you into protective custody, nobody will get to you."

"What, and live in a crappy apartment somewhere out west? Nah, forget it."

It was time to play my last card.

Chapter Sixty-Two

I clicked on the link and requested to join the meeting. A box with the number of participants in the virtual room appeared. There were a lot of names, but Pembroke wasn't one of them.

Barrio said, "Five people? This was supposed to be confidential."

"It is. Don't worry, you have a signed proffer agreement."

A bunch of windows opened. My gaze went to the one with Romney French. I said, "Mr. French, thanks for organizing this meeting."

"Hello, Frank, hello, Mr. Barrio. Also on this call is the inspector general for the Treasury, Miriam Scone, and the IG for Homeland Security, Martin Blase. As well as the respective counsels for both departments."

"Hello, everyone."

A chorus of hellos were returned.

French said, "Let's get this started. Mr. Barrio, you've signed the queen for a day document."

Barrio looked at me. I said, "That's the informal name for a proffer agreement. Nothing you say today can be used against you."

"Okay. I get it."

"That's correct, Mr. Barrio. With that in mind, we'd like to hear what you know about the laundering scheme and your relationship with Mr. George Pembroke. What you tell us today will determine whether we can grant you immunity and protection."

"And what about the whistleblower reward?"

"Yes, that as well. If the information is actionable, you'll be granted protective custody and immunity as well as be compensated under the whistleblower provision."

"Where should I start?"

"At the beginning."

"Well, I got a job with Noble Metals about four years ago as a buyer. I'd deal with the mines and middlemen buying gold that we'd refine and sell. Part of the territory I was assigned to was Mexico."

"Is Mexico a large supplier, of legitimate gold?"

"Yes, they're the ninth or tenth biggest producer in the world."

"I didn't know that. Go on."

"Well, like a year into the job, I was promoted and was told Peru was moving up in terms of the amount of gold they were mining. Now they're even bigger than Mexico. So, we went down to Peru to see the people at the Cuajone mine—"

Someone laughed. "Cuajone? Are you kidding?"

"No, no, it's not the same as the slang, for you know, a man's . . ."

"Go on. You said *we*. Who went to see the Peruvian mine?"

"Me and Matt Walker. He's a buyer too."

"And what happened?"

"Well, we went to the mine and made a deal to buy ten tons from them as a kind of trial. Then, the day before we leave, somebody comes to the hotel, saying they want to talk to us about selling gold. Well, we meet this guy, he said his name was

Ruffo, but we found out later his real name was Vicente Blanco."

"Do you know who he represented?"

"At the time no, but later on, we found out he was working for the La Familia cartel."

"You struck a deal with him?"

"Not right there, we had to go to the owners of Noble Metals, but I knew they would buy because of the discount."

"How much of a discount were they offering?"

"Twenty percent off the raw market."

"Why would they offer such a low price?"

"I asked the same thing, and though he didn't come right out and say it, it was understood that it was coming from illegal mines."

"How do you know this?"

"Like I said, we got the impression, as he was dodging around—but hold on a second, and I'll get to that. So, we went back to the owners, and they jumped on the offer, like we knew they would. I mean, we were happy about it because we got bonuses based on the volume we bought."

"Did the owners know it was coming out of illegal mines?"

"We told them what we thought."

"Who did you tell?"

"The brothers who own the place, John and Cesar Medina."

"You said you later discovered for certain the supply was illegal."

"Yes, we were going down to Peru pretty often, and we were like a big deal, you know. Next thing you know, we're asked to buy from two other mines. It was exciting, but in the back of your head, you know something is off."

"And who were these people looking to sell gold to you?"

"They were related to the cartels."

"How do you know for sure?"

"Because we ended up going to three of these mines with

them, and believe me, you wouldn't get close to them if you weren't a part of the cartel."

"You have the names of the people you did deals with?"

"Yes, I gave Frank, uh, Mr. Luca, a list of the names."

I cut in. "Yes, I have them and will share it with you."

"When you discovered the source of the gold you were buying out of Peru was coming from illegal mines, ones controlled by cartel members, did you alert the management of Noble Metals?"

"Yes, both brothers were told."

"So, they knew the gold was illegal?"

"Yes."

"And they did nothing?"

"No, basically they avoided talking about it. It was never mentioned, not to me anyway. But, and I know it sounds self-serving, but it started bothering me more and more. These mines destroy the environment. You have to see it for yourself."

"Yet you did nothing?"

"I don't need the reminder."

"What role did George Pembroke play in all of this?"

Chapter Sixty-Three

"Mr. Pembroke approached you?"

"Yes. Let me set it up for you, or it won't make sense. So, we were doing more volume with the Peruvians . . ."

"The illegal mines connected to the cartels?"

"Yes. It was going really well, and they kept coming up with more supplies. We found out they were mining in Colombia as well."

"Illegally?"

"Yes. In the south, near the border with Peru."

"We understand. Go ahead."

"Well, it was all good, but we started having a problem selling what we bought and refined."

Bradley's report on the dramatic increase in gold coming out of Peru popped into my head.

French asked, "What kind of problems?"

"There's not too many buyers who can take all the new supplies of gold we had. Management said to hold off taking any more because of cash-flow issues. And I told the Peruvians we wanted to take more but the buying side was softening. I said we'd need six months or so to see where the market was going."

"How did they react to that?"

"They seemed to be disappointed but said they understood. Then the next day, Vicente calls me saying he has a solution, and I'm like, excited, you know. And I asked what it was, and he said I'd be hearing from an associate when I got back home."

"That's how he characterized George Pembroke? As an associate?"

"Yes, that's what he called him. So, the day after I got home, I was walking in South Pointe Park. It's right by the apartment I rented when me and my wife separated. And a guy comes up to me and says there was someone that wanted to meet me. I was like, are you kidding me? I said no thanks, and then he said he was working with Vicente Blanco."

"The man you met down in Peru?" French consulted his notes. "Who originally said his name was Ruffo?"

"Yes. I was caught off guard but still wary, you know? So, I said, 'What is this about?' And the guy said, 'To buy gold.' So, I knew it was real because Vicente said someone would contact me."

"What happened then?"

"He told me to come back in two days at five o'clock and to walk to the end of the pier. He said there would be a man fishing who would be wearing a white baseball cap."

"And who was he?"

"It ended up being George Pembroke, but originally he said his name was Sam. He never looked at me. He kept his eyes on the water, like he was fishing."

"What did he say?"

"He said he could help with buying gold from Noble. I asked who he represented, and he said the United States government. I was like, what? I couldn't believe it and asked if it was some kind of joke. He said the Feds were huge buyers of gold, and he could open the doors if the price was right. I was like, *okay, here comes the bad news,* but he said they'd buy big volumes but needed a five percent discount. I said it wasn't a problem because I knew we were buying below the market in the first place."

"And that was it?"

"No, he said we were to charge the full market price to the Feds and give the five percent discount to the sellers."

"You were buying at a twenty percent discount, correct?"

"Yes. So, it basically became fifteen percent."

"And who benefited from the reduced discount?"

"The way I understood it, Pembroke and Vicente split it."

"Are you certain?"

"I never saw any money change hands, but that's the way it was told to me."

"By who?"

"Vicente."

"Did George Pembroke know the gold was being sourced from illegal mines?"

"He had to."

"Did you tell him it was?"

"No, but Vicente only worked with illegal mines. Everybody knew that."

"Did you or anyone at Noble Metals deal directly with Mr. Pembroke?"

"I wasn't involved in the selling side."

"How did this arrangement come into being?"

"He told me to contact a George Martin at the Treasury Department. That he was the guy who handled the buys for Fort Knox. I asked if there was any approval process or something like that. And he said he would handle what was needed to get Noble to be an approved vendor."

"Do you believe George Martin was a part of this conspiracy?"

"I honestly don't know. I never spoke to him. The next day I went into the office and told Cesar we had a chance to sell to the government, and he was super excited. Then a couple of days later, Cesar brought me into the office and said I was going to get a huge bonus for putting together the deal with the Feds."

"Cesar Medina?"

"Yes, one of the brothers who own Noble."

"Did you tell the owners how you came upon this opportunity?"

"I didn't tell him about Pembroke because Pembroke said not to mention him to anyone. So, I told them a friend of a friend introduced me to Martin."

"Did you get the bonus?"

"Yes. It took about a month before we shipped to Fort Knox."

"How much was it?"

"Three hundred thousand."

"Is that everything you received?"

"From the selling deal, but I was making a lot of money from all the buying we did."

"What did you make on average each year?"

"A million and a half."

"And you considered this normal for the type of work you were doing."

"There was a lot of travel and stress. It destroyed my marriage."

"You didn't think it was unusual?"

He shrugged. "Yeah, it wasn't all good. I know it sounds like bull, but it was really getting to me, and I was drinking way too much. My wife wanted me to go into rehab, but I didn't want to. I probably should have because she left me and filed for divorce."

The Inspector General for the Treasury Department said,

"Mr. Barrio, what date did the meeting with the person you believe to have been George Pembroke occur?"

"September twentieth."

"Are you certain?"

"Definitely, it was my mother's birthday."

"Thank you."

French said, "Hold on a minute, gentlemen, we're going to mute this for a moment."

The sound dropped out, and French and the others began talking to each other. Heads were nodding, and Barrio said, "What are they talking about?"

"What you told them."

"Do they believe what I said?"

"Yes. Don't worry. Where on the pier did you meet Pembroke that day?"

"Kind of like in the middle."

"Looking at the water, the left or right side?"

"The right side."

After five minutes French took the mute off the call. "Thank you. Mr. Barrio, why don't you take us through this again. From the beginning."

Barrio repeated how he got hooked up with the cartel that ran gold mines, eventually meeting with Pembroke. When he finished, French said, "Okay, Mr. Barrio, I believe we have enough to grant you immunity and to pursue a whistleblower claim. Let's discuss how to move forward."

We said our goodbyes, and just before ending the call, French said, "Frank, I'd like to talk to you offline. Please give me a call when you're available, but give me a couple of hours first."

Chapter Sixty-Four

"It won't be long."

"Are you sure they're going to get me the whistleblower money?"

"They should."

"If they don't, I'm not going along with all this."

He was in too deep to try and walk away. "Don't worry. If we run into a problem, which I don't think we will, I have a couple of cards I can pull."

"Really?"

"Yes."

He exhaled. "That makes me feel better. Thanks, man."

"Look, grab a couple of days' worth of clothes."

"Where are we going?"

"Not me, you. I think it's a good idea for you to stay in a hotel."

"You're probably right."

The fact he didn't fight the idea meant the risk was there. "Hustle up, I have to drive across the state to get home."

He went into the bedroom and a couple of minutes later came out with a duffel bag.

"Okay. There's a Westin that's pretty nice."

"What else is around here?"

"A Courtyard and a Hampton Inn."

"Let's do the Courtyard. They usually have efficiency units."

"Okay. Let's go." Barrio swept the bottle of tequila off the counter and stuffed it in his bag.

"If you've got a problem with alcohol, it's better you deal with it now. Go into rehab before you testify."

"I don't have a problem. Let's go."

He seemed to be in denial, but now wasn't the time to get into it.

After dropping Barrio off at the hotel, I navigated onto Route 75 and called Mary Ann.

"Hey, I wanted to let you know I'm on my way home."

"Good. How did it go?"

I filled her in, and she said, "That's great."

"I know, it went as good as I expected, but I'm not feeling good about it."

"Why? What's the matter?"

"I guess I'm doubting this whole plea thing. I mean, Barrio, he broke all the rules, made a ton of money helping the cartels. And now he's not only going to get off, but he's going to get something like five million as a reward?"

"I understand, but that's the way it's done. We did it that way working for the sheriff's department."

"Only when we absolutely had to."

"That's true, but Barrio lost his wife and is going to be in witness protection. He won't be able to see his mother."

"I know, but—"

"Look, you're going to put a dent in the laundering operation. That's what you set out to do."

"You're right."

"Plus, you're going to take down a corrupt official. That's a big deal, Frank."

"There shouldn't be one to take down. This is the United States, not some third world country."

"You're being unrealistic, Frank. We've got plenty of corruption right here in America. It's sad, but it's a fact."

"You had me feeling better, and now you go ruining it?"

She laughed. "I glad this is coming to an end. If it went on any longer, it might have made sense to get a condo in Miami."

"There's a lot of nice spots. I like the color of the water there. In a lot of places, it looks like the Caribbean."

"What do you know about the Caribbean? You never went there."

"Are you trying to rope me into another vacation?"

"Oh, speaking of going away, Melissa from the travel agency just sent a couple of hotel recommendations. They're really nice, but they're not cheap."

"Nothing is these days. We'll look them over when I get home."

"How long will you be?"

"About an hour. I have to call Washington, so I'll see you in a bit."

It'd been close to two hours since Romney French closed our video conference with asking me to call him in a couple of hours. I checked the mile marker. I was on 67.1. I waited until I passed the marker for 71 before dialing his number.

"Mr. French, it's Frank Luca. You asked me to call you."

"Yes. Yes. By the way, I think it went very well today."

"I agree, sir. He's the real deal. I hope we'll be able to get Pembroke."

"Miriam, the Inspector General at the Treasury, confirmed Pembroke was in Miami on September twentieth."

"Wow. So, we got him."

"We're going to need more. He can deny meeting Barrio."

"I understand, and I'm working on something that will seal the deal."

"You know, George and I go back about ten years. It's difficult to see what he's gotten involved with."

"It sure is."

"He has it all. His family is very well off, and he's got a job ninety-nine percent of the population would kill for."

"Greed is a powerful motivator."

"That's true. I'm curious, did George ever ask you about Jay Adams?"

"He did. I had to agree to investigate him to get Pembroke to authorize this mission."

"I'm not surprised. George has a real hate on for Adams. George believes he'd prevented him from moving up the ladder and resented all the success Adams had after he left."

"He said there was some funny business going on, like what happened with Madoff."

"It may be, but it's just as likely George wanted to cause him some trouble. I used to kid him, saying he had Irish Alzheimer's because the only thing he remembers are grudges."

"Wow. I don't know what to say."

"There's nothing to say. Oh, before I forget, I wanted to let you know that I reached out to the commissioner of customs regarding the Noble Metals case."

"You did? What did he say?"

"I asked him to put the original investigator back on the case, and he agreed."

"JD is back on it? We have to be careful. They're going to tip off Pembroke."

"I hope they do. We're watching Pembroke, and if he tries to interfere, it'll only add more evidence to the corruption case against him."

"That's true. I'm curious, what did you tell him?"

"That we were working a human trafficking case that involved the illegal gold trade."

"Excellent. I like the cover."

"We're tapping Pembroke's phone and tracking his movements."

"Thank you, sir."

"No. You're the one who deserves the thanks. If it weren't for your instincts, this would never have come to light."

I couldn't deny the acknowledgment, it felt good. I thanked him and hung up. When the call ended, my phone, which was attached to the dash, displayed the home screen. The picture of Jimmy, Stevie, and Jessie destroyed the high from French's compliment.

If the plan to get the Fisherman to face justice failed, it would not only overshadow the success of the laundering scheme, but it would also eat me alive.

Chapter Sixty-Five

It'd been two days since I tracked down who was responsible for the surveillance systems at the South Pointe Pier. Bryan Jordan was Miami-Dade County Parks and Recreation Department's head of security. He'd promised to send the video a day ago, but I was still waiting. Earlier that morning, I'd sent an email, but he hadn't responded to it. Normally, I'd have gone in person, but I was heading to Texas in the morning.

I punched in Jordan's number. A familiar voice said, "Miami-Dade Parks."

"Is this Bryan Jordan?"

"Yes. Who is this?"

"Special Agent Luca. We spoke a couple of days ago about the surveillance video of the pier."

"Sure. How are you doing?"

"Pretty good, but I'll feel better if you'll send me the footage I asked for."

"Oh, right. It got a little busy around here, and I've got to say, it slipped my mind."

"I understand, but this is important to the case we're running. In fact, it will probably clinch the deal for us."

"What kind of case?"

"I can't talk about it, but you'll be reading about it in the paper."

"Wow. That's cool."

"I'm leaving town on another investigation in a couple of hours, and I really need to tie this up. Can you send it now?"

"You're a special agent, so you work on big cases?"

"Yes."

"Man, I'd love to hear about them. I'm really into the true crime stuff."

"I'll tell you what, I'm in Miami twice a month. How about I stop in, and we grab lunch one day?"

"Oh, man, that'd be cool."

"I'll tell you about some of the nutty cases we've had."

"I can't wait."

"Look, like I said, I need the pier footage for September twentieth, from four p.m. to six p.m."

"I'm on it. You'll have it in ten minutes."

Doubting his measure of ten minutes was the same as mine, I made another call. This one to Homeland Security's Romney French.

"Hello, Frank, what's on your mind?"

"I was watching the news last night, and they had a story on the case involving the Chinese front company that was shipping hi-tech goods to China without a license."

"Crimson Technologies."

"Yes, that's it."

"What about it?"

"Well, I know we want to prevent sensitive technologies like the new semiconductors that powerful computers need from falling into the hands of our enemies."

"Yes, and that's one reason why we require exporters to get a license before shipping them. We want to see what the product is and who is getting it."

"This might sound silly, but why don't we have the same thing for imports?"

"Well, we do. On certain goods, like arms and some agricultural products, licenses are required."

"I could be way off here, but why couldn't we require one to import gold? We'd be able to drastically cut down the number of illegal shipments."

"Well, that's an idea. There'd be pushback from the legitimate producing nations."

"Couldn't it be country-specific? Say for Peru, Colombia, and Mexico, for example?"

"That's possible. I'd have to give this some thought. Thanks, it's a good idea."

Rather than ask why customs hadn't thought of it, I thanked him and hung up.

My inbox pinged, and attached to the park's email was an MP4 video file. Scooting my chair closer, I double-clicked on the attachment.

The footage was grainy and black-and-white. I fast-forwarded to 4:50 p.m. and hit play. A constant stream of tourists and locals enjoying the view from the pier entered and left the screen. At 4:55 p.m., a man carrying a fishing pole and bucket came on-screen.

Wearing a white baseball cap, he kept his head down and angled away from the camera. It had to be Pembroke. He leaned against the railing and cast his line into the bay.

I replayed the section slowly. But it was impossible to get a clear view of his face. Pembroke knew there were cameras and avoided them. I let the video play, and at 5:01, Barrio came onto the screen.

They never shook hands, and Pembroke kept staring into the bay. Trying to read Barrio's lips was a waste of time. The meeting ended at 5:09, less than eight minutes. Barrio walked away and Pembroke reeled his line in. He cast again and continued to pretend he was fishing for fifteen minutes.

He grabbed his pail and scooted about twenty feet further down the pier. It looked as if he was finding a new place to fish. After casting twice, he reeled the line in and tugged his cap lower. He picked up his pail and left. Pembroke kept his head down while he walked off camera.

It wasn't worth the effort to check other cameras as Pembroke knew how to avoid detection.

I popped my head out of the den. "Mary Ann! Can you come here?"

"What's the matter?"

"Take a look at this."

After playing the video for her, I said, "If you had to identify the guy fishing, could you?"

"No. You can't make out his face."

"This is a complete waste of time. The video is useless. That bastard Pembroke thinks he's slick."

"That's who that was?"

"Yeah, it's when he met Barrio, the guy who worked for Noble Metals."

"Oh, now I get it."

"Yeah, but we're screwed. I was counting on the surveillance video to prove Pembroke met Barrio. Now, we got nothing."

"You'll get something. Right now, stay focused on getting Jimmy's killer."

"I know, but I thought we'd be able to nail Pembroke."

"What time are you leaving tomorrow?"

"I have to be at Naples Airport at the crack of dawn. French said the flight to Texas would leave at six."

"Look at you, they're sending a plane for you."

I didn't want to tell her going to Texas was the easy part. I joked, "Yeah, I'm a real big shot."

After an early dinner, I said, "Let's go for a walk."

The sun was shining, and a soft breeze was blowing as we hit the street. Mary Ann was going to the right, and I said, "No, let's go the other way."

I was afraid we'd run into Connie. "Okay."

We waved to a pair of neighbors walking their dogs, and Mary Ann said, "Maybe we should get a dog. What do you think?"

"I don't know, it's a lot of work."

"It's not that bad. It'd be fun to have around the house."

"If anything, we should wait until we get back from our trip."

"You're right. So, you're good with doing the Italian Rivera, Lake Como, and Venice?"

"Is that what you want to do?"

"There's so many places I want to go. Everybody said we should do this trip and save the Amalfi Coast for another time."

"Sounds good." About a dozen houses away, a man walked off his driveway into the street. I pointed, "Looks like Sal is back in town."

"Yeah, that's him."

I stopped. "Oh, man."

Mary Ann said, "What's the matter?"

"I got it."

"What? What do you have?"

"Hold on, let me think this through a second."

I smiled.

"Frank, are you going to tell me what is going on?"

Chapter Sixty-Six

I ripped off my sneakers, tossed them aside, and was halfway into the house when Mary Ann said, "Frank, what is going on?"

"Give me a little time, and if I'm right, I'll show you."

"And if you're wrong?"

I closed the door to the den and opened my laptop. George Pembroke was one of the top dogs in the Treasury Department. In his role, he made a fair number of public appearances.

Going straight to YouTube, I put Pembroke's name in the search bar. A long line of videos populated the screen. I weeded out several with him behind a podium and clicked on one of him at a roundtable discussion.

Five empty chairs were arranged in a semicircle under a large sign proclaiming Economics and the Developed World. I hit play.

The participants were announced one by one, and they walked to their chairs. I identified Pembroke after he took two steps from behind a curtain.

I smiled as I noticed Pembroke was wearing a dark suit and a yellow tie. Rewinding it, I watched it three more times. It was unmistakable.

Next, I opened the video of Pembroke appearing with the Treasury secretary. Pembroke was behind a podium. He was in a supporting role, making opening comments before introducing the secretary.

Pembroke walked toward the center of the stage to greet his boss. What I saw was irrefutable.

I copied the URLs for both videos, along with an MP4, and sent them in an email.

Opening the den's door, I said, "Mary Ann, can you come in here?"

"I'm coming."

I plopped into my chair as Mary Ann came into the room.

"Come around, I want to show you this."

Hitting play on the first YouTube video, I said, "Here's Pembroke at an economic forum."

She looked over my shoulder. "Okay."

"And this is him introducing the Treasury secretary. Wait until he goes to greet her."

"What are you getting at?"

"Hold on." I cued up an MP4 video. "Now, remember I showed you this? It's the surveillance video of Pembroke at South Pointe Pier when he met Barrio."

"Yes, I remember it."

My finger was poised over the play button. "Tell me who you think this is."

I dropped my finger and fast-forwarded. As soon as the man fake-fishing started to walk off the pier she said, "That's the same man in the other videos. It's Pembroke."

"It sure is. His gait matches perfectly."

"How did you figure this out?"

"When we were walking, as soon as I saw Sal walking, I knew who it was. We both did. His gait is recognizable, as is Pembroke's."

"Gait identification is somewhat controversial."

"Yes, but it's admissible in court, and we've got Barrio, who was there, saying it was Pembroke."

"What are you going to do?"

I palmed my phone. "I sent Romney French at Homeland the videos. He needs to drive it from here."

"Good luck."

I punched in French's number. He answered on the first ring. "Frank, I can see you've been busy."

"I'm trying to wrap things up before I head to Texas."

"Texas?"

"For another case. Did you see the videos?"

"Yes. You can clearly see it's George."

"It'll support Barrio's testimony, and with the circumstantial evidence, like Pembroke interfering in the Noble case, I think you have enough to nail him."

"It's time to show the prosecutorial team what we have."

Part Five

United States-Mexico Border

Chapter Sixty-Seven

We were sitting on the edge of a runway that had weeds growing out of the cracks in the asphalt. Sitting in the copilot seat, I said, "I still can't believe you didn't use instruments to fly here."

"It's always good to have backup instruments to fly, especially if the weather changes. But it was a short flight, and when you're flying visual only, you don't need to file your route and altitude."

"Good job. But I don't know if I'd ever be comfortable sitting in such a small space."

"You get used to it."

"I wouldn't."

The pilot pointed. "Is that them?"

I pulled my sunglasses off and squinted. "Yes. If you talk to them, treat them like any other passengers. And remember to use Spanish."

He smiled. "Ningun problema."

I got out of the cockpit seat. Crouching, I stepped onto the top step of the stairs. The captain stood behind me.

I waved as they approached. "Bienvenido."

My chest tightened as they climbed aboard, I asked, "Sin equipaje?"

They said they didn't have any baggage. The captain returned to the cockpit. I pulled up the stairs and locked the door in place.

I asked them to put their seat belts on and advised them the trip was going to take around twenty minutes.

They declined my offer to use the restroom, and I retreated to the cockpit. Settling into my seat, the pilot asked, "Everything good?"

"Yes. Let's get in the air."

We taxied onto the runway. He picked up the handset and, using Spanish, informed the passengers we were going to take off.

Engines revving, he thrust a mechanism forward and the plane sped up. The nose lifted. As the end of the runaway came into view, the wheels left the pavement. The engines whined as we climbed higher and higher.

I said, "Let me know when it's good to go."

"We're going to level off in a minute. We should cross into Texas in under five."

Rehearsing what I was going to do for the twentieth time, the pilot pointed out the window. "You're good to go."

Taking a deep breath, I unbuckled the seat harness. I got up and patted the Glock holstered to my ankle. I could hear the passengers chatting in Spanish.

I opened the cockpit door and stepped into the cabin. Both looked up. I said, "Debe usar del bano."

Steadying myself with a hand on the back of a seat, I made it to the narrow bathroom door. I squeezed into the space. Banging my head on the tiny sink, I grabbed my pistol out of the holster.

I counted to thirty and hit the lever, flushing the toilet. As the noise died out, I put the gun in the waistband by the small of my back. Softly closing the door behind me, I stepped into the cabin. Two rows ahead, the passengers were talking to each other across the aisle. Both men looked toward the back of the plane.

I smiled, tucking my shirt in and they went back to talking. Taking a step forward, I reached behind my back and pulled the Glock out. I held it alongside my leg. I raised the gun. Rushing forward, I jammed the barrel of the gun into the back of the Fisherman's head.

He said, "What the fuck?"

"Shut up! And put your hands behind your head! You too!"

The Fisherman hesitated.

"Now. Get them up!"

Acuna was looking straight ahead. I said, "You! Get 'em up!"

I slapped cuffs on the Fisherman and did the same to Acuna. I jabbed the back of the Fisherman's head with the pistol. "Get on your feet."

He rose.

I stepped into the aisle. "Turn around."

He faced the back of the plane, saying, "What the fuck is this? You're dead. You're a dead motherfucker."

"Shut up."

Frisking him, I pulled up the leg of his pants. An eight-inch knife was in a sheath secured to his calf. I disarmed him. The blade had a serrated edge. Was it the one he gutted Jimmy with? Digging into the front pocket of his jeans, I pulled out his phone and wallet.

I put the gun to the base of his skull. "Now, you're going to move to the next row. And do it slowly."

Swearing under his breath, the Fisherman moved. Using another pair, I cuffed the ones he had on to the arm of his seat. I made a show of frisking Acuna and securing him to his seat.

Acuna said, "Who are you working for? Whoever it is, we can pay you double."

"Keep quiet."

I tapped on the door to the cockpit and opened it. "Okay. Get us home."

The Fisherman shouted, "Where the fuck are you taking us?"

"Keep quiet."

"Is this guy from the DEA?"

Acuna said, "I don't know."

"Hey, man. We got rights."

"Yes, you sure do. You'll get your chance to exercise them in a courtroom."

His eyes widened. "You think you can kidnap us? We'll get you and your family."

I stepped toward him, waving the pistol in his face. "Shut up, or I'm going to gag you."

After checking his cuffs, I sat behind the Fisherman and looked through his wallet. Nothing but his driver's license and a credit card. I tried to open his phone, but it was locked.

I got up, approaching the Fisherman.

He said, "You ain't getting away with this. We—"

"Shut up!"

I held the phone in front of his face. I smiled when the face recognition worked, unlocking the phone This was going to be a treasure trove of information.

I hurried to my seat and began scrolling. My hopes deflated. The call log was empty, and there were no texts.

I clicked on the contacts icon and mumbled a curse. It was also empty. La Familia's discipline had put up another wall to climb.

Using the settings, I was able to see his carrier was AT&T Mexico and determine the cell's number. We might be able to get something.

The plane landed in Texas. As we taxied to a corner of Edinburg Airport, I sent a text to Bradley asking him to discreetly check into what we could get from AT&T regarding the Fisherman's cell records.

When we came to a stop close to where a jet owned by Homeland Security was waiting for us, I unbuckled and went up to the Fisherman. "Emanuel Ruiz, you're under arrest for the murder of Jimmy Pearson. You have the right to remain silent. Anything you say can and will be used against you in a court of law. You have the right to a lawyer. If you cannot afford a lawyer, one will be appointed for you."

"Hey, man, I got some heavy info for you to trade if you let us go."

"Keep quiet!"

I turned to Acuna, informing him he was under arrest for distribution of illegal narcotics. Then I read him his Miranda rights and opened the door. A pair of agents oversaw the transfer of both prisoners onto the sleek plane. Once they were secured, the officers and I took our seats.

Acuna kept trying to meet my eyes as we headed to Naples Airport. I enjoyed seeing him nervous. It was icing on the cake for catching the Fisherman.

The Fisherman turned toward me. "Hey, man! I gotta talk to you."

"Save it for the courtroom."

"No, man. This is big. I got information on a dirty pig, and he's way up there. He's the one who told me to disappear."

What did he have? Was he lying to save himself? "Wait until we land in Naples."

The high from catching Jimmy's killer deflated like a balloon. If he was telling the truth, we could weed out a traitor. But there was no way I was going to go along with allowing the Fisherman to escape justice.

Chapter Sixty-Eight

Naples, Florida

I was beat from traveling, but it was hard sleeping with the Fisherman on my mind. I got out of bed well before the sun rose. I padded into the kitchen.

The sliding door was clouded with overnight moisture. I made a cup of coffee and turned my phone on.

There was a voicemail from JD. All it said was to call him. It was ten minutes to seven. I sent him a text.

A minute later, he called.

"Hey, Frank. I tried to call you last night."

"I know. I have enough trouble sleeping without the phone going off, so I've started shutting it off at night."

"That's a good move. My wife keeps hers on, and the notifications drive me nuts."

"What's going on?"

"We seized the load late last night. It was too valuable, and we couldn't risk leaving it on the dock."

"Good to hear."

"I also put a flag in the system on Noble so any future shipments will be scrutinized."

"They should bar them from importing."

"Even though importing is a privilege, not a right, banning an importer is a long process, and the law firm they hired is top-shelf."

"Frigging lawyers."

"We've issued fines and penalty letters on each of the shipments where the documentation didn't jibe. They've got thirty days to respond. I'm sure they'll try to mitigate the fines as they amount to the full value of the shipments involved."

"That should get their attention, but I wish the money was coming out of the cartels."

"That's about the best we can do."

"Well, I'm glad you're doing as much as you can. I just worry the cartels will find another willing refiner to play their dirty game."

"Exactly, or set up a company themselves."

My stomach dropped. "You know, I never thought about that. How easy is it to do that?"

"Too easy, if you ask me. You don't even have to be located in the States. You can be a foreign-based importer."

"That's crazy."

"All you need is a representative here."

"How the hell are we going to stop this kind of laundering with laws like that?"

"Sorry, buddy, but that's above my pay grade."

What was it about this case? Every plus had a minus. We seized the shipment, depriving the cartel of some money, but the import process had a giant hole in it.

I was sure the cartels would create one or more companies to exploit the system. They'd be one step ahead of us, again.

It was frustrating. Why couldn't the government innovate and adapt like criminals did? We were always reacting.

Grabbing my cell, I dialed a number.

"Homeland Security. How can I assist you today?"

"Romney French. Tell him it's Frank Luca."

"Hold on, sir."

Mary Ann came into the kitchen as French answered.

"Frank. How are you?"

"I know I should be feeling good about the Noble Metals case. You got JD back on it, and they seized a gold shipment. And I appreciate it, I really do."

"It sounds like a but is coming."

"Yes. It seems easy for the cartels to find another refiner to work with, or I understand they can create a company to do the importing. It's like a whack-a-mole thing."

"People willing to commit crimes find endless ways to circumvent the law. I'm sure you're aware of that."

"I am, but isn't there something we could do? Like permanently barring companies or not allowing imports of gold from Peru?"

"There would be pushback from the State Department for singling out Peru, or Colombia, for that matter."

"Well, something must be done, or everything we've done by shining a light on this scheme is going to continue. This is nothing but a little hiccup for the cartels, and they'll keep destroying the rainforest."

"I was going to write a memorandum to increase the scrutiny of shipments coming out of Peru and Colombia."

"That's good, but wouldn't they just move it through Mexico?"

"That's certainly a possibility, but it makes it more difficult and costly for them."

"Their margins can absorb it."

"Probably, but it will impact them."

"I appreciate everything you're doing. I just hope it's enough."

"Me too. Okay, have a good day."

I went into the kitchen.

Mary Ann said, "You were talking to the guy at Homeland?"

"Yes, Romney French. Let me tell you, there's a hole in the importing system so wide the moon could pass through it."

"I think they're relying on technology to solve things. Maybe AI can help."

"AI? I don't think so. We need manpower at the borders and ports and robust undercover operations. It's sickening how all the drugs are getting in, and the cash is getting washed. It's—"

"Frank. You're rambling."

"I'm not rambling, I'm just frustrated all the work I put in—"

"The main goal was getting Jimmy's killer, right?"

"Absolutely."

"Aren't you interviewing him today?"

"Yes. I'm leaving in an hour."

"You don't seem excited about it. You used to live for days like this."

"I know, but there's something about this damn case."

"It's almost over."

Was it the fact that the Fisherman claimed to have dirt on a corrupt cop that had me down? Corruption was more widespread than I'd imagined. And just who was he talking about?

Chapter Sixty-Nine

"Thanks. Is the coffee still crappy around here?"

He laughed. "Nothing's changed."

"I'm going to grab a cup. You want one?"

"No thanks."

I walked into the cafeteria and everyone, including my replacement, Donovan, started clapping. I looked behind me; no one was there.

Until someone said, "You're a badass, Frank," I didn't realize the applause was for me.

Putting up a palm, I said, "It's not over yet."

I shook several hands, including Donovan's, and poured a cup of burnt coffee.

Donovan sidled up to me. "Well done, buddy. Since you brought Ruiz in, do you want to do the interview today?"

"I'd be honored."

"It's all yours."

"Thanks, and don't worry, I'm not coming back."

He laughed. "Ruiz and his arrogant lawyer are in room one."

"Did you shut the air off in that room?"

"What?"

"Nothing. I used to screw with suspects by making them wait in a hot room. You know, it gave me an edge."

He looked at me as if I had changed into a bikini.

"It was a little game Derrick and I used to play."

"Okay. Let's get moving."

Donovan opened the door to the interview room, and Ruiz and his lawyer Bill Rudy broke up their huddle.

Donovan said, "Special Agent Frank Luca is going to conduct the interview."

We sat across the metal table from them, and Donovan turned on the recording apparatus. He recited the formalities for the record and turned to me.

Squaring the folder I had put on the table, I said, "Mr. Ruiz, when you were arrested, you claimed to have information on a corrupt law enforcement officer. Before we go into the murder you've been charged with, tell us about the dirty officer so we can determine if it's real and weigh what kind of a plea we can offer in exchange."

His attorney, Rudy, smirked. "You've got serious problems with whatever it is you think you're attempting here. For the record, and maybe it's because you're retired, but the way this works is you dangle an offer, and we consider whether to cooperate before providing specifics."

I wanted to wipe the smug smile off his face. "This is no ordinary case, so, we're going to do it my way. Your client reveals what he has, and we'll consider whether to offer relief. Keep in mind, Mr. Ruiz is in serious trouble."

"It's your case that is in serious jeopardy, Mr. Luca."

"Save your bravado for the jurors, counselor."

Rudy pushed away from the table and stood. "We're going to end this little charade right now."

"Hold on. You can't just leave."

"I sure can. We're filing a motion to have the charges dismissed."

"On what basis? It's not going to go anywhere."

"You illegally detained and transported Mr. Ruiz. Your acts constitute kidnapping under federal law, specifically, the Mann Act. You've broken several international agreements as well, but we'll look past those and will even agree to forgo filing a complaint with the Mexican government, who take transporting persons against their will, over a border, as one of the most serious crimes you could commit."

I looked at Ruiz, saying, "How much are you paying your lawyer? A thousand an hour?"

Rudy said, "My fee is none of you concern."

I flipped open the folder sitting in front of me. "Well, whatever it is, Mr. Ruiz, you're overpaying."

Rudy checked his phone and stood. "I can confirm the motion was delivered to Judge Hollins." He looked at Ruiz. "We'll have you out of here in a couple of hours."

I slid two documents across the table. "Here are two sworn statements from witnesses testifying your client boarded the plane that took him to Texas of his own volition."

Ruiz leaned over, looked at the documents, and muttered, "Fucking Acuna? What did you give him to make Acuna jam me up?"

Rudy lowered himself into a chair. "Mr. Acuna's testimony will be discounted by whatever deal you gave him. Who is Paul Gibbons?"

"The pilot of the plane Mr. Ruiz freely boarded. Sorry, counselor, this wasn't a kidnapping."

Ruiz turned to his lawyer. "Bullshit, they cuffed me on the plane."

"We were in American airspace, governed by US law, when Mr. Ruiz was secured. Now, tell your client to start talking."

Rudy shifted in his seat. "I'd like a few moments in private with my client."

We stepped into the hallway, and Donovan said, "You see

Rudy's face when you gave him the statements? He's such a pompous ass."

My cell started vibrating as I said, "I'm glad I don't have to deal with clowns like him anymore."

It was Bradley. I took a step away. "Let me get this."

I slipped into an empty interview room. "Hey, Bradley, I don't have much time. I'm in the middle of interviewing the Fisherman. What's up?"

"That's why I called. I've got some information for you."

"Go ahead."

"I got Ruiz's phone records from AT&T."

"Any calls or texts with Dillon or anyone at the DEA?"

"No. But there's one from the Collier County Sheriff's Office."

I leaned against the wall. "Are you shitting me?"

"No."

My mind rifled through all the people I'd worked with. "I'm afraid to ask, who is it?"

When Bradley told me, I gasped for air.

Chapter Seventy

"Are you sure it's Sergeant Gesso?"

"Yes. The records show Ruiz receiving a call from Gesso's cell right before the raid, and another one right before he ran off down to Mexico."

I collapsed into a chair. "This makes no sense."

"What do you mean? Gesso is the leak."

"There's nothing else?"

"Nothing involving a law enforcement officer or agency."

"I don't believe this."

"You know him well, right?"

"At least I thought I did. Look, I got to go."

The coffee I drank started backing up. I stood and paced the room. Gesso had been here when I joined the force. When had he gone bad?

Rifling through the hundreds of cases I handled, I couldn't come up with more than three where Gesso had tried to shut down a case. But in fairness to him, the three were problematic.

Stomach churning, my thoughts shifted to the way Gesso

reacted when I asked if we had a leak that turned a raid into a waste of time. He kept telling me to dial back the accusations.

And then with DEA's Dillon, he warned me to tone it down as well. Was he trying to knock me off the path he'd taken?

There was a knock on the door. I jumped up as Donovan popped his head in. "Are you okay?"

"Yeah, yeah. Well, not really."

"What's the matter?"

"Nah, forget it, it's just my stomach acting up. Let's get this done."

Donovan clicked record. He recited the time, date, attendees, and said, "We're resuming the interview of Emmanuel Ruiz, who is represented by William Rudy."

Rudy said, "My client is interested in cooperating provided the deal offered is good."

I said, "Though it pains me to say it, the prosecutors have agreed to forgo the death penalty in exchange for your client's cooperation."

"I'm afraid that is not going to cut it. You've got to do better than that."

"Mr. Ruiz murdered Jimmy Pearson, brutally gutting his body. Furthermore, your client is a member of the La Familia drug cartel. He's engaged in drug distribution and trafficking."

"We're going to need some sentencing relief."

A mixture of bile and coffee splashed the back of my throat. "Surely, you're aware that Governor DeSantis signed a new drug law. That legislation increased the minimum sentences for trafficking in fentanyl."

"There's no evidence Mr. Ruiz was engaged in—"

I leaned forward. "You want me to take you to the morgue? You want autopsy reports? What? What do you want? You want to talk to my neighbor whose son overdosed on the shit your client sells?"

Donovan kicked me under the table and said, "Look, all we can do is see what Mr. Ruiz has to say and then take it upstairs. Maybe they'll shave a couple of years off, but that's about it, so you better take it while the offer is still there."

Then it hit me, it could have been Gesso who told Ruiz that it was Jimmy who had identified him. I jumped up, putting my hand over my mouth. "I got to throw up."

Body in full protest, I ran to the bathroom.

Bursting through the door, I vomited into the sink.

As I was cleaning up the mess I'd made, Donovan burst in. "Frank, are you okay?"

"I must have caught a virus or something. My stomach is killing me."

"Don't worry, go home. I'll finish the interview."

I wasn't sure what was worse, not being there, or hearing what I knew was coming. "Can you reschedule it?"

"I don't know."

"You know, maybe we shouldn't give Ruiz anything. Screw him, he deserves to get the death penalty."

"But what about the information he has?"

"Can we really trust what he says?"

"We can vet it."

"If you could postpone it, I'd appreciate it. My stomach is rumbling, I got to get home."

<hr>

MARY ANN WAS WIPING down the outdoor furniture. I took a frozen bagel out of the freezer and put it in the microwave. I ate half of it before sticking my head out of the slider. "Mary Ann, come inside, I need to talk to you."

She came in as I stuffed the rest of the bagel in my mouth.

"How'd it go with Ruiz?"

"You're not going to believe it, but Gesso was the leak."

"What? Ruiz pinned it on the Sarge?"

"Bradley got Ruiz's phone records, and there are two calls from Gesso, one right before the raid, and the other after I told them it was Ruiz who killed Jimmy."

"Oh my God. I can't believe it."

"Everything is all screwed up. I don't know what to do."

"What happened during the interrogation?"

I told her I had thrown up. After reassuring her I was fine, I said, "What should I do?"

"What do you want to do?"

"Wring Gesso's frigging neck. I just can't believe he betrayed me and Jimmy, everybody."

She took my hands. "You're mad and have every right to be. Why don't you talk to Gesso. See what he has to say before this blows up."

"You think there could be a legitimate reason for the calls?"

She frowned. "Given what you said about the timing of them, no."

I shook my head. "I have to talk to him."

"Good, but promise me you won't get crazy, okay?"

"I won't."

Pulling out my phone, I dialed the cell number of the man I had called Sarge for twenty years.

"Frank?"

"Meet me in Bayfront by the marina."

"When?"

"Now."

"I've got a meeting—"

"I said now!"

"I don't understand, Frank. What's going on?"

"No, it's me who doesn't understand what the hell is going on, so be there in fifteen minutes."

"Okay."

Shoving the phone in my pocket, Mary Ann said, "You said you weren't going to get crazy."

Heading toward the garage, I said, "I had to make sure he would meet now."

Chapter Seventy-One

Surveying the area, I saw Gesso getting out of his car. He scanned the waterfront and nodded when he saw me.

He was moving slower than normal. Did he know I had found out about him and Ruiz?

When he was a couple of steps away, he said, "What's so urgent?"

Seething, I stared at him.

Gesso stepped to my side, saying, "You going to say something or—"

"How the hell do you live with yourself?"

"What are you talking about?"

"How much did Ruiz pay you?"

Gesso face darkened. "Ruiz?"

"Yeah, Ruiz. You tipped him off about the raid and then told him we were onto him about Jimmy's murder. How much was selling out the community, the force, everything we stand for— how much was it worth?"

He looked at his shoes. "I fucked up. Big time."

Full of scorn, I said, "That's an understatement. When did this bullshit start?"

"A year ago. I figured I was about to retire, and it's so expensive to live these days."

"Why didn't you start selling drugs on some corner then?"

"Don't be ridiculous."

"There's no difference in what you did."

"Come on, of course there is."

"You helped them. They're poisoning our kids, and you helped them. I can't believe we're even talking about this. You helped kill Jimmy."

"Now, hold on there. I only told him when there was a raid. It was harmless. These dealers just set up somewhere else the next day."

"Jimmy's dead because of you. I can't believe you gave him up."

"I swear I didn't. I never mentioned the kid's name."

"Bullshit! How the hell did Ruiz find out then?"

"It wasn't from me, but it was out there. I'm pretty sure Pearson told his friends he told you."

"What? The kid was scared out of his mind."

"What can I tell you? After you told us he was there when they made the buy, we reinterviewed a couple of other kids, and two of them knew Pearson had told you it was Ruiz."

Though Jimmy was scared, the power of a secret may have doomed him. "I don't know if I buy that. But either way, besides tipping the raid, you helped a murderer get away."

"It wasn't like that. I told him to turn himself in or he was going get to himself killed."

"You expect me to believe that?"

"It's what happened. I did what I did on the raid, but I'd never let a murderer get away with it. I had no idea he would run."

"Come on, you should've known he'd take off."

"I really thought I could bring him in for you."

"So now you were doing me a favor?"

"No. Ruiz seemed to trust me."

"Trust you? Have you lost it? Ruiz is a cold-blooded killer."

"I didn't know that. I just knew him as a lower-level dealer."

"He was working for a cartel."

"I didn't know, I swear."

"Well, you should have, especially if you were going be helping them."

"You have to believe me. I would never help a killer. I really screwed up with the raid, but that's all it was."

"You did more than screw up, you threw your entire career and reputation out the frigging window."

"What do you think is going to happen? I can't go to prison. They'll kill me within a week."

"You should have thought of that before you sold your soul."

"Frank, is there anything you can do for me?"

"You're something else."

"For old times' sake, Frank. Please, Marilyn is gonna go to pieces."

"Hand in your papers."

"Now?"

"Yes."

"But I only have seven months to full retirement."

"That's too bad. Get out now and get yourself a good lawyer. You're going to need it."

"Are you going to tell anybody we spoke?"

"I haven't made up my mind."

"Frank, please. I'm begging you."

I turned and walked away.

I NEEDED to speak to someone else. Derrick had been a cop, and that colored things.

Dr. Bilotti worked closely with law enforcement but wasn't

a part of the force. He was also older and had proven to be wise. I called him and he agreed to meet.

Bilotti was waiting for me in front of the medical examiner's low-slung building.

"Do you want to talk in my office?"

It was always cold in his office. "Why don't we sit over there?" I pointed to a bench in the shade.

"Sure."

It smelled like cigarettes by the bench. Before sitting I said, "What I'm about to tell you is confidential."

"I understand."

I took a deep breath and said, "Gesso is dirty. I don't know how bad, but for certain he tipped off the dealer who killed my neighbor's kid."

"Boy, I never saw that coming. Are you certain about this?"

"Yes. We have two phone calls between Ruiz and Gesso. One right before the raid, and the other before he took off. I talked to Gesso, he admitted to the first one about the raid but claims he was trying to convince Ruiz to turn himself in."

"Does anyone else know about this?"

"Not yet. We were interviewing Ruiz, and it was going to come out because he was looking to trade what he had on a bad cop for leniency, but I got sick and we postponed the interrogation."

"And you want advice on what you should do?"

"Yes. I know I'm putting you on the spot, but it's . . ."

"Of course, it's confusing. You've worked alongside Sergeant Gesso for years and had an excellent relationship with him."

"He put Mary Ann and me together because he thought we'd make a nice couple."

"I remember you mentioning that. He was right on that."

I nodded. "It's tough processing all this."

"What did you say when you confronted him?"

"I told him to retire, immediately."

"You're conflicted as to whether to participate in getting all of this to the surface?"

"Yes. I mean if he really tried to get Ruiz to turn himself in, it's a whole different ballgame. I mean, I'm not forgiving him for tipping off the raid. That was a violation of everything we stand for. And he said he wasn't the one who told Ruiz it was Jimmy who had fingered him as the dealer."

"Do you believe him on that?"

"I kind of do."

"Can you make the connection from the raid to the murder?"

"Not directly, but if the raid was successful, we could've gotten lucky and arrested Ruiz. Jimmy told us Ruiz was the one who sold the drugs to Steve when he overdosed."

"You're angry at Gesso, but at the same time, your relationship with him is preventing you from going after him, right?"

I nodded. "I feel like I should, but if this was a one-time thing, and he really did try to bring Ruiz in, should everything he did in his career go down the drain? At least half of me says yes. What should I do?"

"Considering you're not part of the sheriff's office any longer, you are under no obligation to do anything. You said Ruiz was looking to trade what he knows about Gesso for a plea of some kind, right?"

"Yes."

"Then it's going to come out anyway. Gesso will have to defend himself for whatever he did and suffer the consequences. You won't have to be involved and suffer any guilt if you participate."

"So just walk away?"

"Why not? You don't need to see a man ruined up close. You did your part by bringing him in. It took enough out of you, didn't it?"

"It sure did, and Mary Ann would be happy if it was over."

"So, that's it. Let Donovan handle it from here, and you go back to being retired. Go on the trip you promised your wife."

Bilotti was right. It was painful enough knowing what Gesso had done. He'd retire and face whatever charges were brought against him.

Chapter Seventy-Two

My cell vibrated. It was Derrick.

"Hey, Frank. Did you hear?"

"Hear what?"

"Gesso turned his papers in and retired early."

"He did?"

"Yeah, something doesn't make sense. He had less than a year left."

I hesitated before saying, "Well, you didn't hear it from me, but there were rumors he might have crossed the line."

"What line? What do you know?"

"I heard it's something to do with the Fisherman and the tip-off about the raid."

"Holy shit. And you thought it was the DEA guy, Dillon."

"Don't run with this. It's only speculation at this point."

"You're involved, you'll get the scoop."

"Not any longer. I did my part bringing Ruiz in, and I'm done with this."

"Really?"

"Yes. I did what I set out to do, and that's all I'm going to do."

"How much did you get for getting the Fisherman?"

"Nothing but satisfaction. I wouldn't take a dime from Jimmy's murder."

"But what about the gold laundering case? You had to make some big bucks on that."

"I did okay."

"You're not going to tell me?"

"Why? You had every chance to join me?"

"Come on, give me an idea so I know what I missed out on."

"Ten million."

"Wow. That's a not a bad payday."

"Half is going to the Fallen Officers fund, and the rest we're putting in a trust for Jessie."

My phone vibrated. "Derrick, I have to go, the guy from Homeland is calling."

"Mr. French, how are you?"

"Good, Frank, and you?"

"All is well. What's going on?"

"I wanted to bring you up to speed on the Noble Metals case."

"I was wondering what the status was."

"It seems like trying to criminally charge the Medina brothers is too tall a mountain to climb. Barrio isn't the most credible witness, and he's the only one claiming the owners knew the gold was illegally mined. Neither brother traveled to Peru, and neither had direct contact with the sellers."

"Damn. So, what is going to be done?"

"A couple of things, in addition to some hefty fines. One is making sure the rest of the refining industry is aware of the trouble Noble got itself into. To address that, the Medina brothers have agreed to fund a five-year advertising campaign to get the word out in the industry's major publications."

"I hope that's effective, but greed is powerful."

"It is, and thanks to your idea, we're going to require import licenses for gold importations out of Peru and Colombia."

"You are?"

"Yes, it won't be perfect, but the process should put a damper on the flow of illegal gold coming into the States."

After finishing the call, I went into the kitchen. Mary Ann said, "You've been busy this morning."

"Word is getting out on Gesso retiring."

"I was just thinking, it's been quiet about what he did."

"You can't keep it hidden. It'll come out, it's just a matter of how bad it will be if Ruiz doesn't say Gesso tried to convince him to come in."

"Still not good that he was talking to him while Ruiz was the number one suspect."

I exhaled. "It sure isn't. I just can't get my head around what he did."

"I feel bad for Marilyn."

I didn't know if what I was feeling for Gesso was anger or sadness. He was someone we'd considered asking to be Jessie's godfather.

Gesso had orchestrated Mary Ann and I as partners because he thought we were a good match, romantically speaking. I felt indebted to him for life for that.

My cell sounded. It wasn't a recognizable number but had Washington, D.C.'s 202 area code.

"Hello?"

"Mr. Luca, it's Jack Pierce, DEA headquarters."

An image of the overweight analyst I'd met when I got to Washington popped into my head. "Oh, hi. What's going on?"

"I figured we owed you an update. Is this a good time?"

"Sure. An update on what?"

"The La Familia cartel. We've been able to get high-value intelligence from the two members you brought into protective custody."

"Javier White and Ernesto Carmen?"

"Yes. White provided good information on the money flows and laundering efforts, and Carmen filled in the blanks on their distribution network and members in the United States."

"I hope they gave enough to warrant witness protection."

"We're in the early stages, but we'll make arrests over the next several months, and their testimony will be critical. Oh, and White's brother Tonino paid the price for Javier's cooperation; his body was found a couple of days ago."

"I have limited sympathy for any of these people."

"I hear you. You know, I have to say, when you came to see me in Washington, I didn't take you seriously. I know you had a career in enforcement, but these cartels are something else, and I've seen a truck load of officers try to do something, but you're the only one who had an impact."

"My mother raised me to back up my word."

"She did a hell of a job."

"Thanks. Have a good one."

Mary Ann said, "Who was that?"

I filled her in, finishing by saying, "He said I proved him wrong and did what no one else could."

She said, "Don't let it go to your head."

Mary Ann didn't have to worry; any success I had was already tarnished by the loss of Steve and Jimmy. And now, because of what I'd uncovered, there was Gesso's downfall.

Chapter Seventy-Three

She came in holding a dish towel. "When is it going to be on?"

"French said it was going to be the lead story."

Dressed in a light-blue dress, the anchorwoman smiled, welcoming viewers to the six o'clock broadcast.

"Tonight we lead with a story out of Washington that has become far too familiar."

She was replaced on the screen by an image of Pembroke being led out of the Treasury Department. His suit jacket was draped over his handcuffed hands.

"George Pembroke, one the most senior members of the Treasury Department, was arrested earlier this afternoon. It is alleged that Mr. Pembroke engaged in an international scheme involving a Mexican cartel that was engaged in illegal gold mining. The scheme involved the shipment of raw gold to a refinery in Miami, laundering the proceeds of drug sales. It is alleged that Mr. Pembroke arranged sales of the refined gold to the US government in exchange for a percentage of the proceeds."

Mary Ann said, "I hope he gets fifty years."

"He'll probably cut a plea deal, especially if he knows a lot about the La Familia cartel."

"He'd have to go into protection."

"His family is high-profile. It won't be easy, but it's either that or a long stint in prison."

"I can't believe he took such a risk letting you pursue this whole thing."

"Pembroke was blinded by his hatred for Adams. He paid me lip service about me going after money, but Pembroke never respected me. I was convenient for him, an outsider with a proven record."

"It was a good cover."

I nodded, "But he made a mistake figuring me for someone he could control. Romney said Pembroke told him he expected me to quit chasing this down and, don't forget, he had Sears try to shut us down when we followed the money into Peru."

"And he interfered when you looked into the refinery."

"Exactly. At the end of day, Pembroke is like a lot of smart, successful people; they think they can control an investigation."

Pembroke going to jail didn't bother me in the least. His type of crime was more dangerous than the street type. He could rot in prison, but I was torn about Gesso and the possibility he'd be behind bars. It was impossible to understand why he did something so stupid.

FOR AT LEAST THE fifth time, we were watching *The Usual Suspects*. As the credits began to scroll, I grabbed the remote. "Let's go to bed."

"Wait. I want to see the weather. Connie said there's a tropical storm heading our way."

"I didn't hear about that."

"That's what she said."

Saying, "Tell her not watch so much TV," I put on WINK news.

After a story about the Naples film festival, weatherman Matt Devitt came on. He was standing to the side of a colorful map. "Everybody is asking about what's brewing in the Caribbean. Is it going to affect us? Stay with us, the current models and our predictions are coming up."

I said, "It's too late in the season to be anything serious. The Gulf is cooling off."

"It's probably hype."

The anchorman appeared on screen. "We're bringing you a WINK news exclusive. Sources inform us that a high-ranking member of the Collier County Sheriff's Office has been questioned in regard to possible collaboration with a Southwest Florida drug ring.

The person is believed to be Sergeant Vincent Gesso, who has been with the department for twenty-four years. WINK News tried to get a statement from Mr. Gesso, but he declined."

A video of Sergeant Gesso and his wife being trailed by reporters in the Coastland Mall's parking lot played.

Microphone in hand, a reporter asked, "Mr. Gesso, why did you retire early? Is it connected to the rumors you're about to be indicted?"

"No comment."

Gesso's wife, whose head was down, snapped, "Leave us alone!"

The anchorman said, "We've asked the sheriff's department to comment on the allegations."

Mary Ann said, "Oh my God. I can't believe this is happening."

"He did it to himself, but seeing this makes me sick."

The anchorman replayed the Gesso footage. "We'll update you on this developing story. Now, let's find out what Matt can tell us about a disturbance that could be heading our way."

With a storm already raging in my head, a tropical one, hundreds of miles away, was minor.

I tossed the remote on the couch. "I'm going to brush my teeth."

Lying in bed that night, I reviewed the murder and laundering case. It was a success but bittersweet. Steve and Jimmy were gone, and Gesso, a good friend, had become collateral damage.

Knowing the sting would never go away, I batted around two loose ends. I knew I had to deal with one and would tend to it in the morning.

———

Rinsing my mug, Mary Ann said, "Don't forget, Melissa is coming over at nine."

"Who?"

"The travel agent. She wants to drop off a bunch of material on tours for us to consider."

I didn't want to see too many churches, but said, "Whatever you decide, I'm good with."

"No, Frank. We're doing this together. I don't want you complaining."

"Me? Complain?"

"That's right, remember you in Rome? You kept moaning about going to too many churches."

She really could read my mind. "They have one on every street there."

"That's the way Europe is."

Heading for the den, I said, "I've got to make a call."

I sat behind my desk and stared at my phone. I wanted to change the home screen picture of Jimmy, Steve, and Jessie but hesitated. It felt disrespectful.

Making this call was supposed to be easy, but I'd given my word and didn't break it easily. But like everything else in this case, there were two sides to it.

I pulled up Dillon's number and placed a call to the Fort Myers DEA office.

"Frank, how's it going? Hey, I heard about Gesso."

"Yeah, we'll see how bad it is."

"Damn shame. Who would've thought 'the' sergeant for Collier County was on the take?"

I knew he was giving me back some of the crap I'd given him about the DEA being dirty. "Trust me, I'm still recovering."

"I'm sure that's not why you're calling."

"No. I wanted to provide some inside information on a major distributor."

"I'm all ears."

"Farro Acuna, aka Cherdo. He was key in helping me get the Fisherman. I told him we'd leave his operation alone, but that isn't right."

"What do you have on him?"

I detailed what I'd learned. Dillon thanked me and promised to act immediately.

That left one rock in my shoe. And that was Rico, the corrupt CIA operative I'd met in Peru. I didn't know what to do about him, but I couldn't let an infection go unaddressed.

It might take time, but time I had.

The doorbell rang.

Mary Ann said, "Frank, she's here."

I waited until I heard the lady leave. When I came into the family room, Mary Ann was studying a glossy brochure.

"Oh my God, Frank. Look at this, it's the Italian Riviera. This is Portofino."

She handed it to me. The cover featured a picture of a

couple our age. They were framed by bright red bougainvillea bushes and were overlooking the ocean.

Now there was a home-screen picture if I ever saw one.

"We have to go there and take a picture just like this one."

———

The End

———

Thank you for reading, ***The Golden Sellout: A Luca Thriller.*** We hope you enjoyed this book in the Luca Series. You can find a complete list of the authors work on the following pages, and on his website where you can subscribe for his newsletter of future books, story insights, and on very rare occasions special deals and recommendations.

www.danpetrosini.com

Dan is a USA Today and Amazon best-selling author who wrote his first story at the age of ten and enjoys telling a story or joke.

Dan gets his story ideas by exploring the question; What if?

In almost every situation he finds himself in, Dan explores what if this or that happened? What if this person died or did something unusual or illegal?

Dan's non-stop mind spin provides him with plenty of material to weave into interesting stories.

A fan of books and films that have twists and are difficult to predict, Dan crafts his stories to prevent readers from guessing correctly. He writes every day, forcing the words out when necessary and has written over twenty-five novels to date.

It's not a matter of wanting to write, Dan simply has to.

Dan passionately believes people can realize their dreams if they focus and act, and he encourages just that.

His favorite saying is – "The price of discipline is always less than the cost of regret"

Dan reminds people to get the negativity out of their lives. He believes it is contagious and advises people to steer clear of negative people. He knows having a true, positive mind set makes it feel like life is rigged in your favor. When he gets off base, he tells himself, 'You can't have a good day with a bad attitude.'

Married with two daughters and a needy Maltese, Dan lives in Southwest Florida. A New York native, Dan has taught at local colleges, writes novels, and plays tenor saxophone in several jazz bands. He also drinks way too much wine and never, ever takes himself too seriously.

He puts out a twice-a-month newsletter featuring articles, his writing and special deals and steals.

Sign up at www.danpetrosini.com